A Needful Heart

by

J. M. MADDEN

Also includes a bonus novella by
author Donna McDonald

EDITION NOTICE

This book is a work of fiction. Names, characters, places, and incidents either are the product of the author's imagination or are used fictitiously. Any resemblance to actual persons, living or dead, businesses, companies, events, or locales is coincidental.

This book contains content that may not be suitable for young readers 17 and under.

Cover art by Viola Estrella and The Author's Red Room
Edited by The Comma Cabal

Acknowledgements

As always, I have to recognize my husband for being the fantastic man he is and supporting me in everything I want to do. He is my hero.

I have to thank the girls of KYRW and KIW for being awesome critique partners and sounding boards. You ladies are the best!

And to my parents, all of them, for being super supportive. I love you guys.

Here's your print book Mom.

Chapter One

Matt hoped for, yet dreaded, the possibility that Gina would brush against him as she strode down the hallway to the next exam room. The hope nagged at him. The dread, on the other hand, gnawed out his stomach and almost swamped him. What if she did brush against him? What if she glanced up at him with that gut-turning smile she had and said something to him, and expected some kind of response?

His worries stalled as she bypassed him completely and went into the small lab room directly across from where he leaned. He blew the stale air from his lungs and tried to settle his thudding heart. The peaches and cream scent she wore wafted to him, teased him with her freshness and sent a fresh jolt of awareness down his body.

Once a month for the past four years Matt had brought his neighbor George in for check-ups following a liver transplant. While George waited to be seen, Matt devoted his time to watching Gina and storing up images of her in his mind to tide him over till the next month. The shape of her ass in pink scrubs as it swayed down the hallway, the way her curly hair blew under the vent at the far end, the way her smiles came so easily when she greeted people and the way her ice-blue eyes crinkled at the corners.

Every time they left the doctor's office, Matt was frustrated and furious at himself for not talking to Gina about something other than George's next appointment or the pills he was on. But nothing ever came to mind. She'd tried to start conversations before, and he had totally locked up. She had to think he was the village idiot. Or the Shelbyville, Indiana, idiot.

Clenching his fists in frustration, he vowed to himself he was going to say *something* to her coherent, even if he had to stay here all day to do it. He needed to talk to her just to prove to himself that he could. Besides, it wasn't like she'd respond. Her pristine little life didn't have room for a roughneck like him in it. She'd give him a generic smile and dodge around him like she always did, and maybe he could get over this thing he had for her. Determined, planning words in his head, he stepped into the lab room doorway.

Just as Gina started to exit.

Head down, she was scanning a chart in her hand, totally oblivious. She plowed into him folder first. Papers flew and her arms wind-milled as she tried to keep her balance. Matt reached out to grab her but missed her arm. Horrified, he could only watch as she crashed to the hard tile. One of her tiny hands went down first to try to break her fall, and Matt heard the snap as soon as it hit. Her cry of pain made his stomach clench.

Oh, fuck! I've broken her.

He was on his knees in an instant, but the damage was done. Gina's eyes were awash in tears as she struggled to sit up. He put a trembling hand behind her back to support her. "Gina, I am so sorry," he began. His chest was tight with fear at what he had done and the urge to throw up was almost more than he could swallow down.

Her fly-away brown hair shone in the light as she shook her head and looked up at him with a tight smile. “No, Matt, it wasn’t your fault. I wasn’t watching where I was going.”

She moaned as she cradled her right wrist. It was quite obviously broken. Matt had had enough broken bones in his life to know the sound. Then the instant nausea, the disbelief.

Man, why hadn’t he just stood against the wall?

Gina cradled her arm protectively as footsteps approached. Dr. Hamilton stepped in, saw her on the floor and dropped to her other side.

“What happened?” he demanded. Gently, he took her wrist in his hands to examine it.

“I knocked her down,” Matt admitted.

Gina laughed, or tried to. “No, you didn’t, Matt. You were just standing there. *I* ran into *you.*” She gasped as the doctor turned her arm over.

“Definitely broken. We’ll get a splint to bind you up so you can go to the hospital. Any other injuries?” The older man peered into her eyes over the tops of his bifocals.

Gina turned her head and tested the rest of her body parts, but everything seemed to work correctly. “I think just my wrist. I put my hand down to catch myself.”

Madison, one of the other RNs, came in the door and almost tripped on the group on the floor. “Oh, my God. What happened?” She knelt down and rested a hand on Gina’s knee. “What did you do, Gina?”

“I fell and broke my arm. Klutz that I am.”

Matt rumbled deep in his chest, fists clenched. Why was she taking the responsibility? It was his fault, not hers. He must have looked truly alarming, because Gina reached out and rested her good hand on his arm. "I did it, Matt. Not you."

For the first time, Gina got a good look at Matt's face under the bill of his cap, and it worried her. He was pale, a tic in his jaw was pounding overtime and every one of his impressive muscles were clenched. The expression in his eyes made her think of a wild horse. Spooked. Shaken. "Matt, look at me." She waited until he did. "You did not do this. I did. Just like the five other times I've broken a bone. It was all me."

Something must have gotten through to him, because he eased back a bit on his haunches. Some of the fierceness left his bold face. He looked down where her hand rested on his tattooed arm, and Gina couldn't tell if he was surprised to see her touch him or what, but the expression on his face broke her heart. If the adrenalin wasn't beginning to wear off, and her arm wasn't beginning to throb, she would have probably taken more time to explore it.

"We need to get you to the hospital, Gina," Dr. Hamilton manipulated her arm into a soft splint as he spoke, and Gina gasped at the pain. Her eyes welled with tears as he gently strapped it on. He checked the circulation in her fingertips and guided her to hold her hand up, across her chest.

"Ok, it seems good. Let me get one of the nurses to run you over to the hospital."

"I can walk over. It's not that far." It was only actually a quarter of a mile, but Gina dreaded every step even as she made the offer.

"I'll take her."

Matt's voice brought all eyes to him. His skin took on a ruddy cast at the attention, but his eyes stayed determined.

"George still has to be seen. I'll take her over and come back for George."

Dr. Hamilton hesitated, his kind eyes shifting between Gina and the big man. "I don't know..."

"I'll take her," he repeated, and Gina could hear the determination in his voice.

Dr. Hamilton reached out to clap him on the back but changed his mind at the last second. "Ok. Thank you, Matt."

Before she knew what happened, Gina was gently lifted her to her feet and guided down the hallway. Madison retrieved her purse from the break room, promised to check on her later, and out the door they went. Matt made her wait at a bench out front and jogged to get his truck, a big black dually. He bumped the curb and pulled it right up to the bench.

Gina laughed at his total disregard for propriety, but she appreciated not having to walk any further than necessary because every step caused a ripple of pain to slide up her arm. He was so very gentle as he handed her up into the truck. Gina knew if she faltered, he would catch her in a heartbeat.

"You don't have to do this, Matt," she told him faintly. The pain was really beginning to get to her.

"I'm already doing it."

In less than a minute, he had pulled up in front of the emergency room doors. Gina tried to juggle her purse and grab the door handle with her left hand, but all she managed to do was drop the bag upside down on the ground. Contents scattered everywhere. Her lip gloss and mascara rolled away under the truck, and her credit cards fanned across the concrete.

"Damn it!" Frustrated tears filled her eyes.

Matt appeared in front of her as she prepared to drop to the ground to retrieve her things.

"Just hold on a minute," he grumbled. Leaning down, he snatched up all the items and shoved them in her purse, then zipped it closed when he was done. Gina was dismayed to see her cell phone in his big hands, in several pieces. "This didn't survive. I'm sorry."

The new, shiny, red phone had been an extravagance, and it made her sad to see it broken. Great, just great.

Slinging the purse strap over her shoulder, she left the pieces lying on the seat. She had other things to worry about right now.

Matt held onto her good arm as she slid down out of the cab, and Gina appreciated the help. It was bad enough having to go to the emergency room like this. Sprawling on the concrete was not something she wanted to do in front of so many people she knew. Delores Jones manned the front desk, as she had every day for twenty years, and Gina sagged into her arms gratefully as she came through the doors. Concern darkened the older woman's eyes.

"Oh, girl, what did you do to yourself?"

"Tumbleweed strikes again," Gina mumbled, cradling her arm. "I fell."

"We'll get you fixed right up, honey."

As Delores hustled her into the emergency, Gina turned to thank Matt for bringing her, but he was already gone.

Though everybody tried to be gentle in their care, Gina was frazzled and in pain three hours later when she tried to sign her release paperwork with her left hand. Delores was still at the front desk. Her smile creased her kind face until she saw the bulky blue cast on Gina's right arm and the sling that looped around her neck.

"Oh, dear. You poor thing. And look how whipped you are."

Gina forced a smile at her concern, though it took more energy than she cared to expend. She was so tired.

"Delores, can I get you to call me a cab? I'll have to get my car later."

"Oh, no, dear. No cab. Your lumberjack chauffer is here. " She waved a hand at the farthest, darkest corner of the waiting room.

Matt dwarfed the molded plastic chair he sat on. His ball-capped head was bent over his folded hands, and he was running his thumbs over themselves. Gina could understand why Delores had called him a lumberjack. The red and black plaid shirt strained across his broad shoulders.

The waiting room was crowded, but there was a cushion of several empty chairs around him, as if the people waiting felt the antagonism that rolled off of him.

She glanced back to Delores. "Has he been here all this time?"

The older woman smiled as she looked across the room. "He took George home, then came back to wait for you. He's been here about two hours."

"Thanks, Delores."

Gina shook her head in wonder. Why had he done that? Surely it wasn't guilt for knocking her down. It wasn't his fault she hadn't looked where she was going. She headed across the room.

Matt looked up at her approach, and Gina was sure she saw relief cross his heavy features.

"Matt, you didn't have to come back. I'm fine. Delores is going to call me a cab, and I'm heading home."

Her neck craned as he stood up in front of her. Jeez! She'd never looked up at him from this perspective before. She'd always just kind of dodged around him in the hallway at work, or spoken to him through the reception window. Now that he stood in front of her this way, she realized exactly how big he was. He was easily a foot taller than her. And his chest! There was no way she could ever wrap her arms around him.

Matt was a carpenter, but Gina knew he also laid brick. Surely the brick was responsible for all the rounded muscles. Her glance flicked down over his trim waist, heavy thighs, and the bulge at the apex of those thighs.

Gina was surprised when a tingle of attraction danced down her spine. Matt Calvin had a pretty awesome bod. She dragged her eyes back up to his face and realized he wasn't bad looking there, either, though not normally the type of guy who appealed to her. A little too grim, and controlled, and definitely too unapproachable. A brown beard lightly shadowed his jaw, and Gina tried to remember if she'd ever seen him clean shaven. She didn't think she had.

Overall, an aura of intimidation rolled off him. The dragon tattoo wrapped around his right forearm and disappeared under the rolled cuff of the flannel. She wondered how high it went.

He'd been coming into the office for a long time, but she didn't know a lot about him. She didn't think she'd ever seen him smile. Though she'd felt him watch her. A lot. Everybody at the office seemed leery of him, but she didn't know if there was a reason for that reserve or if they just reacted to the emotion they probably sensed inside him. He was so quiet when he brought George in. Never in the way.

Actually, he'd seemed embarrassed when George requested he stand outside the exam room rather than wait in the waiting room. But the old man was a little shaky on his feet, and more than once Gina had watched

Matt save him from a fall.

Looking at him now, Gina totally understood why the old man would be so secure in those strong arms. Matt didn't intimidate her, really. With little provocation, she herself could probably burrow into his embrace. Especially now, as weary as she was.

"Don't worry about the cab. I'll drive you home." His face was implacable, but his gaze flared with some emotion.

Gina eyed him. "Ok, Matt, I'll let you drive me home. Actually," she said with a tired sigh, "I would love for you to take me home."

Her acquiescence eased the tight lines around his eyes, and Gina noticed they were a pretty light grayish-green. The sawdust covered cap usually shaded his face, and Gina couldn't specifically remember noticing his eyes before.

Hmmm.

Towering over her, Matt guided her out of the hospital and to his truck, parked just a few spaces away. Gina had to use the running board to get up inside the big vehicle, and she automatically reached for the safety handle with her right hand, in spite of the sling she wore. Pain sliced through her arm and up into her shoulder, stealing her breath. Matt's big hands gripped her waist and guided her into the seat. For several long seconds, they lingered there, before finally pulling away. She shivered with reaction. She'd almost fallen again.

Gina forced a smile to her lips. "Thank you."

His head tipped forward until the bill shaded his face. "No problem," he mumbled. Slamming the door, he circled the front of the truck.

Gina cradled her bulky arm to her chest and leaned back against the seat. For as big as it was, the truck rode surprisingly smooth. Gina felt her eyelids drifting down.

She was so tired. Forcing herself up, she focused ahead deliberately. She needed to tell Matt how to get to her house.

"If you turn left at Alber. . .," she told him firmly, before relaxing her posture for just a moment.

Matt couldn't help but smile as he looked at the sleeping woman beside him. She had literally fallen asleep in the middle of the sentence. Not that he needed directions to her house. He knew exactly where she lived, less than five blocks from his own house. He'd known the first week after he'd seen her at the fair. One of the men working for him at the time had asked her out, but the date had gone sour. Matt's impression of Gina had gone up at the rebuff. The man had been slime.

He braced her shoulder with his hand as he turned right. He couldn't help but feel how small she was. And fragile.

And breakable.

Guilt ate at him. He should have been able to catch her when she'd fallen. Hell, he'd been right there.

Memories of his own mother in the same position had dogged him for hours. The only difference was, Matt's father had deliberately shoved her down. And Matt had been too small to catch her, even though he had been close enough. She'd left not long after that.

Matt shoved the memories aside and focused on the drive to Gina's house. As he pulled into the gravel driveway of the little two-story cottage, she mumbled something under her breath, but stayed asleep. Matt turned off the ignition, slid out and slammed his door deliberately. She never roused. Circling to her side, he opened the door. She had melted into a boneless heap in the seat and her head rested on her purse in the middle. Her broken wrist was cradled to her chest.

Matt thought she looked incredibly appealing, lying

there all soft and unguarded.

He squeezed her shoulder. She never moved.

"Gina."

He shook her. Still no response. Matt debated for several seconds before he finally dug her overloaded keychain from the depths of her purse. He needed to get her into the house. His legs brushed top-heavy flowers as he walked by and took the few porch steps two at a time.

Unlocking the door, he peeked inside long enough to ascertain there was a couch in the living room he could lay her on, then returned to the truck. Gina hardly roused as he turned her over and lifted her in his arms, her head to the left and her feet to the right. She mumbled, and he almost thought he heard her say his name.

Matt's steps faltered a bit as she wrapped her tiny fist into his shirt and nestled her face into his chest. Need roared through him at the innocent contact, and he couldn't help but squeeze her to him. What a tempting creature she was. He couldn't believe he actually held her in his arms, something he'd dreamt about for so long. Unable to deny himself, his steps slowed as he ascended the stairs.

As he maneuvered them through the doorway, he took care not to bump her head or feet. Gina sighed as he laid her on the tan couch, sinking into the cushions. Matt pulled the afghan from the back of the couch over her, tucked her in, and settled into an upholstered chair opposite the couch. Maybe he would just wait for her to wake up. He could watch her as she slept and imagine for a heartbeat of time that he belonged there, with her.

Chapter Two

Gina woke to pain in her arm and something tantalizing her nose. Blinking, she was surprised to see she was in her own house, lying on the couch. The hassock to the chair was wedged up against the front. Tossing the afghan away, she sat up. She didn't remember moving the stool over or covering herself with the blanket. Those pills had really knocked her out. The pain in her arm was manageable though.

She swung her legs to the floor and stood, then headed toward the kitchen. Who on earth was cooking?

She thought she'd see Laurie from a couple houses down or maybe Madison from work. She certainly wasn't prepared to see Matt Calvin standing at her stove, stirring what appeared to be soup.

"Matt?"

Red soup splattered on the white smooth-top stove when he jerked around. "Gina! I didn't know you were up." He dropped the spoon to the counter and moved toward her. "Are you feeling okay? Do you need anything?"

Gina smiled at the big man's concern. "No, I'm fine. A little achy, but I think that's just the pain pills wearing off. Those little suckers work good. I don't remember anything after giving you directions to the house."

Matt ducked his head and brushed at a spot on his nose. "Well, you kinda didn't even get through the directions before you passed out."

Gina stared at him, dumfounded. "What?"

He nodded once at her wide-eyed stare. "You passed out right in the middle of a sentence. I had an idea where you lived, though. I found your keys in your purse and brought you in."

"You carried me in? Oh. My. God. You carried me in the house."

Gina felt the blush start at the tips of her toes and move to the top of her head. How humiliating! No, she wasn't fat, but she certainly couldn't be considered lightweight either. Curvy was a better description. "Matt, I'm so sorry. No man should have to do that."

His pale eyes met hers for a long, intense moment before they slid away. "I enjoyed it actually."

Once again that energizing tingle washed through her. Had he just hit on her? Big, scary, tattooed Matt? Kind of? Hell of a change from this afternoon when he couldn't even talk to her.

She was distracted when he placed a bowl of tomato soup in front of her, followed by a perfectly grilled cheese. Gina didn't even realize she was hungry until the smell reached her nose and her tummy growled.

"Thank you," she sighed.

Matt turned away before she could see his face. She reached for the spoon with her left hand, but fumbled the thing. It plopped into the soup with a splash.

"Damn it!" she gasped as soup landed on her scrubs top. Right arm cradled to her stomach, she breathed deeply for several long seconds. When she looked up, Matt had knelt beside her chair. His dark brows were furrowed in concern. Gina shook her head and smiled ruefully.

"This is going to take a while to get used to, I guess."

Nodding his head, he pushed to his feet. Gina was fascinated by the play of muscles in his tree-trunk sized thighs. He had to have done some serious lifting for them to be that massive.

With her left hand, she took a bite of the buttery, gooey sandwich. It melted in her mouth. Matt stood at the counter, his back to her. "This is wonderful, Matt. Thank you so much."

He turned to acknowledge her thanks, and Gina was surprised to see him eating from the counter.

"Oh, sit down, please. Why are you standing to eat? I won't bite, I promise."

Matt regarded her for several long moments before he turned with his plate to sit across from her. He settled gingerly in the wooden Captain's chair, and Gina wondered if finding one sturdy enough was a problem. He was a huge man, barrel-chested and brawny. Sometimes he deliberately intimidated people, she thought, so that he wouldn't have to talk to them. But that size was what made Gina feel safe. He had a bowl of soup as well, and a single sandwich. Surely it took more than that to fill him up?

"Was George okay today?" she asked.

Matt nodded his head. "He was fine. Blood work was fine. As ornery as ever."

Gina smiled and shook her head. "You know, that man actually pinched my butt the last time you brought him in. And cackled about it."

"That sounds like him. He's always been like that."

Gina took another bite of sandwich. "How long have you known him?"

Matt looked off in the distance for a few moments,

thinking. "Hmmm, at least twenty-five years or so. He was a drinking buddy of my father's. After Rick died, George helped me out."

Gina thought it was curious that Matt referred to his father by his first name. If what she had heard was correct, there would definitely be a distance. One of the girls at the office had gone to school with Matt, and she remembered many times when he'd come in with bruises darkening his face. Paula remembered he'd dropped out when he was sixteen, but she didn't know what had happened to him after that.

"When did your father die?" she asked.

He looked at her from underneath the bill of his cap, and it was pretty obvious this was not something he wanted to talk about. But he answered.

"Ten years ago. Got drunk off his ass and plowed head-on into a tree. Killed him instantly."

"I'm sorry," she said.

Matt waved a rough hand in the air. "Don't be. It was a relief."

Gina could only gape in surprise as he stood and gathered their dirty dishes to take to the dishwasher. Things must have been really bad to cause that kind of resentment. She just couldn't imagine the life he must have had to make him almost happy that his father was gone. Her family was the heart-stone of her life.

She groaned as she thought of her mother. If she didn't do damage control, and quick, Mom would be down here in a split second to take care of her. And as much as she loved her family, she treasured the independence she had gained when she'd moved away.

"What's wrong?"

Once again, Matt was at her side, ready to help her do anything. With her left hand, Gina pushed her messy hair away from her face. Heck, she thought, how was she even going to do her hair? Or go to the bathroom?

Pushing the worries aside, she focused on Matt. "My mother is going to want to come down when she finds out about my wrist. And if she finds out from somebody else about it, she's going to think I'm hiding something from her. I have to call her."

Matt nodded and reached for the phone hanging on the wall. Passing her the handset, he offered to punch in the numbers. Gina let him, simply because she didn't want to drop it and break it like her cell.

Matt pressed the numbers, then disappeared into the living room to give her some privacy. Gina listened to the ringing at the other end of the line, and her stomach tightened just a little more with each ring. The sixth ring was cut off mid-way.

"Hello."

Relief rolled over her, and tears clogged her throat as she heard her father's gruff voice. "Hi, Daddy."

"Hey, Pumpkin, how are you? Haven't talked to you for a while. Had that golf thing last Saturday, so I missed your regular call."

"I know, and that's ok. I didn't have anything in particular to talk about." Gina paused and took a deep breath. "Uh, Dad?"

"Yeah, Pumpkin?"

"Is Mom around? I mean, is she in the room?"

Her father was silent for several long moments. "No," he said finally. "Why?"

"Well, I, uh, kinda hurt myself, and I don't want her to go off the deep end about it. It's just my wrist. I fell at the office and broke it. It's a clean break, no shards or anything. I've already got the cast on and everything."

"Which arm was it? And when did you do it?"

"It's my right arm, which is going to be difficult, and I did it this morning at work. A, uh, friend of mine took me to the hospital to get the cast. I'm fine, though. They did blood tests just to make sure, and my bones are fine. No more brittle than the average person's, they said."

Relief eased her father's voice. "Good, good. So, I guess you want me to run interference with your mother?"

"Yes," she said firmly. "There's no need for her to drive two hundred miles just to look at my cast. I'm fine. Besides, I'll be up there next weekend for Charli's sweet sixteen party."

"Hmmm," her father mumbled. "Okay, Pumpkin, as long as you're sure you're all right."

"I am, Dad, I promise."

"Okay. You better be. If you're not, your mother will tan my hide."

Gina smiled at the familiar complaint. "I love you, Dad. See you next weekend."

"Love you too, baby. See you then."

Gina was smiling as she crossed the kitchen to replace the handset. She loved her dad. He was always willing to let her spread her wings. Her mother, on the other hand, worried incessantly.

"They upset with you?"

Startled, she turned from the counter. Matt stood just a few feet behind her. "Jeez, you scared me. For as big as you are, you move very quietly. No, they're not mad. Actually, that was just my dad. He'll let Mom know what happened. He was just concerned."

Matt nodded his head like he understood, but Gina was sure he didn't. "When I was a child," she told him, "I had leukemia. Took me years of radiation, drugs, and chemotherapy to get over it. Mom was right there with me the entire time. I've been in remission since I was about eleven. She still worries, though, a lot. It was after I broke a bone that we found out I had the cancer. Heck, she may still come down if Dad can't convince her otherwise."

Matt frowned fiercely. "So, could this mean your illness is coming back?" he demanded.

Gina raised her brows at the tone. "No, no. I had them check my white cell count while I was in there, and it's fine. I'm fine. Really. Just more clumsy than the average human."

Matt still looked worried, and Gina thought it was endearing. She glanced down at his heavy fists. They were clenched, as if he wanted to punch something. That emotion she sensed under his implacable expression was a little closer to the top now. She hadn't known that the thought of her being sick would upset him so much. It was sweet, though, actually. Made her heart warm.

Where had this man come from? Six hours ago, he had been an obstacle in the hallway at work. Now he was very close to being a friend.

She glanced at the clock, surprised to see it had crept toward evening. Man, being drugged out of your mind really made the time fly. "Matt, I'm so sorry. Am I keeping you from something? I just kind of wrecked everybody's day, didn't I?"

Matt shook his head and tugged on the bill of his cap to shade his eyes. "Nah, you're not keeping me from anything. And you didn't wreck my day."

He smiled slightly, surprising Gina with the hint of charm in his smile. The man was so reserved; she couldn't remember him ever smiling at her. Or anybody else for that matter.

"Are you sure nobody will be waiting for you? Your girlfriend or wife or anything?"

Blazing heat spread across her cheeks. Why on Earth had she asked that?

Not that he noticed. Matt's head tipped even further down, until all she could see was the button on top of the faded blue hat. "No, ma'am. Actually," he said, standing from the chair and towering over her, "I need to go. Let you get some rest."

Gina looked up at him and found it hard to believe she had never noticed him before. He seemed like a very nice man, in spite of the ink on his arm and his prickly nature. Quiet. Was the dragon that decorated his forearm a turn-off? Not really, she decided. It was actually kind of pretty.

She was surprised to realize she didn't want him to go, but she didn't know how to make him to stay.

"Well, okay." She followed him out of the kitchen and down the hallway, wrist cradled to her chest. Gina was struck with how he dwarfed everything. He was almost too broad to fit through the doorways. Automatically, he tipped his head as he walked under the doorjambs. Gina didn't think he was actually tall enough to hit them, but he had probably done it enough to learn to be cautious.

Her eyes drifted from his broad shoulders, down to his narrow hips and settled on his tight ass. Damn! How had she never noticed *that* before? She was a butt-woman all the way, and Matt Calvin had the finest tush she'd seen in years. A tingle of heat spread through her belly. Followed quickly by guilt. He was here to take care of her and she was checking out his butt.

Matt swung the front door open and ducked through. He didn't say anything, and Gina wondered if he would leave without telling her goodbye. Or without even looking at her.

"Goodbye, Matt. And thank you for everything you did. I really appreciate it."

The big man paused for just a moment at the front of the black truck. "You're welcome." Tipping his hat, he continued on around the hood and climbed in. The big vehicle roared to life, backed out of her driveway and took off.

Gina stared down the street for a long time after he disappeared. Inside the house, her phone rang. Sighing, she turned and let herself into the house. "Coming, Mom," she muttered.

Matt took his first deep breath of the night when Gina's house faded from sight as he accelerated away. Claustrophobia had eaten at him. The entire time he'd been inside, he'd been worried about breaking something, or, God forbid, bumping into her while she was in pain.

He gritted his teeth at the thought of what she was going through. Because of him. She could explain it away all she wanted to, but he knew the guilt rested solely on his shoulders. If he hadn't tried to talk to her and been in that doorway, she never would have fallen in the first place.

The tears in her ice-blue eyes had been the worst. For somebody like her, with a regular life, that pain was an anomaly, something they didn't feel every day. In a heartbeat, he would take it away and just merge it in with his own. Hell, a broken wrist would be a drop in the bucket compared to what he was used to.

He looked at his fists. The thumbnail on his left hand was black from a distracted hammer strike and would probably fall off soon. His knuckles were scraped from moving concrete blocks yesterday. There was a cut on the meat of his right hand that just would not seal and the fresh coat of superglue had broken open.

Those tears had made her eyes sparkle, though. Prettier than anything he had ever seen before. Even with her kinky hair a mess around her face, she appealed to him like no other person ever had. It was difficult to look at her very long because he lost his train of thought and found himself floundering.

Hell, not like that was anything new.

What the heck was he doing though, seriously? After talking to her, and seeing her pretty, feminine house with the family pictures plastered over the walls, the differences between them could not be more clear. A white trash grunt like him had no business even being near her. For four years he had watched her, leery of making any kind of move because he didn't know whether he had anything she needed. Now that he had spoken to her and gotten a glimpse into her shining life, he knew for a fact he had no business being there.

A sparkle of red caught his eye and he glanced down at the truck seat. Her phone was there, sadly scattered in three pieces. A crack split the touch-screen almost perfectly in half. Picking up one piece, he held it to his nose experimentally. Peaches and cream tickled his senses. She had been so heartbroken that it had shattered.

With a heavy sigh, he snatched up his own phone and punched in a number by memory.

"'lo." The word was muffled, as if the speaker's mouth were full.

"Are you eating, Monroe?"

There were noises at the other end of the line. "Mmmm hmmm. Wassup?"

Matt shook his head in the dark truck. Anderson Monroe had been known to close down buffet lines at night because they were out of food. The man was a walking trash compactor and his best friend in the world.

Actually, he was one of the few people Matt considered an actual friend and the only person who knew about his infatuation with Gina Carruthers. "I tried to talk to her today."

There was silence on the other end of the line for several long seconds. "And how did that go?"

"Oh, wonderfully. Ended up knocking her on the ground and breaking her wrist."

Monroe choked on the other end of the line. "No fucking way! You're not serious."

Matt sighed and pinched the bridge of his nose. "I wish I wasn't. We crashed into each other in the damn doctor's office. She fell to the ground and snapped her wrist like a toothpick."

"What'd she do? Is she pissed? Oh, you're in jail and I need to come get you, huh?"

"No, she's not pissed. I drove her home and she seemed to appreciate the help. I feel guilty as hell, though. Totally didn't happen the way I wanted it to."

"Well, yeah, I guess not." Monroe laughed and took a swig of something. "So, are you done crushin' on this girl now or what?"

Matt sighed and rested his head against the seat rest. "I guess." He cleared his tight throat and sought a different topic. "So, where are you right now?"

"Boulder. Chasing a wildfire. Been on for way too long. This is my first chance to get some food and rest."

For the first time Matt noticed how raspy his buddy's voice was. Guilt swamped him.

"Hell, Monroe. I'll let you go, then. Call me when you aren't chasing fires and sucking smoke. Maybe we can catch a game or something sometime."

"Sure thing, Matt. Maybe it's good this happened, though. This girl wasn't the one for you. I'll holler at you when I get back in the state."

"Okay. Later."

Monroe had already hung up. Matt tossed his phone

to the seat and stared out the dark windshield. Monroe was right. She wasn't the one for him.

Gina hung up the phone in relief. Her mother would stay home, reassured after talking to her daughter. It had been a close thing, but Gina had promised to see her next week for her sister Charli's sixteenth birthday. Then reminded her mother pointedly that she had a lot of plans to pull together before the party itself. Mom had agreed she still had a lot to do, and if Gina was sure, she would just see her in a few days.

Gina was sure.

Not that she didn't appreciate her mother's concern, because she did. But sometimes it was a bit...too much. And it all stemmed from her illness years ago.

When the leukemia had been discovered, her mother had cleaned the house obsessively, and Gina had been quarantined in her room, basically, for months at the height of her treatments. She hadn't been able to see her friends at all. Family only sporadically. The summer of her ninth year had been the loneliest time of her life. Upstairs in the back bedroom of her parent's house, she had journal after journal sitting on the shelves, full of a sick young girl's fanciful dreams. It had been the only escape she'd had.

Her mother had meant well, but it had still been difficult.

With a sigh, she looked around the kitchen. Dishes were going to have to wait. The throbbing arm thing was really starting to get to her, and she needed to take a pain pill.

Her purse was in the living room, probably exactly where Matt had dropped it when he'd brought it in. She found the prescription bottle on the bottom and read the directions as she headed back to the kitchen.

Running a glass of water from the fridge dispenser, she fumbled the lid off the bottle, downed a pill, and hoped it would work quickly. She looked at the dirty dishes again and cringed. Tomorrow. Maybe.

Climbing the stairs reminded her how tired she was. She debated taking a bath but finally decided against it. She would probably fall asleep and drown. Wouldn't that be the perfect end to a perfect day?

Instead she wet a washcloth, wiped her face down and used the toilet, then went into her bedroom to find her nightgown. The sling took forever to get off one-handed. She doubted she'd be able to get it on again without some major finagling. Her bright pink, tomato-stained scrubs went into the dirty clothes basket beside the door and she settled her long t-shirt over her hips. It was soft cotton and immediately made her want to curl up in bed to sleep. But she delayed and crossed to the window.

No lights were on in the house next door, but that could just mean that Chuck had forgotten to pay the bill again in his drunken stupor. Sticking her head out the window into the moist night air, she whistled softly, then waited to see if anybody came to the second story window directly across from her own.

There was a scrabbling in the dark below her and she was surprised to see Gabe in the bushes below her window. "What are you doing down there?" she whispered at him.

Gabe glanced back at his house, as if he expected Chuck to come running around the corner any second. "Can I come in?" he whispered back.

Gina motioned him inside. Gabe knew where the hidden key was. She had shown him the day she'd found him huddled under her porch in the rain. If she was around, though, he always asked to come in.

Gina awkwardly pulled on a pair of sleep pants then waited at the top of the stairs for him to come up. The young boy was nine years old, but his slight form was more the size of a seven year old. And as he slipped up the stairs in the shadows tonight, he seemed even smaller, curled in on himself. "What's wrong?" she asked, as soon as he crested the stairs.

The boy hung back, afraid to leave the last shadow to step closer to her. Gina took the step herself and rested a hand on his shoulder. "What's wrong, Little Man?"

He flung his arms around her waist and buried his face in her T-shirt. Gina felt tears come to her eyes and struggled to push them away. If Gabe saw her cry over him, he would man-up and not come to her any more. As young as he was, he had an amazing amount of pride.

That same pride made him pull away within just a few seconds. He avoided her eyes by looking at the floor. Swiping at his face, he glanced back down the stairs as if he thought somebody were after him.

"You relocked the door, right?" Gina asked.

The boy nodded his head firmly and met her gaze for the first time.

"Okay, then. Let's go in your room and watch some tube, want to?"

Once again, his bright blond head bobbed up and down, and he allowed Gina to lead him into her spare bedroom. It wasn't his actually, but any time he needed to get away from the tension in his own house, he was allowed to come here and chill out. Gina turned on the small light beside the door and motioned to the futon. "Park it, my man."

Gabe crossed the room and melted onto the mattress in a slump. Gina frowned as she retrieved the remote control from the top of the TV. This was a little unusual, even for him. Normally he was all tough-guy, nobody messes with me. Tonight he seemed, well, defeated. She sat down beside him. "What's wrong, Gabe?"

He shrugged his shoulders and glanced up at her. "Nothing really." His eyes fell to her wrist on her lap and he gasped. "What happened?" he demanded.

Gina told him about plowing into a mountain named Matt and the resulting broken bone. His wide blue eyes barely blinked as he listened to her story. Holding the heavy thing out, she turned it over for his inspection. The movements hurt, but it was more like the weight of the cast hurt.

"Did he do it on purpose?" Grim resolved tightened his young face.

"No, Gabe. Of course not. It was an accident."

Gabe didn't look convinced. Of course, he knew about 'accidents'. His parents had died in an accident and left him in the situation he was in now. She actually didn't think his situation had been much better before they'd died. Gina tried to distract him from their troubles by pressing a button on the remote. She flipped to Animal Planet and the popular cop show they liked was on. "Is this okay?"

Nodding, he settled against the back of the futon, but he reached out a hand to touch her knee. Just a fingertip, but it was a connection. Gina rested her right arm across the back of the couch and let her casted fingers rest in his hair. She couldn't move them much, but again, it was a connection.

The night was long and arduous for Gina. She just could not find a comfortable position to lie in. The drugs helped a little, but there was still an ache that couldn't be touched.

At six AM she went downstairs to get breakfast and start the day. Gabe was gone and the door was locked, so she assumed he had gone home. She hoped Chuck would work this weekend and the little boy would have some peace. She hadn't seen anything physically wrong with the boy, but the verbal abuse seemed to be escalating. He'd been positively needy last night and it broke her heart.

Patrice, her friend at Children's Services, told her they could not technically do anything until some kind of abuse manifested in the home. So far Chuck only screamed. And occasionally forgot to buy food for the boy. From Patrice's perspective, though, any relative was better than no relative. Gina knew better. Gabe was suffering, so she did anything she could to help him out.

It was Saturday, so she didn't have to go into work, but her body didn't know that. She had several things she needed to do today. Retrieve her car from the office, buy groceries she'd been putting off getting for the last week, and look at new cell phones. None of which she actually wanted to do. Her eyes were gritty, her hair wild, and she was overall tired.

And she didn't feel any better when Madison stuck her head in the front door and called out a hello. Her friend looked glorious today, long, dark hair in an artfully messy knot on top of her head and her gray eyes twinkling with humor as she dropped a drive-thru bag on the kitchen table. She accepted Madison's hug and sat across the table from her to show her the cast.

"I swear, Gina, you could get hurt in a padded room."

Gina laughed because she was totally right. "I know. At least it wasn't my leg or my tailbone like last time. This should be easier to deal with."

Madison laughed at her. "Right. You'll just have to switch everything you've done right handed all your life to your left. Easy as pie, huh?"

"Well. . ."

"So how did you get home? I tried to call your cell phone but it kept ringing busy."

"I broke my phone at the hospital. Dropped it in the parking lot and it shattered, so I'll have to get another one in a couple days. And Matt Calvin drove me home."

For several long seconds, Madison just stared at her. "He stayed that long just to drive you home?"

Gina shrugged. "He took George home after his check-up then came back for me. I think he feels guilty for hurting me."

"Huh. I never would have thought he'd do something like that. He doesn't seem the Good-Samaritan type. Too frickin' intimidating." Her eyes brightened. "He does have a nice ass, though."

Gina knew her cheeks were turning pink when Madison hooted and pointed a finger at her. "Uh- huh, you've noticed."

She shrugged, totally guilty. "Just last night, actually, when he was walking out the door."

She didn't tell Madison that he had pretty green eyes, or that he didn't intimidate her like he used to.

Madison glanced at her watch and grimaced. "I have to run, dear. I promised Slade I'd meet him for a round of tennis."

"Slade? His name is actually Slade?" Gina couldn't help but curl her lip.

Her friend nodded. "I know. Bad, huh? Actually, I think he picked it himself. Because he's just that special." Madison winked, and Gina knew the relationship was going nowhere. Madison went through men like she did shoes and none of them ever seemed to work out.

They walked to the door and hugged as Madison let

herself out. "If you need anything, give me a call. Have you talked to the boss yet?"

"No. I'll call him later."

"Okay. I'll check on you Monday if I don't see you at work."

Gina waved her off and immediately deflated. Madison was a ball of motion and Gina just couldn't keep up with her today like she normally did. She walked back into the kitchen and wrinkled her nose at the take-out bag. It turned her stomach to even smell it. She tossed in into the fridge.

Maybe a shower would wake her up. But even that was going to be a hassle. She dug beneath the kitchen sink for a trash bag and wound the thing around her cast. She secured the excess with a heavy duty rubber band. Twisting and tugging, she managed to get the thing pretty tightly secured. Then realized she probably should have put the trash bag on *after* she had gotten undressed.

Gina clomped up the stairs and decided everything in town could wait until tomorrow. Tiredness dragged her down. The car wasn't going anywhere. There were security cameras mounted in the lot, so she doubted anything would happen to it. She would get her shower done and lay down for a nap. Hell, she thought, as she crested the top of the stairs, panting. Maybe she would nap first. Stripping off the bag and rubber band, she fell across the mattress and pulled the covers over top of herself.

Chapter Three

Several hours later, she was downstairs loading her washer when somebody rang her front door bell. It wouldn't be Gabe, because he usually knocked quietly on the back door when he knew she was home, then let himself in. Smoothing her hair behind her headband, she navigated through the house.

She certainly didn't expect to see Matt when she opened the door. The brilliant burst of happiness at the sight of his big, bulky body and cagey eyes surprised her with its intensity. "Matt! What are you doing here?"

"I, uh, brought your car for you."

Gina frowned and looked at her little driveway beside her house. Well, damn, it *was* there. The big dually was backed in front of it and there was a car dolly on the back. Her little Toyota was dwarfed by the big truck and Gina thought Matt probably could have picked the thing up and put it in the bed of the pick-up himself. She laughed at the imagery and turned back to Matt.

"I can't believe you did that. I was going to go get it tomorrow. How did you get inside it?"

He rubbed his scraped hand over his bristly chin. "Well, you don't really need to get inside when you haul it on a dolly like that. I just strapped up your front tires and went."

Gina felt warmth spread in her chest at his actions. That was so sweet. "Matt, thank you so much. That is so far beyond being nice. You didn't have to do that."

His big feet shifted on the boards of the porch and he settled his thumbs into the corners of his hip pockets. Pale, grey-green eyes flashed up to meet her own. "I know, but I didn't think you'd feel like going to do it in the next couple of days. Broken bones ache pretty fierce when they're first broken."

Gina nodded her head in agreement. Stepping back, she held the front door open for him. "Please, come in. Can I get you a cup of coffee?"

Matt stepped inside, careful not to bump against her. He crossed to stand at the base of the stairs and shoved his hands into his hip pockets. Today he was wearing a dark blue Carhart t-shirt that strained across his body and well-worn, baggy carpenter jeans. The same faded blue ball cap was on his head. Gina thought he looked pretty darn cute.

"No, I don't need coffee. I, uh, won't be staying long."

Gina was disappointed and she knew it showed on her face. "Are you sure? I can throw us together some lunch or something."

Matt shook his head and reached deep into his right pocket. For several seconds he played with something in his hand before he finally pulled it out and shoved it at her.

Gina reached out to take the red thing from him.

"My phone?" she gasped. She looked at the device in disbelief. It had been shattered. The screen cracked. "How did you do this?"

Matt shifted on his big feet and glanced at her. "I have a similar phone, so I took it in and they replaced it.

Switched your SIM card. You should be ready to go, but you need to try it to make sure."

She touched the screen and all her contacts came up. Tears came to her eyes, and she didn't try to hide them. "You did this for me?"

Matt felt like he was falling as he looked at her blue eyes all awash in tears again, but for a good reason this time. He shrugged uncomfortably. Maybe he should have just left it on the car seat or something. No, he did right by bringing it to her. If this happiness shining in her face was the last thing he saw before he left, it would be enough.

When Gina stepped forward and wrapped her arms around him, resting her curly head against his chest, Matt was floored. And humbled. And shamed. She was beautiful, and sweet, and had more friends than he had nails in his garage, and she was wrapped around him like he meant something to her.

For the briefest second he wrapped his arms around her and squeezed, then stepped back. Or tried to step back. With his feet already up against the bottom stair, he couldn't get them untangled fast enough from hers. He felt his weight shift and knew he wouldn't be able to keep them upright. Swinging his right arm out to break their fall, he encountered the base post of the banister. Clenching fiercely, his muscles strained as he tried to keep them both vertical.

It was no use. Under their substantial combined weight, the post snapped.

Matt landed on the stairs hard, with Gina clutched to his chest. He didn't even care that he had fallen. His foremost concern was for her and her recent injury. So, even though he had stairs digging into his back and a four inch by four inch post had conked him on the head, he cradled Gina as protectively as he could.

Gina looked down at him in a daze, her left hand clutched in his t-shirt and her right held against her chest. Her eyes were wide with fright and her hair more wild than normal. Their legs had gotten tangled and her right leg was over his lap. Looking down, it was easy enough to imagine another, more intimate situation, and in spite of the crazy circumstance, his body responded. Even as he tried to ignore the tempting picture she made, his dick hardened.

"Uh, wow," she laughed. She tried to adjust her leg, and Matt knew the exact second she noticed his erection. All movement stopped, and a pink tinge colored her cheeks, but she looked up with a smile, which surprised him. "We, uh, need to quit meeting like this. Really." She pressed a quick, hard kiss to his chin before she scrambled off his lap. She took several steps back and surveyed the damage.

Matt could see the dismay on her face when she saw the mess and he felt his face heat with embarrassment. He pushed the base post off his shoulder and levered himself up off the step, then turned back to look.

God, it was bad. These cookie-cutter houses had been here for a long time, and the age showed in the frailty of the wood. The old base had snapped at the bottom and ripped up two of the hardwood floor boards. The post was still attached to the banister, but six of the spindles had broken as well and were leaning in over the stairs. The only good thing he could see was that the long banister itself was not one piece. It was two sections. In his mind, he had already begun the fix.

Humiliation gnawed at his chest, and his face felt as red as it had ever been. Sweat broke out on his forehead and ran down his cheek. "I am so sorry," he choked out. Disgust beat at him. He clenched his jaw so hard his teeth creaked. He had turned out exactly as Rick had said years ago. Big, stupid, clumsy ox. The man had been dead for years, but Matt could still hear his voice as if he stood next to him. *No good for anything*.

Taking a deep breath he dared to glance at Gina.

She smiled up at him gently. Her brows were raised in humor, and her left hand was propped on her hip. The right was nestled between her breasts. But there was no censure in her eyes. She shrugged her shoulders and giggled. "We just can't seem to have a normal conversation, can we?"

Unable to believe that she wasn't mad, Matt shook his head. "No, ma'am."

Her gaze suddenly zeroed in on something and she reached up with her left hand to grasp his chin, turning his head to the right. Gentle fingers lifted his hair off his head and Matt realized his hat was on the floor. He hadn't even noticed it being gone.

"Oh, Matt. Come on."

Gina clutched his hand in hers and tugged him toward the kitchen. Once there, she pulled a chair away from the table and swung it around in front of the sink. "Sit down, please. You conked your head pretty good with that post."

Matt reached up and probed the area. He pulled back bloody fingers. He hadn't even noticed he'd been hurt. Wiping the side of his face with a paper towel she shoved at him, he realized it was blood running down his face, not sweat. Once he recognized the blood, the area started to throb in pain.

Gina rummaged in a low cupboard, most of her body buried inside. It was the first time Matt had ever seen her in jeans and he had to admit he liked them much better than scrubs. They cupped her ass to perfection.

When she backed out and stood up, she had a white first-aid box in her hand. Popping the latch one-handed, she ripped open a square gauze pad and pressed it to his head. Matt winced at the thought of getting her dirty and tried to put his hand in her place. "Hold that there a minute," she told him.

She rummaged in the box again and ripped open another gauze square with her teeth. Peering in yet again, she set out several sterile cotton swabs in paper. Matt couldn't help but pull away a bit as she ripped them open and reached for his head. Gina paused and looked down at him. "I'm not going to hurt you."

Matt felt like a heel. It was second nature to pull away from anybody. "I know. Just habit. Go ahead."

Gina reached forward again, slower this time, and Matt just felt plain stupid. It wasn't her fault he had been raised to expect being hit.

She lifted away the gauze pad and he was startled to see how much blood was on it. Gina must have seen the look because she pressed the second one to his head gently and tossed the used square onto the paper it had been originally wrapped in. "Head wounds always bleed a lot. You probably just have a tiny cut. We'll hold this here for a minute and then clean it and see what we have."

Matt tipped his head into the pressure, praying that the thing would stop bleeding sooner. Gina stood so close, he could smell peaches. It had to be her shampoo or body lotion.

For the first time, he realized his eyes rested on her breasts, directly in front of him. He slammed his eyes closed, but he could still see the gentle swell of the purple T-shirt stretched thin over the heaviest part of them and the shape of her nipples at the crest.

Blood began to head south and it was all he could do not to tug her to him. He crossed his hands over his lap and the erection that hadn't completely gone away, but it did no good. He was hard as a board as she pulled the second pad away and tossed it to the counter. She stepped away for a moment to retrieve the swabs, then came back to stand in front of him again. This time, though, she leaned forward to look at the wound even closer.

Matt felt his breath stall in his lungs as he was blasted by the heat of her body and the scent of her skin. Only this time, her breasts were mere inches from his face. He had no idea what size they were, but he knew if he shaped his hands to them, they would fill them perfectly. It was a battle to keep his hands clenched together.

"Now this may hurt a bit," she warned as she reached across with her casted hand to pull the hair away from the cut.

Good. It did hurt a little bit, but not enough to distract his body from what was directly in front of his face. He closed his eyes again and tried to breathe slowly, but her scent was all around him, keeping him on edge.

"Well," she said suddenly, "looks like it's just a little spot. It could probably use a stitch, though."

"No stitches," he grumbled.

"You may have a scar if we just bandage it," she warned.

Shrugging, he pointed to his right eyebrow, which had a line through the middle of the brow where his father had tossed him against the coffee table. "I'm used to scars."

He'd probably shock her if he showed them all to her.

When she pulled back and looked in his face, Matt wished he had kept his damn mouth shut.

"How did you get that one?" she asked.

Yep, stupid, that's what you get. "Coffee table when I was a kid."

Gina seemed to know there was more to the story than he was saying, but she didn't press. Pulling the swabs from their paper sleeves, she cleaned his head. It was difficult for her to place the butterfly bandages with the cast on her hand, so he held his own hair out of the way. With a last swipe of a pad, she was done and stepped away.

Matt took his first deep breath in several minutes as she cleaned up the bloody paper mess, and his brain cleared. He had other things to worry about.

"I'll fix the banister," he said.

Gina smiled at him over her shoulder. "I know you will. I never had any doubt. Honestly, that thing has been loose for a long time."

Matt frowned at the lie. She was trying to make him feel better. The post had been sturdy. Until he'd grabbed it, that is. "I'll go get my tools. I'll shift my jobs around that I had planned for this weekend. Are you going to be home for a while?"

Gina nodded and crossed to wash her hand and the tips of her fingers on her casted hand. She dried them on a dishtowel that hung from the oven door.

"Yep. Oh, wait. I may go get a few groceries, but I'll leave the front door open. I'll be home by—," she looked at the digital clock on her microwave, "—eleven o'clock."

"I'll be back then." He turned and walked through the door before she tried to put him off.

He wasn't actually work-free, but he would shuffle everything to get her banister done first. The sooner he got away and out of her life, the better they both would be.

Gina heaved a huge sigh and leaned against the sink as he walked away. Finally, she could breathe. It had been all she could do to bandage the poor man's head without straddling that incredible boner. The entire time she had stood over him, he'd watched her breasts. Looking down, she saw they were finally beginning to relax. They'd been hard for so long. Her panties were soaked.

What was it about the quiet man that appealed to her so strongly? And why so suddenly? Other, better looking, more eloquent men with a lot less baggage usually appealed to her.

But the longer she was with Matt, the better looking he became. He seemed to be a gentle soul, even though it was pretty obvious he hadn't had a gentle life growing up. He actually reminded her of little Gabe, worried and solemn, leery of everything. He surveyed his environment with cool eyes and reacted little. Actually, he reacted; you just had to watch very carefully for the tightening of his lips or a slight flinch around his eyes.

Gina wondered for a moment if this was her mothering trait coming out to try to make things better for him, but she discounted that quickly. He was too freakin' hot to mother. And the way she reacted to him was definitely *not* mother-like.

When the post had broken, he'd been mortified and angry with himself. Gina felt terrible, because it had actually been her fault. Again. She was the one who'd made him trip. Her clumsiness had spread to an innocent bystander.

She headed out of the kitchen. Her new phone was at the base of the stairs, thankfully unscathed, and another little thrill went through her. It was exactly the same as what she'd had before, just without some of the extra bling she'd added.

And her car. She couldn't believe he'd brought her car home for her. That consideration floored her and she promised herself to make it up to him.

She glanced down and decided she was decent enough to go out. The grocery store was calling.

Powering through the store, she found herself buying larger packages of food than she normally would. She stared in surprise when she realized her cart was heaping full. Was she secretly hoping Matt was going to stay to dinner? Or more?

Gina got home right at eleven, and Matt was parked on the street in front of her house. Several pieces of machinery were on her porch, but he was still sitting in his vehicle, windows rolled down to let in the fall breeze. The sun was shining warmer today, but Gina knew it wouldn't be long before the weather began to cool. Actually, it had been a warmer October than normal for Indiana.

Matt got out of his truck when she pulled in the drive and was waiting for her to pop the trunk by the time she got out.

"I told you you could go in."

Matt glanced at her as he grabbed the bulk of her grocery bags in his big hands. "I know."

Gina tried to catch his gaze, but he avoided her look. Gathering the lone bag he didn't get, she slammed the lid on the trunk and crossed to the porch. Gina was surprised by how much stuff was there. Boards and saws, a big carpenter's bag full of hammers, pencils and nails, and several cases with equipment. She smiled to herself as he stepped through her door. Matt would be around for a while.

As soon as he dropped the grocery bags in the kitchen, he started on the staircase. A tape measure was suddenly attached to his hand and whipped this way and that. He pulled a small notebook from his pocket and began to make notes with a square carpenter pencil. Gina watched him for a few minutes before she went into the kitchen to unload the bags. She debated what to have for dinner. Her freezer was a little overloaded, so she pulled out a bag of meatballs and a jar of tomato sauce, then threw the lot into a pan to simmer. They could have subs later. Quick and easy.

Stashing everything else, she attacked the dishes. Most of them just went into the dishwasher chunky, because it was too difficult to clean them off in the sink without getting her cast wet. Even as she dropped the silverware into the crate, her ears were super alert to any noise in the entryway. So far, she had heard a pencil drop, a tape measure snap six times, and several heavy thunks as something was dropped into a bucket.

Gina called herself a fool when she realized her movements had stalled as she remembered how soft Matt's hair had been under her fingers. She blinked the thought away and looked up just in time to see a little head disappear below the kitchen window-sill.

Gabe was already around the corner of the house by the time she stuck her head out the back door, but he came running when she whistled. He slid to a stop in front of her. "Hey, Gina."

"Hey, Gabe. What are you up to today?"

The boy's narrow shoulders bounced in a shrug. "Nothin', really. I heard noise over here and thought I'd see what you were doing."

Gina stepped back and opened the door wide to let him slide by. "Well, we had an accident, and Matt is here to work on the railing we broke. Come on in and I'll show you."

She led him down the hallway and stopped outside the living room doorway. Matt was removing a spindle but paused when she came out. Gabe's eyes widened when he saw the damage to the railing then widened even more when he saw Matt. Gina could understand his reaction, because even sitting folded over on the step the way he was, he could tell Matt was a huge man. Probably intimidating to a small boy.

"Matt, this is Gabe. He's my next door neighbor and a buddy, so you may see him over here every once in a while."

Gabe looked at her in surprise when she called him her buddy, and it was difficult for Gina to hold in a smile.

Matt nodded his head to Gabe, then turned back to un-mount the spindle. Gina was dismayed by how much he already had done. The broken post was outside on the porch and the rest of the spindles were in a pile at the bottom of the stairs. At this rate, he'd be done within a day or two.

"So, how did you break that?" Gabe questioned, motioning to the post on the porch.

Heat washed up through her face, but she smiled. "Well, I kind of hugged Matt and we tripped and fell down. You know how much of a klutz I am."

Gabe looked at her strangely, as if he didn't believe what she told him. He glanced up at the stairs and Matt nodded, agreeing with her.

"Wow." There was awe in the boy's soft exclamation.

Gina laughed and ruffled his hair. "He took his hug about as well as you do yours."

Gabe dropped his eyes to the floor and studied his ragged shoes. Gina felt like a schmuck for making him self-conscious. Desperate for a change of topic, she asked him if he'd had lunch. He continued to avoid her eyes as he shook his head, and Gina had to wonder if he had even eaten breakfast. "Want a meatball sub?"

He nodded and headed for the kitchen when Gina motioned in that direction but avoided her hand on his bony shoulder. "Matt, can I get you a sub?"

He glanced up only long enough to shake his head and give her a hard stare. "I'm fine."

But he was lying. She could see it in his eyes. The smell of the marinara drifted through the house now, and even Gina's mouth was watering. She didn't challenge him, though. She just went into the kitchen and dished out meatballs for the boy. They weren't actually warm enough, so she threw a bowl into the microwave to heat them all the way.

Gabe was starved. She knew as soon as she set the sandwich in front of him. He waited long enough for her to spread mozzarella on it and sit down with her own sandwich, then he dove in. Within minutes, the sandwich was gone and he was working on his second one. This one he savored, though, as if he knew it was going to have to hold him for a while.

"Thanks, Gina."

Smiling gently, she crossed to the cupboard and pulled down a box of granola bars. She passed him a handful. "Here, put these in your pockets."

Gabe looked like he was going to argue for a minute, but his stomach must have overruled his head. He shoved them into the pockets of his jeans with a mumbled thank-you and disappeared. The screen door slammed shut behind him and Gina wondered what he was going to do the rest of the day. He hadn't said whether Chuck was home or not. Probably not. Chuck refused to let him come over if he was home.

Dishing up more meatballs, she made two subs and sprinkled them with mozzarella.

Matt didn't say anything as she walked out and put the meal on his toolbox lid, with a cola beside it. "I know you said you didn't want any, but I didn't want to have to put away left-overs."

Swinging a straight back chair out of the living room, she sat down in the hallway. He looked at her dubiously as he brushed off his hands and reached for the plate. He turned and sat on the step with one leg stretched out.

"How's your head?" she asked.

"It's fine."

Gina felt her eyes widen as she watched him eat the first sandwich. It was the same as with Gabe. He ate so fast. As if somebody was going to come along and steal the food from his hand.

"How's your wrist?"

The question surprised her. "It's not too bad. I'm trying to avoid the pain pills. I don't like feeling so loopy. I take ibuprofen every few hours and it seems to work."

Matt nodded and started on his second sandwich, but he glanced at her occasionally. Gina struggled for something neutral to talk about. "Where did you learn to work with wood?"

Matt didn't say anything for a long time, and she was just about to ask again in case he hadn't heard her. "From Rick, I guess."

"Your dad?"

He frowned as if he didn't like the title of who the man had been. "Yeah."

Gina tried to lighten the atmosphere. "You know," she told him, "I think what you do is pretty artistic."

Matt glanced at her with one brow raised. "What do you mean?"

"Well, I've seen the children's toys you make for the Christmas auction every year." She motioned to the wooden spindles. "And I have a feeling you're not going to put blocks of wood there."

"No, I'm not. You can buy spindles at Lowes."

That stymied her for a moment. Maybe she was wrong. He handled the wood as if it were fragile and precious, and she noticed he completely avoided the toy reference.

"Well," she said finally, "I'm sure whatever you do will be very nice."

Matt smiled slightly and took pity on her. "I actually do turn my own spindles."

She laughed and smacked her hand against her knee. "I knew you would."

Curiosity tightened his brows as he looked at her. "How did you know?"

Gina smiled and looked pointedly at the precisely piled wood. Nothing was thrown or ripped. It had all been dismantled as gently as possible. "You treat that staircase as if you were undressing a woman."

Matt's greenish eyes flared with heat, and he stared at her for a long moment. Gina's breath stalled in her lungs as the tension built between them.

"When I undress a woman," he said, whisper soft, "she will be treated more delicately than any piece of wood."

Gina felt her skin flush and she gasped in a breath of air. *Oh, hell.* Her heart raced, and she clenched her hand around her casted fingers to remind herself where she was. Desire tingled down through her belly and settled low. He was talking to her. Specifically to her. A smile spread across her lips as she acknowledged the need that spread through her.

"I'm sure you would," she murmured, trying not to squirm in her chair.

Matt seemed to realize what he had said, because he turned to his plate and shoved the last bite of sandwich into his mouth. He set it carefully back on the toolbox and brushed his hands off, then picked up the small crowbar lying beside him. "Thank you for the food."

Gina knew he was trying nicely to dismiss her so he could work. She hoped he thought about what he had said. She was certainly going to. Forcing herself to her feet, she collected the plate, carried it to the kitchen and loaded it into the dishwasher.

She was honestly surprised by his solemn words. Matt was quiet and reserved, but that statement had been daring. And sexy. Totally out of character. As she went through her day, she had to wonder what else Matt was hiding under that intimidating demeanor and faded blue ball cap.

Chapter Four

Matt waited until Gina was in the kitchen before he expelled a heavy breath. What the hell had he been thinking, telling her that? As if he didn't have enough issues without stoking the tension between them. He'd already decided not to pursue anything with her, but when she perched on that chair with the sun highlighting her kinky hair, it was all he could do not to toss the damn sandwich away and grab her.

In the deepest part of his heart, he allowed himself to admit that there was nothing he wanted more than to mean something to Gina Carruthers.

For four years, fourteen hundred and some odd days, he'd wondered what she liked to eat, and what her favorite color was, and who she talked to when she went home at night. He'd seen her out with men before and wondered what he could do to be like them, to make her want to smile at him the same way.

But he was man enough to admit he was scared, too. He knew his life was not normal. His upbringing had damaged him to the point that he retreated as much as he could. What right did he have to even contemplate bringing Gina into it? Hell, if she knew how about some of the things he'd done and gone through, she'd probably kick him out of the house and slam the door behind him.

Then again, maybe not. That boy she'd introduced had been so familiar. To himself. Not physically, of course, but his demeanor had been the same. Hunted and leery. Distrustful of anything given to him. But at the same time, so very needful.

Sitting on the step, he rubbed at the ache in his chest. Every time he saw her, he wanted to be closer to her. His eyes flicked around her house, from the cream-colored furniture to the bright paintings on the wall. Black picture frames full of laughing people marched down the hallway in an artful sweep. Even her house appealed to him more than any other he had ever been in. It was lived in and friendly. It was an actual home.

Running his hand over the spindle beside him, he vowed that the work that would be done here would be an honor to her.

Monroe would laugh his ass off if he could see how conflicted Matt was.

The front door cracked open and the tow-headed boy in dirty clothes from earlier peeked in. Stepping inside, he raised his head and straightened his narrow shoulders, standing firmly at the base of the stairs. His blue eyes met Matt's directly.

"You need to be nice to Gina," he said firmly, "and quit having accidents." His little fingers put quote marks around 'accident'. "If you're not nice to her, I'll call the cops."

Matt's brows furrowed as he looked down at the boy. The kid thought he had mistreated Gina.

The thought sickened him as guilt washed through him. He *had* been responsible for her injury.

And the damage to the stairway. "I hope you do. Gina

is a good woman. She deserves to be protected that way."

The little boy's eyes narrowed, as if he couldn't believe Matt agreed with him. Some tension eased out of him as he took in Matt's earnest expression. "Well, ok. I will."

Matt nodded at the boy and turned back to his work, glad to see she had at least one staunch protector.

Gabe stayed for a couple of hours, asking questions here and there about what he was doing, and Matt found he actually liked the company. They didn't dig into anything important, just made small talk. Gina brought out iced tea and chocolate-covered cookies and they all took a break. Matt realized he and Gabe were much the same, soaking up Gina's brand of sunshine.

When a car door slammed, it all shattered. Gabe paled and for the first time appeared to be the scared young boy Matt knew him to be. "He's back," he whispered, clutching Gina's hand.

Gina didn't look any better, but she forced a smile for Gabe. "Let's go talk to him. It'll be okay."

Tugging him along behind her, they went quickly out the front door. Matt followed, but stopped on the porch.

A bearded man was getting out of a beat up Crown Victoria, case of cheap beer hanging from one hand. When he saw Gabe walking across the yard holding Gina's hand, anger slid over his sallow face. "What the hell you doin' out of the house, boy? I told you to stay inside."

Gabe dropped Gina's hand like it had burned him. "I know, sir, but. . ."

"No buts," the man yelled. "I tell you to do something, you do it. You understand me?"

Gabe nodded, eyes to the ground.

Gina stepped in front of the boy, drawing the man's

attention. "Mr. Freeman, it's my fault Gabe is out of the house. I had an accident, you see—" she held up her cast, "—and I asked Gabe to come over. This is my strong hand, and there are several things in the house he's been helping me with."

Chuck's glazed eyes sparkled with meanness when he saw the cast. "Ha, somebody probably finally put you in your place. What'd you do, stick your nose in somebody else's business?"

Gina looked down at the ground, deliberately, Matt thought, looking small. "I fell, actually."

"Right," he drawled, as if he didn't believe a word she said.

"I would like to hire Gabe for a little while, to help me out. I could pay him a few dollars a day and he would be out of your way when you came home at night."

Greed narrowed the man's eyes as he looked at the boy. Matt wondered how long that money would be in Gabe's possession before it disappeared. He had never met Chuck Freeman before, but he knew the type. He was just like Rick Calvin.

Matt realized his fists were clenched and his heart thudded heavily. He wanted to go out in the yard and beat the shit out of Chuck. Give him back some of the grief he had been giving the boy, it looked like. But he held himself in check. As long as they were safe, he would stay out of it.

"Fine, but just for a little while. He's got chores to do at the house."

"I'll get them done," Gabe promised in sullen tones.

"You better," the man threatened, before turning to stomp into the house.

Gina turned Gabe and hustled him up the porch steps. Matt stepped back so they could come in the house and shut the door behind them.

Just inside, Gabe turned into Gina's arms. She lowered to the floor, holding him to her.

"It's okay, buddy," she whispered.

Matt's throat was tight. What if things had gone down differently and he hadn't been here? Gina was tiny compared to Chuck and he could have pulverized her with a single blow. Unable to help himself, he knelt down beside her and gripped her shoulder.

"Why did you do that?" he demanded. His voice was harsh, but he couldn't help it. "You could have been seriously hurt."

Gina looked up at him, and her eyes were bright with tears. "I know, but Gabe didn't have a chance. We usually have him home before Chuck gets back from work. We lost track today, didn't we?"

Gabe pulled back and nodded his head, wiping his face furiously. "You shouldn't have done that, Gina. He'll just wait until I'm not coming over here anymore, and it'll be that much worse when I go back. He just yells a lot right now. He's never actually hit me."

Gina clutched at the boy's arm and leaned down to look him in the eyes. "Do you think it's going to stop there, though? It's a progression, and it starts with yelling and emotional abuse."

She snapped her mouth shut. She must have realized what she was telling the nine-year old. That the hitting would be next.

"Gabe, you have to be prepared to run if he ever comes after you. You just need to get out of the house and call me if I'm not home. Go to the hidey hole under the stairs and lock yourself inside. Remember? I will come get you."

Gabe nodded as if he had heard the warning before. "I know. I will. I promise."

Gina leaned forward and clutched him to her again before she released him.

"Why don't you go make some chocolate milk, then I'll put you to work." Her pretty blue eyes smiled, though. Work indeed, Matt thought.

Gabe walked to the kitchen to do as he was told.

Gina sat on her butt with a sigh. Matt removed his hand and sat back as well.

"Thank you," she said with a slight smile. "I really appreciated you watching us from the porch. You kind of gave me the courage to confront him. I'm sorry if it's a little presumptuous, but I had a feeling you wouldn't let anything happen to us."

Matt glowered at her words. His being there had gotten her into another dangerous situation. Great. "I wouldn't have let him lay a finger on you. Actually, I think I would have enjoyed kicking the shit out of him."

Gina grinned and nodded, her eyes gleaming vindictively. "I know what you mean. The man is damaging Gabe, and there's nothing I can do about it. His parents were killed two years ago in an auto accident and sweet old Uncle Chuck was appointed guardian. I've filed a report with children's services. They did an investigation, but nothing ever came of it."

"I'm not surprised," he rumbled. Thoughts of his own jaunts in foster care tumbled through his mind. Rick had lost custody of him half a dozen times, each time for about six months before he'd gotten clean enough to petition the courts to get him back. Matt used to pray that he would just leave him in the home and forget about him. But he always came back.

"What can I do?" she pleaded as she turned to face him. "I protect him as much as I can, but I'm afraid my interference is just going to get him into more trouble."

Matt felt like crap because there was nothing he

could say to ease her mind. The system sucked and the kids were always the ones to pay.

Gina must have seen the truth in his face. Her eyes clouded over and she looked away. Her hair fell forward to shield her face and she was quiet for a long time. Matt didn't know what to do for her, so he just sat beside her.

When she looked up again, she smiled slightly. "You've kind of been thrown in the deep end of my life, haven't you? You just see me at my best, all the time." She choked out a laugh, and leaned toward him. Before he could even think to retreat, she had wrapped her arms around him. "Thank you for not running out of here screaming. It's nice having somebody to vent to."

Matt felt his throat close up at her words. Is that actually what she thought? He pulled back to look down into her face and search for deceit. Her eyes were as beautiful and clear as always, and he was at a loss. Nobody had ever depended on him before. "No problem," he whispered. Then, unable to do anything else, he wrapped his arms around her.

Gina sighed and leaned against him, and it was life changing. Thirty-two years old, and he had never held another person this way. Never had the chance to. Rick certainly hadn't been affectionate and relationships since then had been few and far between. When his body's needs had to be addressed, he went to the adjoining town and found somebody for the night. They exchanged names and that was about it. There was certainly no affection.

This warmth building in his chest staggered him, and his heart thudded painfully. Gina didn't seem to notice because she snuggled down closer to him and melted, with her forehead against his neck. Matt gritted his teeth and forced his muscles to stay relaxed, even as her soft, sweet breath puffed against his skin. What excruciating, delicious agony.

After a heartbeat of time, she sighed deeply. Matt's arms felt the loss as she pulled away and sat across from him on the floor. Looking down at his scarred boots on her hardwood floor, he tried to remember that he was just helping her out for a few days. Just until he got her stairs done. He'd fix what he broke and be gone. He couldn't give her any more than that.

Fighting panic, he lunged to his feet and snatched up his hammer. *Work!* He avoided Gina's hurt expression.

Gabe was a nice distraction after the incident in the foyer. He didn't allow her to think too deeply on why Matt had pulled away from her as if she were poison. Since she had made the assertion to Chuck that she was going to work him, Gabe insisted she give him something to do so that it wasn't a total lie.

She put him to work in the kitchen, cleaning and putting away dishes. She showed him how to start a load of laundry and sweep a floor, and later how to shuck corn for dinner. He was quiet and good natured about everything, but as the afternoon wore on, he glanced at the clock more and more.

"When do you think you should go home?" she asked him finally.

Gabe shrugged. They both knew it probably wouldn't matter.

"Well, why don't you go upstairs and watch some TV? I'll get dinner going. You can go home after that. Okay?"

The boy nodded and trudged through the kitchen door. Gina felt bad for him, having a perpetual threat hanging over his head. She *would* call Children's Services again and see what she could do.

Matt continued to work in the foyer. When she

peeked out the door, he looked well involved into pulling up hardwood floor boards. There was no way he was cleaning up in the next hour, so she started to cook and hoped he would stay.

Gabe came downstairs when he smelled the pork chops frying. Gina directed him to the cupboards and the silverware drawer, then dished him out a plate of food. His eyes widened when he sat down to his plate. Gina couldn't help but laugh. But then she sobered. He was impressed by a meal he should be getting every night.

Walking down the hallway, she was surprised at the reduction of noise in the foyer. Matt had gathered his tools and stacked the wood, but he glanced up when she neared. Gina searched for some hint of emotion in his eyes, but he dropped his head too quickly. *That damn ball cap.*

"I have dinner ready, if you want to come in and sit down."

Matt gave a single shake of his head. "No, thanks. I need to head out. Will you be home tomorrow?" His sharp, greenish eyes glanced up long enough to catch the nod of her head, then he continued to stack tools. "I'll be back around eight. Is that too early for a Sunday?"

"Nah," she told him, pushing her hair back. "I'll be up."

He stood to face her. "I'll be back then. Call me if you have problems when you send Gabe home. Keep your cell phone on you if you talk to Chuck."

He held out a business card with the picture of a level running across the bottom and several phone numbers. When she curled the card into her hand, he turned away, gathered up his tools and headed out the front door.

Gina couldn't resist calling out a small thank-you as he crossed the yard to the truck. He waved slightly but continued to walk. She waited on the porch to see if he looked up when he drove away, but he didn't.

Gina tried not to let his distance hurt her. What had she done to chill him off so quickly? Was it admitting she liked somebody to vent to? The statement had been innocent, but maybe he didn't want any kind of attachments. Some men were like that. The thought depressed her terribly.

When she returned to the kitchen, Gabe had cleaned his plate and was looking longingly at the stove. "If you want more, you can get it."

But he shook his head. "No, you haven't eaten yet."

Gina crossed to the table and retrieved her plate. She realized she was too worried to eat. Dipping out a few spoonfuls of whatever, she returned to the table. "I have mine now. Go get seconds."

The boy did not argue again. He delved into the second plate, hardly taking time to breathe. "This is so good," he mumbled.

Gina laughed. The food was quick and not very inventive.

"What do you normally eat at home?"

He avoided her eyes and his movements slowed. "Soup."

"Soup? What kind?"

He swallowed heavily and cleared his throat. "Ah, noodle soup. The kind in the plastic package."

"Ah," she said. "Ramen?"

Gabe nodded his head.

"What do you eat other than soup?"

He looked up at her in confusion. "That's it. Noodles. Chuck says it's the cheapest thing he can buy."

Anger tore through her, and Gabe crumpled in his

chair, thinking it was directed at him. "I'm not mad at you, Gabe." Gina reached across the table for his hand. "I'm mad at Chuck. A little boy needs more than just noodles."

Now that she knew, though, she could see it in his body; his smaller size, pale skin. "Any time you get hungry, you come over here. Do you understand? If I'm not here, let yourself in and get something. You know where the key is."

Gabe nodded obediently. His eyes flicked to the clock on the wall. "I better go."

Gina agreed. It was only going on seven, but they didn't want to keep him out too long.

She walked him to the front door. "I'll whistle for you in a while, okay?"

"Okay. Thank you for dinner, Gina. It was really good."

Daring to reach out, she gave him a quick hug. "And thank you for the help today." She pulled out a few dollars. "Put this somewhere Chuck can't find it."

Blue eyes glinted mischievously as he nodded once again and headed out the door. Gina watched him until he disappeared into his house. She didn't hear any immediate yelling, so she took that as a good sign. Maybe Chuck was already passed out. She closed and locked the door, then headed for her cell phone. Patrice answered on the third ring.

"Sorry to call you so late, Patrice. Am I interrupting anything?"

"Oh, no. I'm just indulging in a sob-fest on Lifetime and a pint of Chubby Hubby. I certainly don't have anything more interesting to do on a Saturday night. What can I do for you?"

Gina related what Gabe had told her and Patrice sighed over the line.

"Okay. I'll put him on the list for a surprise visit. You did the right thing by telling me. At some point we'll catch him up in something and the boy can be removed. Did you get those classes in?"

"Yes, I did, but I'm worried that my interfering is making his situation worse."

"I disagree completely. What would his situation be like if Chuck didn't have you looking over his shoulder?"

Gina rubbed her forehead with her casted hand, and she had to admit her friend had a point. Chuck's aggression might have already progressed to physicality if she hadn't been around.

"Maybe you're right. It's just hard seeing Gabe scared like that."

"I know, Gina. I have a lot of faith that this situation will get better. We'll do everything we can for him."

"Okay, Patrice. I'll have to accept your word on that."

Patrice chuckled. "Hey, I was in the hospital yesterday on a follow-up, and Delores said you had another accident."

"Oh, God. Didn't take her long to start talking, did it?" she laughed. "Good old Delores. Yeah, I fell at the office and broke my right wrist. I have a nice, ugly, itchy cast on for the next six weeks."

"Um—hm. That actually wasn't the interesting part of the story, though. Who drove you home?"

Gina was curious at the disapproving note in Patrice's voice. "Matt Calvin brought me home. He also carried me in the house when I passed out and cooked me soup and a sandwich."

"Why on Earth would he do that? That man does not seem like the Betty Crocker type."

"No," Gina admitted, "he's not. But I think he felt guilty for knocking me down."

"Wait a minute. He knocked you down at the office

and broke your wrist?" Patrice's voice had risen several octaves.

Gina was curious at the alarm in Patrice's voice. "Yes, but it was an accident. We ran into each other."

The silence hung on the line for several long seconds. "Gina, you need to be careful. Everybody in this department knows about Rick Calvin. It was long before my time, but the stories carry on. And I'm sure they've had an effect on Matt. Don't take anything from him."

Frowning, Gina shook her head. "Patrice, I know he had issues growing up, but I honestly think he's a good guy."

"Well," she sighed, "just be careful. And if you need anything, call me immediately."

"Okay, I will."

Gina disconnected and then just sat at the table. Patrice's warning had seemed from the heart, but Gina did not believe Matt would ever intentionally hurt her. She clomped upstairs to bed, thoughtful.

Matt waited until the lights flipped off one by one downstairs before he started the truck and pulled away. There was no visible activity at the boy's house next door.

He snorted at the craziness of the past two days. In his wildest imaginings, he never would have thought he would be involved in Gina's life this way. He was fascinated by her and the life she had built for herself, but he was uncomfortable with his own reactions. He liked being with her *too* much. What would happen when the house was fixed?

Pushing the troubling thought aside, he turned for Lowes. He had supplies to pick up.

Chapter Five

Eight o'clock Sunday morning, Matt rang her doorbell. Gina dashed down the stairs, hugging the wall at the bottom due to the missing banister. Tightening her robe around her waist, she took a second to finger comb her crazy hair, which was harder than hell to do with her left hand. She huffed in frustration and swung the door wide.

Matt wore a faded red Carhart t-shirt that hugged his body like it was sewn on him. Well worn carpenter jeans, frayed at the leg, and dusty old leather boots completed his outfit, and appealed to her more than she ever thought possible. Dragging her eyes away from his legs and up to his face, she smiled at him. Then gasped. "You're not wearing a hat!"

A frown settled over his face immediately, and Gina felt bad she had blurted that out. "Sorry."

"It's all right. I lost it somewhere and can't figure out where."

Her brows rose at the admission. "Well, I think you look good without it," she told him firmly.

And he did. The hat was an easy shield, and he used it to hide his face and emotions. Without the covering, she was surprised at how damn good looking he was. His hair was shiny damp and combed down, hiding the butterfly strips, and his sharp jaw shaved clean of stubble. It looked like he had taken extra care with his appearance because the hat was not there.

He'd been checking her out as well. Gina pinkened when she realized her robe had gaped open a bit in the front. She tucked the right side in with her casted hand and straightened the other side with her left. At the same time, she raised her shoulders and pressed her breasts out. If he was going to look at something, might as well give him something not slouchy and rumpled.

Matt cleared his throat and glanced down at the toolbox in his hand. "Did Gabe make it home okay?"

"Yes," she answered. "I whistled for him at my window and he said everything was quiet."

He looked back up at her, a question in his expression. Gina was surprised at how bright and clear his eyes were. A dark curl lay at the corner of his forehead. "We, uh, have corresponding rooms at the top of our houses. I check on him at night before we each go to bed."

Matt's full lips softened into an almost-smile.

"That's nice. You know," he said thoughtfully, "you watching out for him is really considerate. Not a lot of people would get involved."

Gina tried not to let anger sour her morning.

"I don't check on him to be nice. Well," she conceded, "not totally anyway. I check on him because he's a child and he has nobody looking out for his interests. I grew up in a very large family, and children are treasures. I never wanted for anything when I was little. Every child should know that security."

Matt snorted and shook his head. "Not everybody feels the way you do."

Gina shrugged. "I know. But they should."

Matt looked at her for a long moment before sliding by her to the stairway. Gina felt like there was a lot being unsaid.

"What about your family?" she asked. "Do you have any siblings or cousins?"

"Not that I know of."

"Nobody?"

He shook his head.

"No distant relations anywhere?"

"I don't know," he answered shortly. The lid to the toolbox snapped open and he started to pull out tools. Gina thought he was just doing something so he didn't have to look at her.

"Your parents never told you?"

"No."

"Aren't you curious? You may have blood relations out there."

With a sigh, he turned and glared at her.

"My mother left when I was about six, I think. Can't remember exactly. I know nothing of her family. My father was one of several brothers, but they had disowned him. Rick died when I was sixteen. I was sent to a foster home because nobody claimed me, even though they had been notified several times. Rick's father returned the state's letters unopened. Does that answer your questions?"

Gina felt like shit. She knew his relationship with his father had been bad, but she'd had no idea it reached through his whole family. "I'm sorry, Matt. I shouldn't have pestered you."

She slid by him up the stairs to get dressed. The man was helping her out, and in return she badgered him about things he didn't want to talk about. *Smooth, Gina.*

Curiosity had gotten the better of her. She peeked

out the window and saw Gabe in the backyard next door moving branches. She wondered where Chuck was. Normally, he worked Sundays, but his car was in the driveway. Too passed out to do anything, probably.

One-handed, she pulled on jeans and a t-shirt. If she braced the elbow of her bad arm against a wall, she could turn her body enough to fasten the button and pull up the zipper without it hurting too much. She dragged a brush through her crazy mop of hair and managed to pull it to the base of her neck with a scrunchy. Not the classiest look in the world, but it would do. Her wrist ached, so she swallowed a couple of ibuprofen to take the edge off and headed down to eat some breakfast.

Matt sat on the steps, staring into space as if he had the weight of the world on his shoulders. He stood up when she stopped behind him and turned to face her. Being two risers above him actually put her at eye-level with the big man. He blocked her path.

"Listen, Gina," he said finally, shoving his hands in his pockets. "I'm sorry I went off on you earlier. My family is just not something I like to talk about."

Gina blinked in surprise. She certainly hadn't expected an apology. *She* was the one who had been digging. "Don't worry about it, Matt. I shouldn't have been nibby. I just—," she sighed deeply and met his eyes "—I was just curious about you, is all."

Surprise flared in his grey-green eyes, and his brows furrowed in disbelief. "Why on earth would you be curious about me?"

The look on his face would have been cute if it hadn't been so earnest. He honestly didn't understand her attraction.

"I like you. I think you're a nice guy. I wish I'd have talked to you sooner in that hallway, rather than just dodge around you. I'm sorry about that. I made assumptions about you like everybody else does. And they're wrong."

Matt's face had gone slack, as if he didn't dare believe her words, and she couldn't help but reach out and run a finger along his shaved jaw line. His gaze zeroed in on her gently smiling mouth. It was absolutely natural to lean forward and press her lips to his.

Broad and surprisingly soft, Matt's lips remained still as Gina moved her mouth against his. She pressed harder, daring to touch the seam of his lips with her tongue. From deep inside him, a growl rumbled forth, and his lips began to move with hers. Gina slipped her arms around his neck and held on as he pressed back in earnest.

Gina leaned harder and opened her mouth wide to invite him in. She allowed her body to rest against his and she tunneled her good hand into the short hair at the nape of his neck, scraping her fingernails lightly.

Matt shuddered and came alive in her arms. Cupping her head in his massive hands, he drank from her mouth. His tongue teased at her lips, then slid inside to taste her. Gina couldn't contain her helpless moan as she was suddenly wet and aching with arousal. Her nipples rubbed against his solid chest and it was so very delicious.

One of his huge hands cupped her ass and pulled her into his arousal. Then he did some sexy thing with his hips that ground her pelvic bone into his erection. The second time he did it, he hit her clit. She tore away with a gasp, looking into his hooded eyes. This was moving way too fast.

"I, uh, think we should chill for a minute," she panted out. "Yeah, definitely."

Matt's eyes darkened to an almost storm grey. But

he pulled away immediately at her words. "I'm sorry." He cleared his raspy throat. "Yeah, slowing down would be good."

Even though he said the words, his hands seemed reluctant to let her go.

Gina's knees quaked and threatened to fold, so she lowered herself to the step behind her.

"Wow," she said quietly, trying to settle her heartbeat. When she looked up, Matt had a dazed expression on his face. "Are you okay?"

Blinking, he looked down at her before he took a deep breath and nodded. "Yes."

Gina raised her brows, but he didn't say anything else.

"I didn't expect that, Matt. I mean, you're cute and all, but damn." She laughed and motioned to the step. "You just knocked me on my ass."

Slowly, wondrously, his eyes lightened and his lips spread into a smile. The first full smile she had ever seen. It almost made her cry.

There must have been a strange look on her face, because the happy expression faded into a frown. "What?"

"I've just never seen you smile like that before."

He looked away in embarrassment. Then turned to rummage in his toolbox.

Gina could have kicked herself in the ass. They were headed in the right direction, and she had to ruin it. *Great going, Carruthers.*

"I, uh, better go do something. You know, in the kitchen."

Flustered, she forced her knees to hold her as she took off.

Out of the corner of his eye, Matt watched Gina's beautifully shaped ass disappear down the hallway to the kitchen. It had fit so perfectly in his hands, as if the roundness had been formed exactly to his specifications. His cock twitched in his pants, and he knew it wasn't going to go away until he took care of it himself later.

That didn't help him now, though.

And it didn't help him half an hour later when he pinched his thumb with a crowbar. The erection from hell was interfering with the work he had to do. His brain just wouldn't shut off, let alone his body.

Matt could count on two fingers the number of women he had ever kissed, and neither experience had ever left him craving more. It seemed too personal. Off-putting. He'd rather screw and not deal with all that coddling, girly stuff.

Gina's kiss hadn't had the same effect on him others had. The touch of her lips had ignited a need he'd never felt before and he had thrown himself into it. Hell, he'd have spread her legs right there on the stairs and blown his nut within seconds if she'd have continued to kiss him that way. He kept replaying the scene in his head, going over her every word and movement.

It took a long time for the boner to retreat and for work to continue. His ears were targeted on Gina as she puttered through the house. She had been gone the better part of an hour when a mouth-watering smell began to filter through the air. Other than fast-food, he hadn't really been around a lot of cooking, so he wasn't sure what it was until she brought out a small plate covered with chocolate chip cookies, and a huge glass of milk. His gas station breakfast had been hours ago. He eyed the cookies hungrily.

"Thought you might like a snack," Gina said, holding

the plate out to him. The glass of milk was set on the hallway entry table, then she turned and left.

The cookies were still hot from the oven. Matt broke one open, and the molten chocolate looped down over his thumb. Raising it to his mouth, he licked it off his nail and groaned in pleasure. Half the cookie was shoved into his mouth, and the second half quickly followed. Damn, they were good.

Reaching, he grabbed the glass of milk and chugged some down, then shoved another cookie into his mouth, whole. This one he savored and chewed thoroughly before swallowing. The third took a little longer, and he finally decided he had died and gone to heaven. The dough of the cookie was fluffy and not too sweet, the chocolate decidedly on the bitter side. Walnuts added a dimension that was phenomenal. He'd never tasted anything better.

The fourth cookie he took even longer time with, because he knew it was the last. Damn, that was tasty. Unable to help himself, he headed down the hallway to the kitchen.

Gina was bent over the open oven door, pulling out a tray of cookies. There was a row of paper towels lining her counter, with a few cookies already cooling. She glanced at him, then down at the empty plate, and smiled.

"Liked those, did you?"

Matt set the plate in the sink. "I did. Very much. I think I want to hire you to bake me cookies from now on."

Gina laughed out loud and it made his gut tighten with awareness. She began to remove the cookies from the pan with a bright blue spatula.

"I don't know," she hedged, setting the pan on the smooth top. "I have a lot of requests for my cookies."

"I'll change the oil in your car. Renovate your house. Replace your roof. Something."

Gina laughed and turned to face him, leaning back against the sink.

Matt felt his own lips tip up slightly. "You don't believe me?"

"I believe you. I don't think you have to do all that, though. I mean, they're just cookies."

Matt abruptly sobered. They *were* just cookies, but he was trying to attach a sentimentality to them that wasn't there. Nobody had ever made him cookies before. Looking at her now, he realized she may not have even made them for him. Ridiculous hurt poured through him as he realized he was acting like an idiot.

Gina reached out and rested her left hand on his crossed arms.

"Matt, I'll make you cookies anytime. But you certainly don't have to pay me for them. Or roof my house." A thoughtful look came over her face, and her eyes twinkled. "I may let you change my oil, though. I think I'm a few hundred over."

A rusty chuckle burst from him, surprising them both. Gina laughed with him and wrapped her arms around him in a hug. Matt allowed himself a few seconds to enjoy the feeling, even going so far as to bury his nose in her hair and inhale the fragrance before he pulled back. Gina let him go without complaint. She stepped to the counter, snagged two more cookies and pressed them into his hand. "Here. These should hold you till lunch."

Matt nodded and turned away. He paused at the door. "Gina, I uh. . ." He stopped and shook his head, at a loss for what to say. "Thank you for the cookies."

"You're welcome," she whispered, but he was already gone.

Matt Calvin was tearing her to pieces, and breaking her heart one little chunk at a time. It was so difficult to remain emotionally reserved. Desire danced in her blood, just from that small hug. Gina knew if she tried to move too fast, he would be gone. And she didn't want to spook him.

She finished the cookies and made Matt an easy lunch of ham sandwiches, but she didn't stay to chat. After commenting on the progress of the stairs, she forced herself to walk away.

When she looked at the supplies on the counter, she decided she didn't want anything herself right then. Her arm ached, and her tummy was a little nauseous. She shoved everything in the fridge and popped a couple of ibuprofen as she straightened the kitchen. Tiredness dragged at her and she decided to lay down for a little bit on the couch in the living room. There she would be close enough to hear Matt work, but not in his direct line of sight.

The poufy couch and Matt's noises lulled her into sleep almost immediately.

Gina was roused seconds later when her cell phone rang in her pocket. She fumbled it out and tapped the screen. The display told her she had actually been asleep for almost two hours and this was the second call from her mother.

"Yes, Mom."

Linda Carruther's voice on the other end of the line was nauseatingly chirpy. "Hello, dear. I didn't think you were going to answer. I called earlier."

Gina rubbed her eyes with her casted fingers. "I know, Mom. I was asleep on the couch and didn't hear it the first time."

"Oh, okay." Her mother didn't sound appeased. "Well, did you get my voicemail?"

"No, Mom. I literally just woke up. Haven't had a chance to do anything. What did your voicemail say?"

Sighing the way she always did when everybody else wasn't following along with *her* program, Linda repeated the message, relating party details and an updated list.

Gina was still drowsy, but her ears sharpened when she heard her mother say 'date'.

"Wait a minute, Mom. What did you say?"

"Just that I got you a date dear. A really nice man from the fitness club I go to."

Gina groaned and squeezed her eyes shut. "You didn't."

"Grayson is a wonderful man, and I expect you to be nice to him."

Gina counted to ten, struggling to control her mouth. She knew her mother was only trying to do what she thought was best, but it still pissed her off.

"Mom, I'm not a child. You can't just set me up on a date without asking me. Especially with some guy you don't even know."

"Oh, but I do know him dear, from the fitness club," she repeated. "He's wonderful, actually. A doctor. I've spoken with him several times, and I think he would be perfect for you."

"Mom," Gina spoke through clenched teeth, "I don't care if he's a doctor. I don't care if he's a lawyer. I don't care if he's a multi-gazillionaire. I pick my dates. Not you."

Silence stretched on the other end of the line, and Gina knew what was coming. The wounded, 'I'm just trying to do what's best for you' act. So many times over the years she had heard the same thing.

Gina loved her mother, she really did, but certain things got on her nerves.

"Besides," she said quickly, "I already have a date for the cookout."

Her eyes widened as she realized what she had done. Her mother gasped on the other end of the line.

"What do you mean you have a date? Since when are you dating?"

The doubt was thinly veiled, and Gina had to admit, she hadn't been dating much recently. It had all gotten boring because the men were always the same.

"Just recently, Mom, and he's very nice. A, uh—" Gina gulped before plunging in with both feet, "—carpenter actually. His name is Matt, and he's very nice." Her eyes slammed shut when she realized she'd said he was nice twice. "So there's no need for you to set me up on a date, because I already have one."

Gina realized there was no noise in the hallway and when she opened her eyes, Matt was standing at the doorjamb glaring at her, heavy brows furrowed dangerously. Mortification burned through Gina. It was all she could do to get off the phone with her mother.

"Mom, I have to go, I have, uh, an issue. I'll talk to you later."

She quickly pressed the screen to disconnect the phone and sat up on the couch. Searing heat burned her cheeks as she looked up at him with a forced smile.

"Um, that was my mother."

Matt regarded her carefully, not saying anything. There was a small screwdriver clenched in his left fist at his side, and his knuckles were white.

"She set me up with some schmuck, and I didn't want to do it. I told her I was dating you." A fresh wave of embarrassment burned her cheeks. "Matt, would you mind going to my sister's sweet-sixteen birthday party cookout? With me?"

Matt looked down at the floor and was quiet for a

very long time.

"I don't know that it's a very good idea, but yes, I'll go with you."

Without another word, he disappeared. A power something-or-other started up outside the room.

Stale air burst from her lungs in a rush and the heat in her face receded. Certainly not the smoothest of invitations, but he had agreed to go. The aggravation on his face had been plain to see, but she had panicked. She didn't want to face a pity date.

Shit. That's what she herself had just set up.

Groaning, Gina covered her face with her hands. Why the hell had she said Matt's name? Her mother would be frothing at the mouth right now, dying to know who he was, how they had met, and so many other innocuous details.

She debated calling her back to say she had been wrong; Matt wouldn't be going with her. But that would be the coward's way of dealing. And she wasn't a coward. But she *would* go back on her word if Matt wanted her to.

Saying that in her head over and over, she crossed to the doorway.

Matt had set up a saw-horse on the porch and was just getting ready to cut through a board with a circular saw when she came to the front door. He looked up without saying anything.

"I'm sorry I set you up like that," she told him softly. "I was looking for a way out of a difficult situation and I used you. If you don't want to go, I'll call my mother back right now and get you out of it."

Matt looked down at the saw in his hands. One thumb ran over a gash in the plastic handle.

"Maybe you should listen to your mother. I mean, if the guy's a doctor, you should be open-minded."

Shock rocked her back on her heels. "You want me to go on a date with some guy I don't even know? Just because he's a doctor?"

Matt shrugged and shifted on his feet. Then his face closed down and he looked almost angry. "Yes. Because he's a doctor. You're a great woman. You'd make a wonderful doctor's wife."

Gina decided she didn't know Matt at all. Why would he even suggest that? She knew her mouth was open in shock, but she couldn't seem to get her mind around what he'd said. Hurt came to the forefront as she realized he didn't even want to go on a date with her. Her eyes filled with tears. She turned to the screen door to let herself in. "I'll call my mother, then, to let her know," she gasped out, before she slipped inside.

She jerked to a stop when he grabbed her elbow and spun her around. Matt gentled his touch immediately, but he pushed her back against the entryway wall. His face was contorted with anger.

"No, I fucking don't want you to go out with a damn doctor, but I want you to be happy."

Gina's heart softened, because she knew he meant every word.

"A doctor wouldn't make me happy, Matt. A man who would love me and be there for me would make me happy, and believe me, I know doctors. They work terrible hours and usually have terrible home lives. And if Mom met him at the club, he's either obsessive about his health or vain. Neither of which I can put up with." She smiled at him and motioned to her hips. "He probably wouldn't even let me make cookies."

Matt's expression eased, but he still held her shoulders. Now the hold was gentle, though, as if he didn't want to let her go.

"I want you to make cookies," he admitted.

Her smile broadened. "That's why I like you so much."

Her words made him frown. "Gina, I'm not good for you. I think I would hurt you, whether I meant to or not." His hands fell away, and he stepped back. "I don't do relationships. I wouldn't even know what to do in one."

Gina forced herself to shrug lightly, in spite of her wounded feelings.

"So let's just be friends and see where it takes us. There doesn't have to be any serious talk. Let's just help each other out." Smiling up at him, she winked at him with one eye. "You go to the barbeque with me, and I'll keep you rolling in cookies."

Matt smiled reluctantly. "Okay, I'll go to your barbeque."

Gina made herself stand still and not reach out to hug him in gratitude.

"Thank you. Actually, the grill-out is secondary. It's my sister Charli's sixteenth birthday party. It's a big deal for her, so we're trying to make it special. It's going to be kind of an all day thing," she warned. "I think we'll probably get there in the afternoon, spend the night and drive home in the morning, if that's okay with you."

Matt winced. "I didn't even ask you where it was."

"Outside of Dayton, about half an hour east of the city."

He nodded and stepped even further back. "Just let me know when you want to leave and the details later."

He turned and pushed open the screen door to the porch.

"I will," she answered. He waved as he let the door slam shut.

Gina leaned against the wall and listened to him saw the board he had abandoned. Matt Calvin was a good man, whether he knew it or not. Now she just had to convince him of that.

Chapter Six

Dr. Graham called Gina that night, after Matt had gone home, and asked her how she was feeling. He suggested she start out at half-days on Monday, Tuesday and Wednesday, then full days the latter part of the week. The suggestion worked for Gina, even though she knew the girls would be especially busy without her there. Her arm still ached and had begun to itch now as well.

The stairs were not done yet, but Matt had promised to be over Monday afternoon when she got home from work. He said if he weren't done by then, Tuesday definitely. The deadline depressed Gina. She'd gotten used to his gentle smiles and big appetite and genuinely enjoyed having him in the house.

Gabe didn't come over for a couple days. During the day he was at school and after school Chuck had loaded more chores onto him. Gina didn't like it, but at least she wasn't getting him into trouble. She checked on him at night, just like she always did, and reassured herself he was okay.

Matt called her on Tuesday to reschedule. One of his regular clients had had a tree fall through their house and it was exposed to the elements until Matt could get it repaired. Gina told him to do what needed to be done. Her banister wasn't going anywhere.

She answered his call eagerly on Wednesday, hopeful that he would tell her he'd be over that evening. But it wasn't to be. There'd been a delay and he wouldn't be able to work on her house until the next day. Trying desperately to act unconcerned, she told him to let himself in whenever he could get there.

Thursday afternoon after her first full day of work, she dragged herself in the front door, dropped her keys to the table and collapsed onto the couch. Sleep claimed her almost instantly.

Tugging on her hair woke her up. The afternoon sun shone in her front window. Matt knelt on the floor in front of her. Happiness bloomed in her chest at the sight of his hat-less head and slight smile. His hand withdrew when she opened her eyes. Gina was tempted to close them again just so he would touch her. It felt wonderful, soothing and tantalizing all at once.

Smiling, she pushed her hair out of her face and sat up on the couch. She glanced at the clock on the fireplace mantle and gasped. Six o'clock. She had gotten home at four.

"I'm sorry to wake you up," he told her, "but you've been asleep for hours, and I didn't think you'd get much rest tonight if you slept any longer. I ordered pizza for dinner. Hope you don't mind."

"Really? Awesome!" She grinned at him. "I love pizza."

Gina was touched he had done that. She certainly wasn't in the mood to throw something together for dinner. If it had been just her, she would have eaten an apple or something and gone back to bed.

"Are you done with the stairway?"

Matt got a funny look on his face. "Uh, no. Not yet. Maybe tomorrow."

Gina felt like he wasn't saying something and realized she hadn't heard a sound from the hallway at all. "Did you get a chance to work on it?"

Matt looked down at his hands, dangling between his knees. "No, I had staining to do outside."

"Which was probably done hours ago," she finished.

Matt didn't say either way and Gina felt guilty. He had put off finishing the house because she'd been asleep.

"I'm sorry, Matt. I just walked in the door and crashed. I didn't expect going back to work to be so difficult." She held her wrist out in accusation. "This damn thing caused me to fumble so many things today."

"Is it still hurting?" he asked.

"Here and there." She winced when she remembered her few hours at work. "I smacked it into a door jamb today, so I took one of the loopy pills. And the itching is really what's starting to drive me batty."

Matt had a sympathetic expression on his strong face. "You've only got five and a half more weeks to go."

Gina gasped and burst out laughing, pushing him lightly on the chest. "You suck. I can't believe you had to remind me about that."

The gentle push over-balanced him and he fell back on his butt. The startled look on his face was precious. Gina clapped a hand over her mouth. She couldn't believe she'd done that.

Matt laughed out loud and Gina zeroed in on the sound because he had never laughed with her before. It was deep and dark, laced with genuine humor that made her skin tingle. His eyes crinkled at the corners and gave his face levels of character. She laughed with him and realized it was the most at ease they'd been with each other since they'd met. Perhaps he was as glad to see her as she was him.

Matt levered himself to his feet, brushing imaginary dust from his jeans.

"You're right," he conceded. "It was mean. I apologize."

Gina shook her head at him, pushing her tangled hair away with her left hand. "It's okay. It's the truth." She shuddered as she looked down at her scrubs. "I'm going to go change out of these things. I'll get plates and we can watch some TV in here while we eat if you want."

Gina tried not to hold her breath as she waited for his answer.

"Okay. That sounds good."

The expectation holding her captive eased at his easy response. Before he could change his mind she walked out the door and up the stairs.

Maybe she was making some headway in getting Matt to relax. He certainly wasn't as defensive as he had been at first and he was willing to spend time with her. Gina wondered if she could convince him to cuddle later.

Sighing, she crossed to her closet. She'd just be happy he was staying with her and not expect anything more than that.

Matt watched Gina walk out and struggled to rein in his excitement. As mundane as pizza and a movie was to other people, it was entirely different for him. He'd never actually taken a woman out, anywhere. He'd never wanted to, really, because closeness led to questions he had no desire to answer about himself. About his dad and his childhood. He had lived in Shelbyville all his life, so a lot of people already knew about him and his history, but Gina had moved to town only four years ago. She didn't have any preconceived notions about him.

Most of the women in town looked at him as if he were as crazy as his dad had been, even though he'd never given them reason to. Some remembered him from school, with all the bruises and excuses. They hadn't been surprised when he had dropped out.

How ridiculous was it that a thirty-two year old man had never been on an actual date with a woman? Yes, he'd been *out* with women, as in, met them in bars and accepted invitations to follow them home, but he'd never actually taken a woman out and bought her dinner.

Gina was setting all kinds of records for him, though it was probably a stretch to classify this as a date.

He'd never met another woman's family, either. Actually, the thought of being at the mercy of somebody he didn't even know was chilling. Gina will be there, he kept telling himself. And you'll have your truck, so you can leave any time. If he said it enough, maybe he would believe it.

The delivery man came a bit later and Matt paid for the pizzas. The exhilaration at paying the kid the twenty-five bucks was ridiculous, but it was definitely there.

He crossed the room and positioned the two boxes on the coffee table, lining them up with the corners. Excitement needled him, and he sat on the settee to wait for her to come down the stairs.

I've become a caveman, feeding my woman and taking care of her.

The notion didn't chafe as bad as he thought it would. Gina didn't smother him. Actually, he could see the struggle in her expressive eyes. At times she had pulled back when she knew touching him or saying something would have been too much. He appreciated that.

Straightening on the settee, he looked toward the stairs. Then forced himself to turn away and slouch back as if he were comfortable. He heard her jog down the stairs and cross the doorway.

"I'll get plates and napkins. What do you want to drink? Pop, tea, water?"

"Pop," he called after her.

Seconds later she returned, carrying a blue plastic tray loaded with drinks and utensils. The brand of pop he preferred was on the corner of the tray and he felt his throat get tight. Why would she remember what he drank?

All the knick-knacks on the coffee table were removed, and the pizzas and drinks were spread out. Gina looked up at him across the table. "You're going to sit over there? You can't really see the TV from that spot."

Matt knew she was right, so he moved to the opposite end of the couch from her. The couch itself was good sized, but he still felt like he was going to break it. He sat on the edge of the cushion and waited while Gina flipped open the lids and pulled out several pieces of pizza to put on a plate.

"Do you mind watching the news for a while?" she asked as she handed the plate over.

Matt shook his head. He didn't care what they did as long as he was with her.

Gina filled her own plate, then curled up in the corner of the couch with it resting on her folded knees.

Matt tried not to stare but she was just too cute. The scrubs were gone, replaced by soft black jogging pants and a t-shirt which hugged her breasts. It was an effort to drag his eyes away from her shape to watch the flat-screen above the fireplace. The news droned on about chaos in the Middle-East, but he really didn't pay attention to it. The subtle movements of Gina's body to the left of him were driving him insane.

Shoving a huge piece of crust in his mouth, he tried to concentrate on the screen. And almost choked on the giant knot of dough. Chugging the pop, he forced the obstruction down.

It seemed like Gina was doing her best to distract him. She kept making these little mewling sounds as she enjoyed her pizza and other sounds when she saw something distressing on the TV. He kept the plate over his lap in the hopes to disguise the constant hard-on he had, imagining the sounds applied to some other task. Forcing himself to watch the news, he tried to concentrate on Brian William's words.

The news was depressing, of course; a hurricane skirting Florida, another bank in trouble with mortgages. At the end of the show was an article about the correlation between paternal alcoholism being passed from fathers to sons. *Great, another reason to hate Rick.*

And another reason to stay away from Gina. He would not see her end up like his mother had, bruised and bleeding and eventually walking out the door. Rick's rages had come on suddenly, out of nowhere sometimes.

Matt couldn't remember ever being unable to restrain his own anger in a situation, but he knew the Calvin volatility ran strong in his blood. Rick had always talked about heritage when he'd gone into rages, and Matt knew it wasn't something that could just be brushed aside and avoided. Gina's well-being was worth more to him than his own pleasure.

He was a selfish ass to even be talking to her, let

alone spending time with her like this.

The problem was, his desire to do right by Gina and his desire to be like a normal person with a normal life were at cross-purposes.

Gina shifted forward enough to set her plate on the table.

"That was really good, Matt. I love pizza. And Carlino's—" she motioned to the box top, "—has the best around here."

"Yes, they do. They've been around as long as I can remember."

Gina looked at him in surprise. "That long? Wow. I mean, I've seen the signs at the restaurant, but I didn't realize the 'three generations' was true."

Matt shoved the last bite in his mouth and set the plate aside. "It is," he mumbled.

A sudden flash of memory made him close his eyes as he swallowed. His father had ordered a pizza from there once. Matt had been about ten, then. The mouth-watering smell had pulled him out from his room and down the stairs, to the doorjamb of the living room.

He'd peeked around the jamb, hoping, praying for some nibble. It had been a long time since he had eaten anything. His father saw him as he crept up, and those cunning, bloodshot eyes had known what he planned to do. Rick pulled the pizza box onto his lap and ate every single God-damned piece inside. When he was done, he flung the box at Matt, clipping him in the side of the head.

Matt was too hungry to care, though, and had run back to his room, box in hand, and peeled the melted cheese off the cardboard. Hell, he'd even eaten some of the cardboard. It was delicious.

A soft hand on his shoulder reminded him where he was, and when. Gina had shifted closer, and smiled at him in gentle concern. "You okay? You kind of zoned out there for a bit and got this really strange look on your face."

Matt clenched his jaw and forced himself to swallow through his tight throat. "I'm fine," he growled.

Gina pulled her hand away and started to scoot back, and Matt cursed himself for snapping at her. He caught her hand in his. "Don't." *Pull away*, he finished to himself, but he didn't dare say it to her. Shaking his head, he looked away from her caring eyes. "Don't mind me, just be comfortable."

Relaxing back into the middle cushion, she tightened her hold when he started to pull away and turned his hand over in her lap. The tips of her casted fingers ran over a splinter in his hand he hadn't taken the time yet to dig out, and she tsk'ed at him. "This looks painful."

It was, but he didn't say anything. The pain was so every day and inconsequential that he hardly noticed them anymore. When he tugged at his hand again, she released him, but she didn't move back to her side of the couch. Instead, she turned her body, crossed her legs and returned her attention to the TV.

Matt's whole left side was prickling with heat from her body. His erection was harder than ever. She had to know what she was doing to him, but she seemed unconcerned. He turned his head to the screen and tried to lose himself.

An elbow bumped him in the side. "Reach over there and push the button on the side of the couch. There's a recliner at both ends."

Matt pressed the button and his booted feet flipped up in the air.

"Now scoot those big lugs over."

Gina raised her tiny socked feet next to his on the foot rest.

For the first time in his life, Matt felt like he belonged somewhere. It wasn't true, of course, but from the outside looking in they would look like a regular couple, just cuddling on the couch and watching the tube after work.

Gina got up at one point to use the bathroom and when she came back, he automatically raised his arm to hold her to his side. She paused for a long second, obviously surprised at the invitation, and he started to lower his arm in embarrassment at what he had done. But she stopped his movement and snugged herself in to his side.

"Oh, this is much more comfortable," she murmured.

He agreed.

They watched TV that way for half an hour, prolonging the night as long as they could. They watched one show after another, taking turns on choices.

When the game shows were on, Gina blurted out answers and laughed good-naturedly when they were wrong. Matt preferred more informational programs and was fascinated by an old 'Extreme Home Makeover' with a large Victorian.

"That kind of looks like my house," he admitted.

"Really?" Gina asked, ashamed that she didn't even know if he lived nearby or in town.

Matt nodded and sat up straighter on the cushion.

"Big old thing with so much decorative filigree I dread having to paint it every year."

Gina was surprised he offered the information. It seemed like everything she learned she had to drag out of him.

"Is it in good shape?" she asked.

Matt nodded and eased back against the cushions.

"Surprisingly good condition considering the neglect it's been through."

"Is it your family home?" she dared to ask.

Matt was quiet for a long moment. "No, it was just a house I bought after Rick died. I grew up in apartments and rentals for the most part."

Gina hummed softly in her throat. "A house was probably a big adjustment after that, then, huh? All that space, deciding how you wanted to decorate."

Matt snorted in laughter and looked down at her. "I don't know a thing about decorating. I just bought what I liked. But yes, it was a big adjustment."

Gina rolled her head against his bicep. "I remember when I bought this house a few years ago. It needed work, but I didn't care. It was my first house and I wanted to do so much with it. Still do." One hand waved toward the kitchen. "I want to renovate the kitchen next. I've done my bedroom and bathroom upstairs and I had a blast doing it. I need to landscape outside more, too."

"I think you've done a great job so far. I liked the look of the place when I first brought you home."

Matt's voice rumbled deliciously beneath her ear, and her heart warmed at his praise. "Thank you."

They quieted down after that and Gina shifted to get more comfortable. Turning more on her side, she dared to reach her arm across his flat belly. Matt was flipping channels at the time, but he paused when she moved. It seemed to Gina that they both held their breath for a long moment, before they settled into one another again. Matt's heavy arm rested against her back, pulling her closer, and it was incredibly arousing.

Matt stopped at a movie on HBO she had never seen before. The story was interesting and ended up being a love story. Gina could tell there was a love scene coming, and her heart began to pound. Would Matt leave it on or change the channel?

He left it on. Through her own heartbeat, she could tell he was affected as well. His breathing had accelerated and his arm had tightened behind her back. His hand was open, and he made gentle movements against her skin with his big fingers. Gina realized her own fingers moved along the ridges of his tight belly.

Heat began to build in Gina's tummy. In spite of what she'd told him earlier about remaining friends, she wanted that deep, abiding connection with him. Matt was leery of commitment, she got that, but she couldn't help wanting more from him.

Looking up at him from beneath her lashes, she saw he was fascinated by what played on the screen. His jaw was clenched and his eyes were focused intently upon the actors. Glancing down, she saw the erection straining the fly of his jeans. Wetness pooled between her legs and her breasts tingled.

On the screen, the actors were kissing heavily, and the man had stripped off the woman's shirt. He mounded her breasts with his hands and ripped away her bra.

Matt swallowed heavily and glanced at her out of the corner of his eye.

"I, uh, think I need to turn this off," he mumbled. He pointed the remote at the screen. The images went silent. In only magnified how turned on they were and the noises *they* were making.

Gina took a deep breath to try to calm herself and was surprised when Matt jerked beside her. When she looked up in question, Matt was staring at her breasts from beneath lowered lids. She must have rubbed them against him.

He made a move to get up, but Gina tightened her

arm on him. "Hold on, Matt. I think we need to talk about this a minute."

Matt growled deep in his throat and shuddered. "I don't."

Gina had a split second to decide what to do before he pushed her away, so she moved her hand down to rest on his erection. It was as much of a shock for her as it was for him, and she couldn't believe she'd actually done it.

My god, he's huge.

Matt stilled completely and his eyes slammed shut. Gina squeezed gently and let her fingers span his width. The hard length made her breathing accelerate as she imagined what he would do with all that power. Would he be an aggressive lover or a gentle, slow lover? In her mind's eye, she could see them making love anywhere and everywhere, and that desire urged her to move her hand and unbutton his fly.

Matt panted as her fingers manipulated the closure, but he let her do it. The top button gave her a bit of problem, because she only worked with her left hand, but a sharp tug and a gasp from Matt got it free.

Gina moved to her knees, with her casted hand resting on the back of the couch. Matt looked at her as she shifted. Gina was surprised at the vulnerability she saw in his face. The expression in his eyes was almost sad.

"Gina, you need to be sure this is what you want," he whispered. "I can't promise you anything other than a quick screw. I'm just not built for long term."

She tried not to let the pain his words caused show. Smiling, with the promise of sex in her eyes, she burrowed her hand into the opening of his jeans to cradle him gently. "One day at a time, Matt," she reminded him.

His somber eyes stared at her for a long minute, as if he knew she just said what he wanted to hear, but he didn't challenge her on it. Gina squeezed to remind him what she was doing, and was gratified to see him swallow heavily.

Unable to help herself, she looked down at what she held.

Matt liked plain old tighty-whiteys, which Gina thought was endearing. His jeans were folded to the sides and the erection that stretched the cotton was absolutely mouth-watering. Her hand only covered a portion of what she could see. Her touch eminently gentle, she squeezed up the length of him with her thumb and two fingers.

At the waistband, the head of his cock had pushed away from the restraint. Glancing at Matt for permission, Gina tugged the tight elastic down and bared him to view.

Gina had never seen a man as big as Matt, even as a nurse. The depth and breadth of his body carried through everywhere, and Gina felt a flash of worry at the thought of all that man inside her. Quickly washing the worry away was her stunning flash of need to hold him between her legs. She shifted restlessly, feeling the moisture her body had released in preparation.

Matt watched her with narrowed eyes as she fisted his erection and pumped her fist lightly. His chest bellowed and his cock flushed a lurid purple. Moisture glinted from the slit at the tip. Gina ran her thumb over it.

Matt's hips surged into her hand. Gina gasped and tightened her fist, sliding the thin outer skin along the hardness beneath. His lips were drawn back from his teeth in a grimace. He stared at her as if he had never seen her before.

Abruptly, he pulled her hand away. Twisting in the seat, he urged her to her feet. Gina did as she was directed, more clumsily than normal. Snapping the foot rest shut, Matt centered her in front of him. For a long time, he didn't do anything but hold her there and pant.

Gina's knees quivered as she waited. Desire rolled off of her in waves, and she knew the slightest touch against her clit would set her off. She had had other lovers, and been pleasured well, she thought. But Matt's gentle need had her more aroused than any man ever had before.

With a sigh, he rested his forehead against her belly as if his emotions were too much for him. It was the most natural thing in the world for Gina to burrow her fingers into his hair and hold him to her. For several long seconds, he held her that way, before his fingers started to flex. They rubbed against her gently, feeling the cotton sweatpants against her skin. Raising his head, Matt shaped his hands to her hips. Gina had never felt more womanly, more voluptuous, than when he ran his hands gently up and down her thighs.

Those hands spanned her waist, and for the first time Gina felt almost small. Thumbs at her hem rubbed suggestively, before his fingers slid up her torso. He stopped at the bottom edge of her bra, teasing.

Gina knew her eyes were dazed as she looked down at him, wondering why he had stopped. Matt apparently needed her to watch him as he wedged his hands beneath her underwire and cupped her breasts in his hands. Her nipples were abraded by his rough worker's fingers. Gina had never felt anything so delicious. Even as the elastic bit into her back, the touch on her nipples drove her hotter.

Matt moved too slowly, though. Crossing her arms at her belly, she whipped off the shirt. A twist of her fingers and the bra followed.

Matt's face slackened with lust as his eyes zeroed in on her unbound breasts, then suddenly hardened.

"I was trying to go slow for you, Gina."

Pulling her headband off her head, she shook her hair free. "I don't want slow right now," she whispered. Deliberately, taking her courage in hand, she wedged her thumbs in the waistband of her sweats and shoved them to the floor, along with her soaked panties. Stepping out of them, she stood before him proudly.

Matt lunged to his feet and pulled her to him. He cradled her head in his broad hand and kissed her fiercely. His other hand glided down her body to the apex of her thighs.

Teasingly, he tickled her hair for several long moments before easing a broad finger between her lips. He glided easily and chuckled against her mouth at the feel of her body's readiness. Angling his finger upwards, he plunged it into her depths, grinding the heel of his hand to her clit at the same time.

Gina screamed into his mouth as she came. Her legs spasmed, and if it hadn't been for his other arm that encircled her waist, she would have fallen as she panted through her orgasm. Her eyes fluttered shut and she clutched his shirt as aftershocks coursed through her body.

Matt removed his hand and Gina gasped at that last faint touch. When she looked up at him, he had a smirk on his face that was so out of character, it made her stare. "What?" she asked indignantly. "It's been a while."

His lips spread in a broad grin, and he raised his wet finger to his mouth. He licked the tip and let his lids fall shut as he savored her essence.

Gina almost fainted at the look of his unrestrained passion. The incident on the stairs was nothing compared to the heat that had built between them in the few days they'd been apart.

With one hand, she started to unbutton his shirt. The little disks did not want to cooperate. Shoving her hand underneath his shirt, she ran her it over his pectorals and down his abs. A slight trail of hair led her back to the head of his weeping cock. Pushing his underwear away impatiently, Gina cradled his testicles gently before running her hand up his length. Fisting him, she ran her thumb over the head repeatedly. He needed to be as off kilter as she was.

Matt suddenly groaned. Both hands reached down to tug up his pants long enough to grab a wallet out of the back pocket and fumble a condom out of it. As quickly as he could, he rolled it down over himself. Hard hands then cradled her ass and lifted her straight up as if she weighed nothing. Wedging his hips between her thighs, he adjusted her legs around his sides.

Gina flung her arms around his massive shoulders to hang on. Matt used their proximity to press his lips to hers again. This time Gina controlled the movement. Angling her mouth, she pressed and pulled with all the enthusiasm inside her. Slipping her tongue against his, she caressed the soft inner tissue of his mouth. She stilled completely as she felt the tip of his cock at her sopping wet entrance.

For several endless seconds, he played in her moisture there, taunting her with what was to come. Gina rotated her hips in his hands, trying to reach him. Her body demanded another release and his straining cock told her how very ready he was as well.

Finally, millimeter by millimeter, he lowered her down. Gina gasped as the head of his cock breached her gently. He was going to stretch her beyond what she ever had been before. Down, down he let her slide. Gina wiggled her hips, not to tease him, but to ease his way inside her. She inhaled deeply as her downward glide stopped, easing through the fullness. Her clit was twitching around the fullness.

Matt seemed to be waiting for her to move first, so Gina wiggled her hips against his, pressing kisses against his neck, encouraging him to move. Slowly, he raised her up his body, then let her slide down again, this time even deeper. Gina gasped at the invasion. It was almost too much to contain. Her body just was not used to this kind of size.

"Hold on," Matt whispered.

Backing up, he lowered them to the couch, with him on the bottom and she astride. Gina appreciated what he was doing, even though it had to be killing his control. He had put them in a position where she could control the rate of descent. Wedging her knees to the sides of his hips, she braced her hand on his chest and rocked forward to ease the pressure. Matt's hands settled to her hips and he followed her movements. Running them up her front, he supported the weight of her breasts in his hands, comparing their size to his palms. Rough skin kept her nipples puckered as he massaged.

Gina raised herself up, almost disconnecting them. Matt watched her with narrowed eyes. Tugging at the curls hanging beside her face, he brought her face to his own.

"Come here," he whispered.

Gina was only too happy to oblige. She wanted it too, with a desperation that was unfamiliar to her. She also started to move, because her body had accepted his and demanded satisfaction. Bouncing gently, she set up a rhythm that she could maintain while they continued to kiss.

Again, though, it just wasn't enough. Sitting up, she changed the direction and intensity of his entrance, making him sink even deeper into her body, and it was almost too much. Her body strained to accommodate him.

Matt's movements grew impatient. Guiding her hips with his hands, he braced his hips up as she sank down, forcing her to take all of him. Gina cried out as pleasure twanged through her along with the discomfort. Raising herself, she let Matt slam her down again as he surged up.

Their tempo increased until it was all they could do to stay on the couch. Shoving the coffee table aside, Matt rolled them over onto the floor. Gina moaned as he hit a new pleasure spot and hiked her legs around his hips to encourage him to speed up. Matt didn't need any more encouragement. Already his body had begun to lose the rhythm it had maintained for several long minutes. Gina snugged her arms around his neck and bit into his salty skin, not marking, but pinching.

Matt groaned and lunged, curling himself around her body as much as he could. Gina screamed as climax pushed her over the edge again. Her body twitched and danced in his arms as he continued to slam himself into her. The undulations of her orgasm finished him. Stalling out above her, teeth bared, muscles straining, he spasmed into her body, yelling out. It took him a long time to stop convulsing, but Gina held him to her strongly.

Finally, the tension left his muscles and he melted into her. If she hadn't been post-orgasm, his big body would have been too much for her, but as it was, he was just right. She ran her hand over his sweaty back beneath his shirt and down his flanks, making lazy, loving patterns. Her body still hummed with pleasure.

His still felt as hard as when they'd started. When he shifted, all those slowing neurons started to hum again.

Matt lifted his head and looked down at her in concern. "God, I'm so sorry," he shook his head as he braced himself up on his elbows. "I just lost it there at the end, and I couldn't stop. I had to have hurt you."

He started to withdraw but Gina clamped her feet around his behind, holding him to her.

"Now hold on a minute," she told him.

Matt flinched above her when she moved, and hardened inside her even more. Gina laughed in enjoyment as she clenched the muscles deep inside her body, dragging a groan from him.

"If I'm sore, I'll let you know. You didn't do anything wrong, Matt. On the contrary." She flexed her hips up into his. "I enjoyed everything we just did. And everything we're about to do."

He searched her eyes for truth, and Gina gave it to him. She *had* enjoyed every second of their being together. Yes, she would probably be sore, and have rug burn on her ass, but she'd worry about it later.

Matt reluctantly took her word. Surging into her carefully, as if he couldn't help himself, he closed his eyes. Gina cradled his face in her hands and kissed him gently.

"I love how you make me feel," she whispered.

Matt clenched his jaw at her words and surged into her deeper. God. How did he know she meant what she said?

Maybe it was just words, platitudes.

No. It was possible for a woman to fake an orgasm, but he would bet his best hammer that Gina hadn't. Her body had moved in ways that couldn't be controlled.

She was wet when you touched her. That was arousal.

Wrenching himself away, he used a napkin to dispose of the used condom and dug for a second in his discarded wallet. There was another, thank God, and he rolled it on quickly. He leaned over her and met her eyes. The need he thought he saw there humbled him. When he tried to look away, she held his face with her hands and arched her hips up into his erection.

Matt glided back into her, but kept his upper body still so that she could continue to hold his face. The touch was so foreign to him. Even though the cast brushed against him occasionally, it still felt better than anything he'd ever felt before.

And she tasted as good as she smelled. The touching of mouths and tongues had always deterred him before and he'd never gotten the urge to prolong it with the few women he had been with. Sinking himself into Gina the way he was, though, was pleasure in the extreme, and when they kissed, it bound them together even more sharply. Her mouth was sweeter than anything he had ever tasted. And he had no desire to leave.

Gina raised her legs around his hips, clasping him strongly as she tilted her pelvis up into his cock. Matt pulled away from her mouth to groan into her hair as he rocked into her, harder and harder. Gina panted sweetly into his neck and did some kind of wiggle thing with her hips. Pushing himself to his arms, Matt pounded into her. Gina pulled her knees to her chest, narrowing the point of contact between them to her pussy accepting his cock.

Matt almost came from the new position, but forced himself to plow on in spite of the burning in his balls. With sweat pouring off of him, he pistoned into her until he felt the sweet clutch of her orgasm rock through her. Tossing her head, she let out a high-pitched moan. With a bellow, Matt gave himself up to the desperate need that drove him and felt his body gather itself in a surge, before releasing in a torrent.

Gina panted with him as he came, and held him strongly as he convulsed over top of her. Muscles quivering, Matt lowered himself to his elbows and rested his forehead against the rug at her shoulder as he gulped in air.

Thought escaped him as he tried to regain control of his emotions, cradled in her arms. She had absolutely destroyed him.

They lay there for several long minutes, until Gina shifted slightly. Matt lifted away and looked for signs that he had hurt her. But she was smiling as if she had just won the lottery.

"That was wonderful, Matt, but I think I need to get up."

Matt reluctantly pulled out of her and backed up to give her room. His eyes fell on her glistening folds, and his breath stalled in his lungs. She was soaked, and there was a dark spot below her on the rug. As she sat up, moisture dribbled down her ass cheeks to widen the spot.

Following his gaze, she laughed. "I think I need a shower."

She climbed to her feet and stepped over his sprawled legs. Matt watched the flex of her thighs and traced the line of her butt with his eyes. His stomach tightened with resignation at the thought of going to his cold and empty house and leaving her here. Not being able to touch her again. Not being able to smell her peaches and cream hair.

As she rounded the couch, he forced himself to stare straight ahead. Yeah, they had had fun together, but it didn't mean she wanted him to stay.

"Hey, Matt?"

"Don't worry, I'll let myself out." When he looked up, she stood at the threshold, with one hand on the trim. Light from the foyer made her hair shine in shades of gold and brown.

"Oh, okay." She frowned. "I was going to ask if you could help me with the shower, but if you need to get home, that's okay."

Matt wanted to kick himself in the ass. She wasn't asking him to leave. He pushed to his feet and crossed the room to her. She looked down at his cock and flushed pink. She curled her toes into the carpet.

With a bright smile, she looked back up as he drew near. "I want you to know I had a great evening with you. And I guess—"

Matt didn't let her finish. "I'll help you with your shower."

For a moment, her smile slipped away, but then it was replaced by something more true. "I was hoping you would."

Grasping his hand in hers, she led him up the stairs.

Matt had never been up here before, but he couldn't drag his eyes away from Gina's pear shape to take anything in. He looked up long enough to avoid a couple of doorjambs, but then his gaze was drawn right back to her ass.

When she stopped and bent over in front of him to dig underneath a cupboard, he felt himself harden yet again. Turning with a smile, Gina held a small trash bag out to him to tie around her arm. Almost immediately, her eyes dropped to his lengthening erection.

"Oh, my," she whispered.

Matt felt himself flush. It wasn't everyday a woman was impressed with his body. Actually, it was going on five years now since he had even been with anybody. Once he'd seen Gina, every other woman had paled.

Gina struggled to raise her gaze to his, and when she did, she blushed. "Sorry."

Shoving the bag at him, she turned her head to stare at the wall. Matt bundled her arm and twisted the excess plastic to tuck it underneath itself. "There you go."

Gina headed into the bathroom. Matt heard the shower start and wondered if there was enough room for him to slip in with her. Gina must have read his mind, because she peeked around the door and motioned him in with her good hand.

Matt's heart and cock both warmed as he followed her inside.

Chapter Seven

Gina was beside herself with pleasure. Matt's soapy hands glided up and down her body, slowly and thoroughly. At the top of the sweep, he would massage her breasts, her chest, and down her arms. At the bottom, he would swirl over her belly, into her pubic hair and around her thighs. Then he would swing out and shape the contours of her butt and up her back.

Gina had never felt so cared for. The first time with a man was awkward and embarrassing. Body issues had to be overcome. But there was none of that hesitation with Matt. She could tell by the way he watched her move and touched her that he thought she looked beautiful.

For a minute downstairs, she had thought he was going to leave. It had hurt her heart. If she hadn't seen the flash of resignation in his eyes, she would not have issued the request for the shower. She was so glad he had stayed.

Matt acted as if he had never felt another woman this way before. Surely she couldn't be his first?

No, he knew too much about actually pleasing a woman.

She was loathe to interrupt the full-body massage, but the questions were eating her from the inside out.

Gina turned to face him in the stall while the shower pounded at her back. She raised her cast to rest at the top of the stall door.

Matt didn't stop the massage, he just centered in on her breasts, with the hard nipples he was deliberately keeping aroused. Gina sighed as his big hands lifted and pressed her breasts together and let her eyes fall closed.

"That feels so good," she moaned.

"It does," he agreed, voice deep with desire. There was no missing the erection he was sporting. When he'd stepped into the bathroom with her and shucked his shirt, it had been all she could do to close her mouth. The man's body was more defined than any she'd ever seen before.

"Do you do this for all the ladies you're with?"

His gentle hands paused for a split second, then glided on. "Not hardly."

Gina forced her eyes open to look at his face. "You don't? I find that difficult to believe."

Matt snorted and shook his head. "I haven't been with that many women."

Her eyes widened at his unexpected candor, and she nodded slightly. "I did wonder."

Matt's features fell into a frown, and he shrugged. His hands fell away from her body, and he grabbed a bar of soap off the shower caddy, avoiding her eyes. "I just never got into dating. It seemed too. . .iffy."

Gina felt her jaw slacken. He'd never been on a date?

She must have spoken out loud, because his eyes flashed to hers in the splashing water. Swiping a hand over his face, he shook his head again. "Nope. Not really."

Water landed in her open mouth, but Gina was

beyond feeling it. He had never been on a date. She was floored.

"How old are you?"

Matt looked more uncomfortable by the minute. "Thirty two."

Gina blinked and looked down at the drain to hide her face. Emotions ricocheted through her like crazy. Had he never met anyone to go out with? Surely, in his line of work, he ran into unattached women here and there. Or maybe. . .

When she looked up, he must have read the question on her face.

"No, I don't like men. I just—" he shrugged those broad shoulders, and stared at her earnestly, "—never wanted to get into a situation like my parents had. Rick beat my mother, all the time. I remember that, even though I was little. I never saw one nice word pass between them. When I was old enough, I just avoided all that crap."

The water was beginning to cool, but she was too interested in the conversation to care.

"So, you've been with women before, I mean, for sex at least."

Matt nodded and slicked a hand over his dripping head. "You'd be surprised how little conversation is needed when you meet someone in a bar."

Gina absorbed the words, and all they inferred. Basically, he screwed women, but didn't get emotionally attached. At all. A chill swept over her and she knew it wasn't from the water. Doing a last rinse, she glided the glass door back and stepped out onto her towel. Running it up her legs, she wrapped it around herself, tugged the trash-bag off her arm and walked out of the bathroom to get dressed.

Matt walked out a few minutes later, but Gina was

already dressed in fresh sweats and sitting on the corner of the bed. She didn't know how to proceed. Looking at him standing there in just a towel, with water running down his hard-angled chest, it was hard to tell her body that he wasn't available.

Gina loved sex, but generally every relationship she had been in, there had been some vague hope for something permanent. The men she was with were usually of the same mind, kind of wanting to settle down, but not knowing exactly what they were looking for. When they didn't match up, they parted on friendly terms.

Matt seemed to understand her dilemma because he sat down on the bed beside her. They were far enough away that they weren't touching, but close enough that the steamy scent of her body soap on him tantalized her. He sat with his masculine knees spread, hands folded between them.

"I lost my virginity when I was fourteen, to a hooker Rick hired."

Gina gasped and turned to look at him. "Fourteen?" she repeated. No. He'd just been a baby.

Matt shrugged, and the tips of his ears turned red. "Rick thought I needed to know, but he didn't want to explain it to me."

The situation was beginning to clear. He had been raised into anonymous sex, so it's what he'd continued.

"I'm not a hooker," she blurted.

Matt turned his head to look at her, and Gina was struck by the sadness in his eyes. "No, you're not. And you don't deserve to be treated like one. I just. . ."

He stopped, and she could tell he was looking for words.

"I don't know anything else. I've never tried to be anything different. Never wanted to even try."

Until you.

Those two little words hovered in the air. No, he hadn't actually said them with his voice, but the expression in his eyes spoke for him.

Gina was at a loss. She liked Matt a lot. Enough to know instinctively that he could seriously damage her heart.

"So, what do you want from me? I mean, I try to look at every relationship with potential. I don't just screw guys off the street." She gasped as she said the words and smacked a hand over her mouth. "Sorry," she mumbled.

Matt looked glum at her words, and he dropped his head in his hands. "I don't know what I want exactly. I mean, I enjoy being with you, a lot, but I don't have anything to offer."

Gina thought that was a little harsh.

She smiled at him sexily. "Well, I don't know about that."

Matt smiled, as she planned for him to do, but it was just a small smile. Gina felt petty for trying to make a joke out of the situation.

"Have you ever seen a good, working relationship?" she asked.

Matt glanced up at her, looking at her oddly. "Not really, no. There was this old couple I did a job for, a couple years ago. They'd been married for fifty-some years, had a gazillion grandkids. They seemed happy, even after all that time. But I only talked to them for a couple days."

Gina leaned into his shoulder. "You'll have to watch my parents, then. They've been married thirty-four years and they act like kids together. They're so great. My sisters are brats, I'll warn you now. You'll like my brother, though, if he's there." She pulled back uncertainly. "If you're still going, that is?"

Matt sighed and pulled her back against him. "I'll go, Gina. If you still want me to."

"I do."

They were quiet for several moments, just sitting on the bed together.

"You know I don't think of you like those other women, right? Not even close."

Gina's heart shivered in her chest at his words. She *had* wondered. She pulled back enough to look in his eyes.

"Thank you for that, Matt. And I'll tell you a secret. I really like you. I think you have more to offer a relationship than you know."

He stayed quiet. Gina could tell he was skeptical but still trying to keep an open mind.

"I'll try not to push you," she promised. "If you're uncomfortable with something, just let me know."

Matt smiled slightly, and his eyes narrowed. "Well, I am kind of uncomfortable with something."

Gina pulled back in alarm. "What? Is it the kissing? Because I can pull back on that."

Matt held up a big hand to halt her words. "No, no, it's this towel."

He stood up in front of her and let the offensive terry-cloth fall to the floor, revealing his erection. Gina giggled and reached out to wrap her hand around his hardness. She nudged him over a few inches to stand directly in front of her.

"Oh, we can't have that now, can we?"

Encircling him, she positioned her thumb underneath the slit at the tip, and began to make tiny circles. Matt stilled at her touch and looked down at her with wide eyes.

"Do I need to kiss it to make it better?"

She didn't wait for a response, just leaned in and licked the tip of his cock. Matt gasped above her, and Gina saw his hands curl into fists. Removing her hand, she let her mouth take its place, massaging and gently swirling her tongue around his smooth head.

"Fuck."

Matt groaned and rested one heavy hand on her curls. Gina pressed forward and swallowed as much as she could, then pulled back to the tip. Now that he was wet, her mouth moved more easily as she sank down on him again. She increased her speed until she felt Matt begin to twitch and surge into her mouth instinctively. Gina felt her body cream itself. She loved giving fellatio.

Above her, Matt shifted and angled her head a little differently to press deeper against the back of her throat. Gina groaned around him and used the tips of her casted fingers to fondle his testicles. The movement of his body began to lose its rhythm and Gina knew his orgasm was seconds away. His heavy thighs twitched and his chest bellowed.

She tightened her fist and pulled back for a moment, then swirled around his head again. She forced the tip of her tongue into his slit. Tightening her lips into a ring, she angled her mouth down his cock. She did that movement two more times, quickly, before she felt his body gather itself. At the last minute, he tried to pull her head away, but she stayed on, bobbing steadily.

Matt's cum blasted the back of her throat, and Gina worked her jaw to swallow the hot, salty cream. Matt shouted out above her and strained into her mouth, pulsing uncontrollably. Where before he was trying to push her head away, now he pulled her to him until she almost gagged. Her own nerves tingled, almost enough to come herself.

Forcing her body to accept his, she continued to

swallow, until he finally relaxed with completion. Slipping from between her lips, Matt staggered back to lean against the bedroom wall, panting heavily. His eyes were dazed.

Gina smiled at him as she used her discarded towel to wipe her lips and hand.

"Are you okay?" she asked.

Matt grinned at her fully for the first time. Gina caught her breath in wonder.

"I'm beyond okay, right now," he admitted. "Shit."

His head thumped to the wall as he struggled to catch his breath. He panted raggedly, as if he had just run laps around the house and carried weights up the stairs. When he rolled his head back up to look at her, his eyes blazed with heat and he stalked toward her.

Gina felt that banked tingle in her groin build as he loomed over her, then pressed her back to the mattress. With sharp tugs, he disposed of her sweats and panties, running his hands up her calves, behind her knees and along her thighs. Gina was a very tactile person. She loved touching and being touched, so what Matt was doing felt phenomenal. He gripped her hips in his strong hands and physically moved her up the bed several inches. Then he dropped to his knees on the floor and positioned himself between her thighs.

He explored the hair between her legs, then gently spread her folds. Gina knew she was soaked with need and when he pressed a finger into her channel, he slipped in easily. Gina gasped as he retracted his hand and looped a finger up and around her clit. Her hips shifted restlessly and she clutched the comforter beneath her. She felt Matt shift, then the moist warmth of his breath at her mound. With two hands, he spread her lips once again. Gina held her breath in expectation.

"I've never done this before, so be patient with me."

Gina looked at him in surprise, but he didn't give her a chance to assimilate the words before he buried his face in her heat. His tongue immediately found and glided around her clit, making her squeal. It just felt so good. His tongue wiggled around, slid down around her opening, then back up to circle her clit again. Gina felt his thick middle finger enter her, pressing and retreating, and that wonderful heat began to snowball.

As turned on as she was from sucking him off, she knew it would not be long before she came. She twitched her hips against his mouth and guided him where she wanted him. Matt suddenly snugged his face in and sealed his lips around that volatile bud, sucking hard.

Gina had never felt anything like it and from one moment to the next she was flung screaming over the edge. Matt continued to suck and glide his finger inside her strongly, prolonging her torture. Gina arched on the bed and finally had to push his head away.

"Too much," she gasped. "Too much."

Matt eased away from her body but allowed his fingers to play in the fresh moisture from her release. Gina let her eyes fall shut as she panted on the bed. Her mind was numb and her body quaked. But she finally felt spent.

Matt moved up beside her, lying diagonally across the bed. The mattress dipped as his weight settled onto it, rocking Gina into his side. Normally, she would have tried to put a bit of distance between them, but she was too wiped to do anything.

They lay like that for a long time, in the dark bedroom with only the light of the bathroom shining in. Matt eventually roused and sat up at the side of the bed. "I'm going to go," he told her regretfully.

Gina tried not to be put out, but it was hard. She'd

half hoped he would fall asleep beside her, and they would wake up and go to work like a normal couple. It was not to be, though. She sat up beside him with a sigh, careful not to touch him. If he needed to leave, she would let him. This was probably a pretty overwhelming situation for somebody who'd never been in a relationship before.

Matt stood beside the bed looking down at her for several moments. There was a heavy frown on his face. She could tell he was torn too.

"It's all right, Matt. I understand. I'll see you tomorrow afternoon."

He nodded and snagged his towel from the bed, wrapping it around his hips as he walked toward the door. As he stepped through, she called out after him, "I had a really enjoyable night with you, Matt. Maybe we can do it again."

He looked back at her with a grin and gave her an ornery, charming wink. "Definitely. I'll lock up when I leave."

And he was gone.

Gina stared at the closed bedroom door for a long time before she flopped back onto the bed. Emotions beat at her. She didn't know what to think about first.

Memories of the sex were at the top of her thoughts.

My God that man can screw.

He may not have very much experience, but it didn't mean he didn't know what to do. Her body tingled as she remembered his tongue on her clit. That had been sublime.

And the taste of him had been something as well. Salty and earthy, unlike anything she had ever tasted before. Her mouth watered at the thought of going down on him again.

The door closed downstairs and her breathing

relaxed. Dragging the comforter over top of her, she curled up on her big, empty bed. His smiling grin as he left was the last thing she remembered as she faded into sleep.

Matt checked the house next door as he walked down Gina's steps. Gabe's house was dark and quiet, so he continued on.

Loose hipped, he strode to his truck, more relaxed than he could ever remember being. His body was humming with satisfaction and his emotions buzzed. He felt a smile tip up his lips and laughed out loud when he was locked in the cab of his truck. He banged the steering wheel with his fist and stretched out his legs.

For a long minute, he just sat there, looking up at her house and imagining her lying there on the bed again, spread and glistening. Fuck! That image as he lowered his mouth to her cunt was what he would remember for years after he was gone.

And he would have to leave eventually. There was no doubt. His enjoyment of the night dimmed. She liked him right now because of the sex, but within a few days he would be out of her life and she would forget him. Maybe he *should* let her go with that doctor to the cookout.

The anger that flowed through him startled him with its intensity, and reinforced what he already knew. If this was how he was going to react, she would be better off without him.

Matt tried to remind himself the next day, when he walked in the house and was assaulted by Gina's peaches and cream scent. His fourteen hour semi-erection immediately hardened, and his eyes searched the house for her. Work was forgotten as he ducked his head in the living room. Dishes clattered in the kitchen and he knew where she was. Unable to ignore her, he walked down the hallway and through the kitchen door.

Gina wore her pink scrubs. When she looked over her shoulder at him with a brilliant, welcoming smile, it was all he could do not to rush across the room, bend her over and screw her senseless. Some of what he was feeling must have been on his face, because her eyes darkened with arousal. Gina dried her hands on a towel and stepped across the room to him. When she stood in front of him, she rubbed the knuckles of two small fingers against his stomach, as if she wanted to touch him but didn't want to freak him out. Matt leaned forward and she flattened her hand against him, settling it at his waist. She looked up at him and smiled, obviously waiting.

Matt bent and pressed his lips to hers, nibbling gently. Gina moaned and leaned into him, pressing her breasts to his chest. Matt let his hands glide down her back and inside her scrubs bottoms to cup her ass. Gina did some kind of undulation thing with her hips that immediately cranked his erection into the painful stage, bound by the denim of his jeans. One-handed, she squeezed his dick through his jeans and un-tucked his shirt so she could get to his skin. He nipped at her lip and teased with his tongue, fascinated by her responses.

He couldn't go on like that forever.

Matt walked Gina backwards until she was against the cabinets, then he pushed her pants down over her hips. Gina shimmied them down her legs, along with her panties, and kicked them to the side. Matt slipped a finger into her heat and found her saturated for him. He let his fingers play as he continued to tease at her mouth, and within just a few seconds she was twitching around his hand. "Oh, yes," she moaned. "Oh, oh, oh, yessss—," she groaned harshly as she came on his hand.

Matt almost ejaculated in his pants. She was so damn hot.

Lifting her to the counter, he ripped his jeans open and sheathed himself quickly with a condom. Spreading her legs wide, he cupped her ass and speared himself into her.

Gina panted into his neck and nibbled at the skin. Fingers burrowed into his hair and nails caressed the nape of his neck. Matt shivered and sped up. The counter was the perfect height for sex, and within just a few moments, he was at the edge of his control. Gina leaned back and ripped her shirt over her head, then her bra. The nipples on her heavy breasts were tight with arousal, and the visual of looking down at the mounds pressed against his chest was enough to push him over that edge.

Groaning harshly, he plowed into her, bowing his head to her shoulder. Gina moaned in his ear as she tumbled over again as well, spasming around his dick convulsively.

It was all he could do to stay standing. Matt wrapped his arms around Gina as aftershocks rippled through him.

After a few minutes, Gina leaned back and giggled up at him. "Well, hello, Matt. How are you today?"

He pulled away from her body, startled. Had he ever laughed during sex? "I'm good, thank you. And you?"

Her blue eyes twinkled. "Well, I was a little stressed at work, but I'm much better now."

Grinning, he gave her an earnest expression. "Glad I could help out."

Gina laughed and gave him a smacking kiss on the lips. "You're awesome."

Warmth burst in his chest, and he didn't know what

to say. Nobody had ever told him that the way she just did. It wasn't that he didn't believe her. He could tell she was being honest. It was just strange hearing that sentiment directed toward him. Sure, he'd had buddies tell him that occasionally, but it was kind of a throw away comment. Reaching behind her, he pulled a couple of paper towels off the holder. He handed her two and used one for himself to dispose of the condom. He tossed the wad in the trash.

Gina dropped down to the floor, and he growled at himself for not helping her. He was distracted by her breasts bouncing from the impact. When he raised his eyes to her face, she was watching him watch her.

"You have very nice breasts," he rumbled.

She grinned and bent over to grab her scrubs, shapely butt in the air. Matt knew she did it for him, because she peeked at him from beneath her hair. "You have a very nice ass too."

Gina laughed and pressed a kiss to his chin as she walked by him toward the stairs. "Thank you. You have a very nice ass too. I'm going to go grab a shower."

Matt noted that there was no invitation to join her, so he tucked himself away and walked to the foyer to get to work. His stomach was unsettled. Why hadn't she asked him into the shower like she had last night? Was he already crowding her?

He was almost done with the repairs, but he found himself dragging his feet, working slower, just so he could stay in the house longer. Going home to his big, old, empty place had been hard last night. It had never been a problem before. Gina made him feel welcome here.

For the first time in his life he actually felt comfortable with a woman. He wanted to call Monroe, who had more experience with the opposite sex, but he didn't want to bother him if he was still on that fire.

Long-held protective instincts urged him to get the hell out of Dodge. He was tough, but he didn't think he was tough enough to be in a relationship with her for any length of time, then leave. For four years, he'd thought about her, wondered about her, dreamt of her.

Was she actually as sweet as she looked, and seemed, right now? Did he dare trust his own instincts?

Chapter Eight

Gina wrapped her wrist in a trash bag and climbed into the shower. It had been hard not to invite Matt, but she was deliberately trying not to smother him. If she had her choice, she'd be all over him, hugging and kissing him. Cooking for him. Screwing his brains out.

Gina let her hand drift down her sensitive skin and linger over her tender clit. The man certainly knew what to do with her body.

Her mother was going to freak when she saw him. Matt Calvin definitely wasn't the doctor she wanted for her daughter. The tattoos and muscles presented a totally different picture than who she knew the man to be. And he looked forbidding, not very friendly at all. It was part of the reason she had kind of avoided him at the office. The man was intimidating and threw off an aura of dislike and danger.

George was the only one who had dug enough to know the man beneath the ink and glowers.

She felt bad about that, because she knew in her heart she was a good person. It was hard to accept the fact that she had not wanted any interaction with him because of the way he looked.

What did that say about her?

Resolve tightened her spine as she finished her shower and stepped onto her towel. Now that she knew, she *would* change.

Gina dug to the bottom of her underwear drawer, looking for jade green satin. Ah, there it was. The lacy teddy was not what she normally wore, but she thought it would be a nice surprise for Matt to unveil later. Because she knew there would be a later. The snaps in the crotch were a little difficult with her cast, but she managed, and when she looked at herself in the mirror, she was impressed. Yes, she was a little chunky in the hips, but Matt apparently didn't mind. Hell, he wouldn't pick her up the way he did if he minded, right?

Need coursed through her womb as she remembered the encounter in the kitchen. On the counter? Seriously? That was the sexiest place she'd ever had sex.

She wanted to do it again.

Gina tugged a pair of gray sweats on and forced a brush through her hair. When she jogged downstairs, Matt still worked on the banister, and she was dismayed to see he was almost done. It looked like everything was in place except attaching the banister to the oak pillar at the bottom of the stairs. For one irrational minute, she debated throwing herself against the weak wood to break something.

Matt looked up and smiled at her crookedly. He glanced at the handrail as if he knew what she was thinking. "Almost done."

Gina nodded, clamping her lips together. If she didn't say anything, she wouldn't get herself in trouble. She sat on one of the steps and folded her arms around her knees.

"Today was a full day, right? How'd it go?"

She loved that he was interested in her day. "Not too bad. I'm beginning to tolerate the pain a little better. It's just an ache now." She looked down at the white cast. "You do eventually get used to them. Did you break any bones as a kid?"

His eyes dimmed and she could tell he was remembering some incident. She bit her tongue and wished desperately she could take the thoughtless words back.

"I did. A couple times. Wrist, a couple of fingers. Broke my hand when I was fifteen." He flexed the fingers of his right hand. "Tried to take out the old man's jaw."

Gina fought to control her face, and the dismay she felt. "Did you?"

Matt smiled grimly and shook his head. He rested a foot on the step below hers.

"No. He beat the shit out of me that night for standing up to him. George found me in the parking lot of the apartment complex and hauled me in to the hospital. I stayed with him for a while when I got out. A couple months later, Rick plowed himself into a tree."

"Wow." Gina could only stare at him, fascinated.

"Children's Services didn't think George was a good role model at the time, which he wasn't, so they put me in a home until I turned eighteen." He clamped his lips tight and turned away, sorting through his toolbox. "I wasn't very nice when I was in the home. Actually, I was a shit. Most of the time, on purpose."

Gina recognized the move for what it was—busywork for his hands.

"Well, I'm glad you stayed friends with George. At least you had somebody."

Matt snorted. "I guess. Back then, George was lucky to remember what state he lived in when he drank. It's why his liver was fried and he ended up needing the transplant."

Gina frowned at the words. It was obvious Matt cared for the old man. He brought him to the office every month for his check-ups, and she had seen them speaking quietly together. Maybe he was afraid to admit how much the old man did mean to him.

"So, what did you do when you turned eighteen?"

Matt looked up at her and shook his head.

"Nothing really. Batted around the state on a motorcycle for a while doing labor, joined the Army for a couple of years, got a couple tattoos, but eventually came back here. Rick had left a storage container full of carpentry stuff. It was good equipment. Stuff I'd never been allowed to touch." He held up a well-used hammer. "Makes me happy to pound the shit out of it now."

Gina laughed and leaned down to pat him on the back. "I think you deserve to beat the shit out of his stuff."

He tossed the hammer in the toolbox with a clatter. "I guess."

"My dad is going to want to pick your brain."

"Why's that?"

"He likes to tinker in the garage with his woodworking machines. He makes bookcases and birdhouses, smaller things like that."

Matt pointed at the shelving unit in her living room. It was tall and stained a dark oak to match the rest of the trim in the room. "Did he do that?"

Gina nodded. She wasn't surprised Matt had noticed it.

"Yep. Took him several months to build, but I think he kind of liked getting out of the house and away from Mom. She's come up with all sorts of projects for him to do since he's retired."

"What did your dad do?" Matt seemed genuinely interested.

"He worked at an insurance company for twenty-three years. Started having some heart issues last year, so he decided to retire."

Matt was still kneeling in front of the toolbox, looking at the tools inside. "I'm probably not the kind of guy they expect to date their daughter."

Gina scooted down two steps, so that she could lean in to catch his eyes. "Why do you say that?"

"Their lives, and yours, sound pretty pristine. Ordinary."

She snorted. "Oh, please. Believe me; we're not as ordinary as you think. My brother's in the FBI, my older sister lives in Croatia right now with her military husband, and my mother likes to skydive. Little sis is a brainiac and already has scholarships to college. Dad likes to take off gambling a couple weekends a year. We all have our quirks. I think you may be surprised how well you fit in."

But he didn't look convinced. His full lips were pursed in thought, and he was looking at his boots.

"And then me, well," she let her voice lower to a whisper. "Let's just say I like to collect pretty things."

Matt glanced at her with a mock frown, curiosity in his eyes. "Like what?"

Gina twitched her eyebrows suggestively. She leaned forward enough that the loose collar of the sweatshirt gaped down, revealing her lace-covered cleavage. Matt's face went completely slack for several long moments before he tightened his mouth. His pale eyes darkened with need as he stood up in front of her, staring at her hard.

With one hand he jerked her to her feet and Gina knew this would be an encounter to remember.

"Gina?"

The two of them jerked apart. Gabe stood at the open front door, frowning at them fiercely.

She stepped around Matt and met Gabe at the door, straightening her sweatshirt. "Hey buddy. What are you up to? Just get off school? Do you want something to eat?"

She tried to slow her mouth down, but she was flustered. She could feel the embarrassment in her face, and she deliberately took several deep breaths. Caught almost in the act. Gabe was still looking at her as if she had two heads, but when he turned his old eyes to Matt, he glared. Gina was taken aback at the anger she saw. "Hey, what's wrong honey? Why are you mad?"

"All that stuff he told me was crap. He hurt you. He jerked you up by your hand and I heard you make a sound."

Gina flushed all over again. The young boy hadn't seen the heated embrace, he'd seen a woman being jerked around by a really big guy. "Gabe, he didn't hurt me. We were kind of playing actually."

Gabe didn't look convinced. He continued to glare at Matt. "That's what my mom used to say too, but then she'd come out with bruises all over her."

Sinking down onto her bottom right there in the doorway, Gina urged Gabe to sit down across from her. Her heart broke for the child because all he had ever seen was destruction and anger.

"Gabe, I want you to listen to me. I don't know what you saw with your mom and dad, but I can tell you now that Matt would never hurt me. I know it looks like certain things have happened."

She paused to hold up her wrist and motion to the stairway.

"Matt didn't do any of those things on purpose.

Remember I told you I used to break a lot of bones when I was a kid?"

She waited for him to nod.

"Well, I still fall sometimes. Heck, you've seen me fall going up the stairs, remember? I'm clumsy. I'll always be clumsy. As much as I want to, I can't change that. And what you saw just now? Matt wasn't going to hurt me; he was going to kiss me, which I like very much. I promise you, he has never hurt me. And he never will. Do you understand?"

Gabe stared at her for a long time, weighing her words. He nodded. "I guess." But he still looked leery, and not nearly as friendly to Matt as he used to be. She reached forward and pulled his bony little body into her arms for a hug. Gabe put his arms around her neck and clung fiercely, then let her go.

"Come on, Jitterbug. Let's go find you something to eat."

Gina glanced at Matt in apology for the interruption and he tipped his head to her. They could wait for their play.

And Gabe seemed determined to make them wait. It was as if he was going to personally chaperone the two adults for as long as he could. Gina knew Chuck would be angry, though, if the boy didn't get home soon. She shoved a couple dollars in his pocket for the 'work' he did, and reluctantly sent Gabe on his way. "If Chuck gives you problems, let me know."

Gabe nodded and disappeared into the dark. They heard yelling from the house when the boy disappeared inside, but not so much that they needed to call the police. Gina chewed on her fingernail until she saw Gabe's bedroom light flash on upstairs.

Matt had worked through the afternoon and he joined her at the porch railing.

"I'm done," he told her quietly.

Gina tried to be happy and made appreciative noises when she looked at the stairway, but inside she was desperately sad, almost to the point of tears. Matt now had no legitimate reason to come to her house. The work was done. And with as much time as he had spent with her, she had a feeling his other work had suffered.

She had one more weekend with him, then she had a suspicion he would try to fade out of her life.

Gentle hands settled on her shoulders from behind. She allowed herself to lean back against the hardness of his chest.

"You okay?" His voice rumbled at her back.

"Yeah, I'm okay." She cleared her throat deliberately and snugged her bottom into his groin. "I think you were about to do something earlier, but we got interrupted."

Matt clasped her hips with his hands and pulled her even tighter into the erection growing between them. His stubbled jaw burrowed into her hair, pressing kisses to her nape and sending goose bumps across her skin. She gasped at the sensation and then moaned, letting her hair fall forward.

One of Matt's hands left her hip and burrowed beneath her sweatshirt to rest against her satin-clad belly. He ran his fingers over the fabric several times. "I've never felt anything as soft as your skin in this. I need to see."

And Gina needed to show him. She jogged up the stairs, tugging him behind her. Just inside her bedroom doorway, she stripped off the sweatshirt, then turned to face him.

He paused in the doorway and drank her in. Swaying her hips, she pushed the bottoms down to her feet and kicked them away.

For a long time, Matt didn't say anything, and it actually made Gina a little self-conscious. She moved to cross her arms, but he stopped her. He swallowed heavily.

"Don't you dare cover yourself. I've just never seen anything so beautiful. What is that thing you have on?"

She laughed, even as her heart ached. Nobody had ever worn anything like it for him, apparently. "It's a teddy."

Matt's eyes never left her body as he kicked off his heavy boots and jeans and ripped his t-shirt over his head. Gina caught her breath as she watched those incredible muscles flex. She'd been with other men, but nobody had ever turned her on the way Matt did. Watching his body shift was poetry in motion, and moisture pooled between her thighs. She knew what was coming and she welcomed it.

The underwear stayed on, which frustrated her a little. She wanted to see all of him—every last, glorious inch.

Matt stepped forward and raised his hands to her breasts. The satin merged into lace at the cups of the teddy and left nothing to the imagination. Her nipples were hard as stones, and so very needy as they rubbed against the fabric. Matt took the weight of her breasts into his hands, and squeezed the tender tips with thumb and forefinger. Gina moaned and pressed against him harder. Her hips moved forward, searching for a place to rest, but Matt shifted away, not letting her touch his erection.

His mouth settled on hers and he teased her lips with the tip of his tongue. Gina swallowed him down. She needed to merge with him as much as she physically could. Matthew Calvin was like a drug to her. Kissing him was precious and he used every subtle move he'd learned with her. Nothing could match the intimacy of kissing.

Gina had to revise that sentiment as he settled his hips gently against hers. His cock was pushing out from beneath the underwear elastic, searching for a place to nestle. She reached down long enough to position it straight up between them, then began to undulate her hips into the hardness. Matt moaned and clasped her hips in his hands, grinding against her soft belly.

Her breath tightened in her throat as she accepted the assault. If he moved her hips just a fraction of an inch, he would bump her clit, and at that moment, there was nothing more important.

Backing toward the bed, she gave him a look from beneath her bangs and leaned down to unsnap the crotch of the teddy. Her fingers quivered and she gasped when she bumped herself. She was so ready!

As Gina climbed onto the bed, Matt stripped off his underwear and tossed them away. He ripped open a condom and rolled it over his length. Even as she moved, his gazed stayed firmly on the opening she had revealed. He waited long enough for her to lie down on the bed and he crawled over top of her.

They reached for each other and Gina automatically spread her legs to nestle him between them. Matt was one of the biggest men she'd ever seen, broad and strong, heavy, but as he settled on top of her, he felt perfectly right. Emotion clogged her throat as she wrapped her arms around his neck. It would be very easy to love him.

Who was she kidding? She already did.

One week of being the center of his gentle attention and she wanted it for a lifetime.

Instinctively, she knew Matt would freak if she spoke the words, so she tried to tell him with her body.

Tilting her hips up, she angled to work him into her body, but he wasn't ready to give in. He glided his hands down her sides, shaping the dip of her waist and the curve of her hip. He did it several times, apparently fascinated by the way her body felt in the negligee. Lowering his mouth, he closed it over her lace covered nipple.

Gina arched into the hot suction of his mouth, lost to sensation. When he mounded her breasts together and alternated between her nipples, she thought she was going to have to stop him. The sensation was too much. Fluid was flowing freely from her body and she thought if she really let herself go she could come just from the touch of his mouth on her breast. Her clit was already flexing, searching for some kind of contact to bring on orgasm.

Matt shifted and lowered his head to rest against her belly. Gina was curious at the move, but burrowed her fingers into his thick hair and held him to her. 'I love you' was on the tip of her tongue, but she forced it back. He moved subtly, and she realized he was rubbing his whiskered cheek against the fabric of her teddy.

"I've never felt anything so soft," he murmured.

Gina hummed in her throat and promised herself she would go shopping for more things like this to make him happy.

Matt lifted his head and shifted until he was braced over top of her. He looked down at her for a long time, not saying anything, just tracing his eyes over every bit of her face. She smiled at him gently, raising her lips to his. She wondered if he was as emotionally overwhelmed as she was, but she was afraid to ask.

He whispered his mouth over hers for several long minutes, and Gina was amazed at how gentle he was. Opening her lips, she let him consume her. Nobody had ever taken the time to pleasure her the way he did now. When he reached down to tickle her wet curls, her heart began to pound. Pressing gently, he massaged her plump lips, but didn't slip inside. He ground the heel of his hand against her fleshy mound, and it was just enough to snap her into orgasm. Gasping against his neck, she convulsed beneath him with a high, keening moan.

That was when he slid inside her.

Rather than being too much, his hardness was just enough to prolong the torture. Matt moved slowly, but strongly, plunging into her as deeply as he could. Gina lifted her legs up over his hips, deepening the contact. He gasped in her ear and surged harder, again clasping her satin covered hips in his hands. Contracting her muscles, she encouraged him to move harder.

Matt groaned in her ear as his arousal crescendoed. Fumbling, his lips found hers, and they breathed each other in as their pleasure consumed them.

Gina actually thought she was going to pass out from the orgasm that lit her from the inside out. Spots danced in front of her eyes and her breath clogged her throat. Matt groaned loud and long, arching sharply above her. For several heart-stopping moments, he convulsed before sagging to rest on top of her. The force of his heart pounding was enough to make the bed shake.

She ran her hand down his sweat-slicked back and pressed kisses to the wetness of his neck. Tightening her inner muscles, she tried to keep his hardness within her.

Matt laughed when she clenched around him. "Do that again."

She did and flexed her hips just a bit, even with his heavy weight on top of her. Matt responded by surging into her again, weakly.

"We'll have to explore that more later."

With a final, reluctant kiss, he rolled off the bed to pad to the bathroom. When he returned, the condom was gone and he was heavy-eyed. He settled next to her and straightened the teddy over her stomach.

"I've seen these things in magazines and stuff, but I never realized they were so hot."

"I'm glad you liked it."

He plopped down on the bed beside her and folded his arms behind his head. He was still completely naked, but he seemed very unconcerned with his nudity. She leaned over and blew gently against his still damp penis. The sensitive skin tightened and then relaxed. "I don't think you're going to get anything out of him for a while. He's worked pretty hard today."

Gina grinned up at him and shifted to lie against his chest. "Very hard. I'll give him a break."

Matt lowered his right arm to circle around her back and pulled her tighter to his side. She nestled her head into the dip of his shoulder and ran her palm down his abdomen. She teased the trail of hair with her fingers, ruffling it lightly. An indentation in his skin made her pause. "Is this a scar?"

He was quiet above her for a long time. "Yeah."

"What from? It's an odd shape."

This time he was quiet for a longer stretch of time, and Gina had a feeling she had just shoved her foot in her mouth.

"Cigarette," he answered finally.

Her stomach clenched sickeningly. "Cigarette?" she whispered.

Matt's ribcage expanded beneath her as he sighed. "Yep. One of Rick's many and varied punishments."

Gina clenched her jaw and clamped her eyes shut. She would not cry. "I'm sorry. I shouldn't have asked."

"It's all right. There are a few more around the side, so don't freak out when you feel them. And some scars on my back."

She tightened her arm around him and swallowed heavily. It broke her heart that his childhood had been so harsh. She couldn't even begin to imagine what he had gone through.

As a child, she had been loved and coddled. Anything she'd wanted, she'd gotten. Discipline had been taking treats away, or at the very most a light swat on the behind. Certainly never anything more harsh than that.

The total aloneness he must have felt back then had to have been brutal. "Didn't anybody try to help you?"

Air expanded his chest as he sighed deeply. "One neighbor lady tried to help out, but Rick scared her so bad one day she never came back. If she reported me to Children's Services, I never knew about it. It wasn't until years later that they started to investigate."

Anger and confusion battled in her mind, followed quickly by protectiveness. The man was probably two-hundred thirty pounds, but she wanted to stand up and scream at the world on his behalf. And she couldn't. He could take care of himself, now, obviously, but she wanted to right the unjustness of his childhood.

"I wish I had been there," she told him finally. "I would have done everything in my power to get you out of there."

Matt didn't say anything for a long time, just squeezed her tighter to his side. "Thanks, Gina."

She stared into the darkness for a long time, thinking. Matt's breathing deepened until he fell asleep, but his arm stayed tight around her. After an hour of staring at nothing, Gina got up and went to the bathroom. She peeked through the blinds over at Gabe's house, but he was surely long in bed. The window was dark. She felt guilty that she hadn't checked on him earlier, but things had been a little hectic. Even in the darkness, she could feel her face warm. Other things had definitely been on her mind.

Matt shifted to his side when she crawled back into bed, and he tugged her tight against him when she lay down. Gina nestled into his warmth and prayed he would sleep there, just for a while.

Matt was having the best dream. Gina stood in front of him in a green negligee thing that cinched her waist in tight, but left her hips to flare out, just the way he liked. She faced away and danced in front of him, wiggling her ass. She kept giving him these taunting looks over her shoulder, begging him with her blue blue eyes to fuck her. Grabbing her hips in both hands, he pulled her back and centered her over his cock. He hesitated for a split second, then jerked her down onto him.

Gina cried out and Matt was suddenly awake. He was lying on the bed on his side, with his cock buried in Gina's wet heat from behind. Her high leg was over top of his.

"Oh God, Matt, I thought I was dreaming."

She arched her ass into him, urging him deeper. Matt was relieved he hadn't hurt her, but he hesitated. She was very tight, and he didn't want to rush her.

He reached his hand across her and slipped a finger between her thighs. Gina gasped and jerked, tightening around his cock, but moaning. Her left hand reached back to clutch his hip, tugging him closer. "More."

Matt pushed hard, seating himself even deeper. Gina huffed out a breath and pressed back into him, countering his movements. Flicking her clit with his finger, he buried his lips into the hair at her nape, nibbling. Gina twisted in his arms to press her mouth to his. Her breast pouted straight up, so he took a minute to draw it into his mouth. Working his fingertip in a circular motion around her clit, he sucked in time to his movements. Gina cried out, quivering as her orgasm rolled over her and she was suddenly very wet.

Matt lunged into her, but he wasn't satisfied. He needed it harder. Rolling her onto her belly, he braced himself over top of her and spared just a second to look. There was enough illumination in the room that he could see the paleness of her skin and her hourglass shape.

"You are beautiful," he told her. He pressed his lips against her spine and across her shoulders.

Her ass arched up toward him and he couldn't *not* sink himself into her again. Immediately, he knew he was in trouble. The sensations were totally different in this position, harder, sharper, and the visual of her body beneath him arching up to meet his and the feel of his naked cock gliding deep in her wetness built him up to orgasm quicker than ever before. Pounding into her, he only had a very few seconds before the orgasm crashed over him, destroying all sense. He slammed himself deep, and Gina cried out beneath him, he didn't know in pain or release, but he couldn't control his movements until the orgasm abated. Quivering, his arms gave out. He had just enough control to push to the side and not crush Gina. He panted raggedly, trying to suck in oxygen.

"Gina, I'm so sorry. Are you okay? Did I hurt you? I just couldn't stop there at the end."

She twisted around to look at him, and Matt was reassured by her seemingly satisfied smile. "I'm wonderful. That was freaking hot!"

Emotion suddenly clogged his throat. Gina was soft

and mussed and looked well loved. The fact that she was in bed with him humbled him to his core. "I thought I had hurt you for a minute."

She rocked her head on the pillow. "Not at all. You were working my body perfectly and when you hit deep I came again. I've never done that before. Come twice like that. You just manage to drag them out of me."

She rolled over and slipped her arms around him, pressing a kiss to his lips. "You can wake me up like that any time."

Matt grinned at her, more light-hearted than he could ever remember being. "Really?"

Gina nodded and rested her forehead against his chest. "Definitely."

"You know, I thought I was dreaming." Matt laughed and stroked his hand down her smooth back. "Then I woke up, and I was inside you, and it was better than any dream I could have imagined." He snapped his mouth shut. That sounded so sappy.

Gina looked up at him with a gentle smile. "Seriously?"

He nodded once.

Tightening her arms around him, she snugged into his front. "Thank you Matt. I'll tell you, this all seems like a dream to me. You've really become important to me in a very short length of time." She pulled back enough to look him in the eye. "No pressure, though. You know."

They settled back down together, and Matt let himself soak in the closeness.

Gina woke early the next morning and lay in the crook of Matt's arm, watching him sleep. His dark eyelashes made crescents on his cheeks in the early morning glow, and he snored lightly. Stubble shadowed his jaw, but he was the most relaxed she'd ever seen him. Her eyes traced down his pectoral muscles and the light fuzz of dark hair. He'd lost his tighty-whiteys hours ago, and his cock lay long and flaccid to the right.

The poor thing had to be tired, she thought with a smile. After the rear entry session, he'd woken her up one more time in the night to gently, thoroughly rock her world yet again. She had never been so completely loved.

She slipped out of bed and padded to the shower. They needed to get on the road soon, to her parent's house. Swallowing a couple of ibuprofen, she trash-bagged her wrist before stepping under the steaming water. She had aches from their activities last night and her pussy was definitely on the tender side, but on the whole she was more satisfied than she could ever remember being. Matt was a thorough, gentle lover, in spite of what he'd said about not having relationships.

The object of her thoughts stuck his head in the door and gave her a once-over. Gina shook her head at him. "Oh, no, you don't. I have to get cleaned up. And so do you."

Matt nodded once. "I'll be back in a while. What time do you want to leave?"

"By noon."

Matt flipped a hand in the air and disappeared.

Gina was surprised he didn't climb in the shower with her like he did earlier. It was okay, though. They probably both needed time to decompress. They had a long, potentially crazy weekend ahead of them.

She needed to let Gabe know where they were going to be. She'd flirted with the idea of trying to take him along, but there was no way his uncle would go for it. Besides, they'd only be gone for a day and a half.

Chapter Nine

Gina had enough time to bake a fresh batch of cookies especially for Matt and make her world-famous pasta salad, which her little sister dearly loved. It was a minor miracle she'd even been able to do that much with her arm in the cast. It was bulky and difficult, so she had to make modifications. Rather than wrap the gift she got Danielle, she stuffed everything in a bag with tissue paper and signed a card. For several minutes, she debated whether or not to add Matt's name to the card, but in the end she left it off. She could ask him when they got in the truck if he was comfortable with it or not.

At eleven forty-five, he knocked on the front door, but she didn't hear anything more after that. Curious, she walked down the hallway to see where he was. Still on the porch. She opened the door with her brows raised in question. He shrugged awkwardly and rubbed the nape of his neck.

"I didn't know if I should just walk in or not."

Gina smiled, trying to be reassuring. "Of course, you should. You should always consider yourself welcome here, Matt." Leaning up on tiptoe, she pressed a kiss to his lips. Broad hands framed her face, holding her to him, before he released her. Gliding her hands down his chest, she let them settle at his waist and looked up at him. Then had to do a double-take.

"You look very nice, Matt."

Talk about understatement. She stepped back to get a better view. He looked down-right edible. His curls were slicked down with mousse and recently trimmed. The butterfly strips were long gone, but there was still a pale pink line on his forehead from the post. A pretty, hunter-green button-up shirt stretched across his broad shoulders and buttoned at his wrists. Store-creased khakis encased his legs. A brand-new pair of brown suede shoes were planted in her entryway, without a speck of wood dust on them. Gina thought she preferred his old boots and t-shirts. "You didn't have to get dressed up. My family is pretty casual."

He winced a little. "I just didn't want them thinking I was. . .I don't know." His hand motioned in the air.

Gina didn't like that he felt the need to compare himself to other guys. "Matt, I like you, not because of the clothes you wear or what you do, but because of the person you are. Be comfortable."

The word comfortable seemed to release something in him, because he tugged at his stiff collar and shifted as if his feet hurt. He cleared his throat and looked down at his shoes. Swallowing heavily, he met her gaze. "I didn't want you to be embarrassed to be seen with me."

She looked at the shirt again and realized he'd worn long sleeves to cover up the tattoo. Gina felt her throat close with emotion. "I would never be embarrassed to be seen with you. I'm proud to be seen with you. Anywhere or anytime. I, personally, think you're gorgeous just the way you are. And I have a feeling I won't be the only one. There are going to be a dozen giggling teen-agers at this cookout who are going to think you are the cat's meow."

Matt grimaced, and Gina giggled. She reached out and hugged him around the waist. "Come on, big man. I'm ready to go. Let's swing by your place on the way out of town, and you can change."

Twenty minutes later, Matt guided the truck into his driveway.

"Wow," Gina breathed. She'd actually seen this house before, many times. She just hadn't realized whom it belonged to. On lazy days, she drove past it after work just to look at all the detailed cornice work and the wide wrap-around porch. The house looked immaculate, but the gardens had always needed work. They were overgrown. Several rosebushes dotted the property, but they desperately needed pruned and shaped.

"I've driven by this house before. I love it. I can't believe you own it."

One side of Matt's mouth tipped up in a smile. "Sometimes I wonder why I own it. It's a lot of work to maintain."

"I bet."

Curiosity pushed her out of the truck and to follow him into the house. She didn't ask; she just followed. Matt seemed surprised, but accommodated her. "Just watch. The rooms are kind of full right now."

Gina gasped as she stepped into the entryway. From wall to wall, heavy pieces of wooden furniture were stacked, sometimes one on top of another, sometimes singly. Matt wove through a path just wide enough for him if he turned his shoulders. Gina tried to take it all in. She knew her mouth hung open, but she couldn't seem to help it. She had known Matt was a carpenter, but she hadn't known he was this...industrious. "What are you going to do with all of these?" she asked, finally.

Smiling at her over his shoulder, he led her to a staircase and up to the second floor. "Well, I'm waiting on a truck to come from Cincinnati to pick these up. It's why everything is crowded into the front. About once a year, sometimes twice a year, a company I consign with comes for stock."

Gina followed his broad back down the hallway and tried not to feel bad for him. It must be so lonely not having anybody other than a crotchety old man. He said he went out with buddies occasionally, for ball games and such, but she could tell he wasn't especially attached to any of them. What better than work to fill his time?

There were several closed doors along the hallway, but he led her to the very end to the only open door. Inside was a man's room. Dark, masculine colors on the bed and furniture, nothing decorating the walls. For some reason she expected clutter, but there wasn't any. The room was plain and almost sterile. The one piece of Matt in the room was the oversized bed and headboard. It was handmade, obviously, and darkly beautiful. It looked extra-long to accommodate his size. "Now that's a bed."

Matt smiled slightly, and his gaze tracked her movements as she walked across the room to sit on the edge of the mattress. She bounced experimentally, leaned back on one arm and folded the casted arm across her stomach. She lowered her voice deliberately. "Somebody could have some fun in this bed."

His eyes darkened and he took a step toward her.

"Matt, you probably ought to take those clothes off. It looks like they chafe."

The shirt was tossed one way, then the pants. The

shoes thumped to the floor out of sight. Within seconds he stood in front of her in his plain white briefs. His erection stretched the cotton, and her mouth watered at the thought of pulling that cloth down and swallowing the tip of him into her mouth.

Hell, why not? Crooking a finger, she urged him closer to the bed.

An hour later, they left the house. Matt was in jeans and a nice, more casual, polo, he had his favorite ball cap on and there was definitely a swing in his step. Gina knew she walked more loose-hipped as well and the smile just wouldn't leave her face. Matt carried his repacked bag in one hand and had his other hand around her elbow. After they'd made love in his oversized bed, he'd gently washed her clean in his walk-in shower. Gina felt positively pampered. Loved.

She snorted to herself. It wasn't love. Surely, on his part it had to be fascination. If he'd never had a relationship before, the first time he did had to be stunning, and thrilling. She would actually be worried about it if he did proclaim his undying love.

George sat on his porch at the house next door and called out a greeting. Gina waved, but Matt didn't give her a chance to stop and talk. He handed her up into the truck and tossed the duffle in the back, then circled around to climb behind the wheel. He glanced at her sideways. "We may be a little late."

She shrugged. "I can't imagine any better reason why. Although we may not tell my mother."

Matt chuckled quietly and relaxed back into his seat.

Highway 9 was quiet as they headed north toward 70 eastbound. Yellow Springs was one hundred fifty miles away, so they had almost two hours worth of travel time. Gina eyed the expanse of bench seat between them, and wondered what he'd say if she slid over. She chickened out at the last minute. She didn't want to appear too clingy.

Matt wondered how he could get her to slide across. Setting cruise at seventy-two miles per hour, he raised his right arm to rest along the back of the seat, trying to look accommodating. Gina looked at him and smiled, but didn't slide any closer.

He wasn't too put out, because it meant he could still look at her across the seat. At the doctor's office, he'd only ever seen her wear scrubs. The jeans she seemed to prefer suited her so much better. She had on a frilly, flirty shirt in shades of blue that did fantastic things for her eyes. She'd applied make-up, but one eye had a smudge of black beneath it, probably from their play.

Reaching up, he flipped the sun visor down and motioned to the mirror. "Your make-up's messed up a bit."

Gina peered into the mirror and wiped the blemish away, then beamed at him. "Thank you for telling me. I'd have felt foolish finding that later."

"You'd have still been beautiful." The words were instinctive and heartfelt, but he felt exposed saying them.

Gina smiled, though, and seemed to come to a decision. She unfastening her seatbelt, tossed her purse on the floor and shifted to sit beside him. Matt dropped his arm down around her shoulders and snugged her closer.

"My arm's not too heavy, is it?"

She shook her head and fastened the middle seatbelt across her hips.

"I wanted to do this earlier, but I didn't want to crowd you."

Matt appreciated her consideration. She really was trying not to push him too fast. What they were doing was not too much though. He didn't feel overwhelmed. Actually, if anything, he felt more addicted to her and wanted more closeness. "You're not crowding me."

"Well, if I ever do, just tell me to back off and I will, okay?"

He nodded, appreciating her words. "So, where am I going?"

"Yellow Springs. It's about a half hour east of Dayton."

"Is that where you grew up?"

Gina nodded her head against his chest. "All my life. It's a nice little college town, not too big but decent sized. Columbus and Dayton are within driving distance, and it's actually become a bit of a tourist spot in the past few years. Trendy little shops downtown and stuff."

"Sounds nice. You didn't go to school there, though, right?"

"Right. I wanted to get away from my family so I headed west for school. Indiana State."

Matt couldn't blame her for wanting to get away. If he could have gotten away from Rick sooner he would have.

They talked about inconsequential things all the way to Ohio, and it was one of the most relaxed times he had ever spent in an enclosed space with anybody. As the highway signs began to tick down the miles, though, his anxiety ratcheted up. He had no idea who these people were or what they would think about their daughter dating a tattooed reject. Gina seemed to think they would accept him with open arms, but he knew otherwise. They would look at him with suspicion, lightly concealed by civility.

Half an hour later, he guided the truck onto a gravel driveway and pulled up to a two-story house set back against picturesque woods. Cars lined the gravel and

Gina motioned for him to pull into the yard. "It's fine. We do it all the time."

Matt gritted his teeth and had visions of Gina's insurance salesman father chasing him with a shotgun, but he parked where she directed.

Gina was overwhelmed by people almost immediately. She kissed everybody, and they were all kissing and hugging her in return. It was one of the craziest things Matt had ever seen, all the open affection. A little scary actually. They all clucked over her cast, and he felt a flash of guilt.

A hand was shoved at him, and he shook automatically. A tall, lean man with Gina's broad smiled shifted around a woman. "You must be Matt. We're so pleased to meet you. I'm Eric, Gina's dad."

To say he was surprised was an understatement. Matt had expected a short little man with glasses. Eric Carruthers was none of that. Tall and spare with a trustworthy face, he exuded a laid-back confidence that inferred he could handle anything.

"It's a pleasure to meet you. I hope you don't mind I parked in your yard."

Eric waved his words away. "No worries. We park there all the time. How was the drive?"

"Fine, fine." Matt looked for Gina's curls, and he spotted her crossing the drive to wrap her arms around an older woman with identical curls. Eric motioned for him to follow and they crossed to meet them.

Gina turned when he got close enough and held her hand out to him. Matt felt his throat tighten as she tugged him to stand in front of the older woman. "Mom, I would like you to meet Matt Calvin. Matt, my mom, Linda."

It was obvious Gina got her kinky hair from her mother, and her bright blue eyes. Mrs. Carruthers glanced down the length of him, and he knew she was cataloging his faults. Her eyes snagged on his tattoo and paused for the briefest millisecond, but he had seen the cringe. In spite of the look, though, she smiled brightly at him. "Matt, it's a pleasure to meet you. Thank you so much for driving Gina all the way out here."

"It was no problem, Mrs. Carruthers."

"Call me Linda, please."

Matt tipped his head in agreement, but he didn't know if she really meant the offer or not. Her eyes were a little cool. He looked down at Gina. "I'll go get the bags. Why don't you head up with your mom?"

Gina smiled brightly and leaned up for a quick kiss. Matt had no choice but to meet her partway. The move looked as if she'd done it many times before, though he knew otherwise. "Thanks, Matt. Just set them inside the back door. We'll meet you in the back yard."

He nodded once and turned for the truck. Gina and her mother locked arms and started up the driveway. Eric followed him to the truck, and Matt had a feeling the man had questions.

"So, Matt, did you have problems on the interstate or anything?"

He shook his head and leaned in to the back seat to pull out the duffle bags, the pasta salad and the brightly colored gift bag.

A jolt of excitement went through him as he stuffed the bright pink envelope inside the bag. Gina had offered to put his name on the card in case he didn't have a gift, but Matt had surprised her by producing a cardboard box. Inside a nest of newspaper was a jewelry chest he had made several months ago. It was intricately carved and much smaller than what he normally built, but beautiful all the same. Gina's eyes had sparkled when she saw the box and told him it would be perfect for Charli. It was in the bottom of the gift bag, and his name was also on the card. Matt had felt like a part of a couple as he watched Gina sign his name in the truck.

Kicking the door shut with his foot, he started up the driveway in the direction Gina had gone. Eric offered to take one of the bags, but Matt shook his head. "Nah, I'm good."

Eric led him to the back of the house, and Matt had to stop and stare. Colored streamers hung from the trees and bushes, and there were several decorated picnic tables scattered across the lawn. "I know," the older man laughed, "it's a lot. But she's our youngest child and we wanted to make her last birthday at home memorable."

"Why is it her last birthday at home?" Matt asked, curious.

"Well," Eric sighed, "next year she'll be at college. Did Gina tell you about Charli? She's an extremely intelligent young woman, and she graduates high school next June. She goes directly to college in the fall, assuming she settles on one."

Matt was genuinely impressed. He had dropped out of high school at sixteen. Later, he'd gone back for his GED, but he regretted dropping out of school in the first place. College had been an unattainable dream, then. Now, he took the occasional business course at the community college at night if he thought he needed to know something.

There were two long banquet tables on a brick patio at the back door. He set Gina's pasta bowl on the table and Charli's gift bag on another, then set their clothing bags inside the back door Eric directed him to. He shut the door and looked across the yard for Gina, but he didn't see her.

Eric led him to a group of lawn chairs grouped around an obviously well-used brick fire pit. Matt eyed the canvas chairs dubiously and chose a sturdier looking one to lower himself into. It held and he released his breath. He hated these things. He'd take a wooden chair any day.

Eric offered him a drink from an ice chest, and Matt accepted a bottle of water. Questions were coming, so he might as well have something ready when he needed it. He tried to appear relaxed, though his eyes scanned for Gina. He tugged the bill of his cap down.

Popping the top on his can, Eric motioned to the mess behind him. "If you have kids, you'll do this, too, don't worry."

Matt didn't think he'd ever have kids, so he thought it was kind of a moot point, but he made some kind of noise in agreement.

"Do you have kids, Matt?"

He shook his head. "No."

"How long have you been dating my daughter?"

He smiled slightly. "Just a few days."

Gina's dad actually looked relieved at the information. Matt tried not to feel aggravated.

"And you're a carpenter, right?"

"Yes."

Eric launched into a fairly one-sided conversation about the attributes of each type of wood he used, and Matt promised he'd check out his workshop before he left.

A hand rested on his right shoulder, and he looked up at a smiling Gina.

Her eyes widened theatrically, and Matt thought she was trying to tell him she was sorry for leaving him. Reaching up, he held her hand in his own and tugged a second chair close. Gina settled into it and didn't seem in a hurry to remove her hand. Actually, he thought it tightened.

Gina's dad was watching them carefully.

"So, Daddy, what kind of car did you get Charli?"

Eric smiled and rubbed his hands together. "Well, I debated on several things, but finally settled on a sedan."

Matt watched the interplay between father and daughter and found it fascinating. There was no animosity whatsoever, and Eric was genuinely interested in Gina's life. And vice versa. Gina seemed to know about every project he was working on.

"How did you break your wrist? You never did say."

Gina smiled and glanced at Matt. His clamped his mouth shut, and a hollow feeling settled in his stomach.

"Well, I ran into Matt in the office. Literally. And bounced off of him."

Sharp eyes looked to Matt. "Really?"

He nodded, though it pained him. "I tried to grab her, but she was already beyond my reach."

"Gina." Eric shook his head at her. "You're such a klutz. You have to be more careful, Pumpkin."

"I know, Dad," Gina sighed. "I was reading a chart and had my head down. It was like running into a brick wall, too."

She smiled when she said it though and tightened her hand on his. "I think it was the best thing that's happened to me in a long time."

Matt glanced at her earnest expression. There was no freakin' way she could believe that.

Gina didn't like the caged look in Matt's eyes. His ball cap shielded his face, but she could feel the tenseness in his hand as it clutched hers. Her dad was not very subtle. If he wanted to know something, he asked. Time for a change of direction.

"So how have you been feeling, Dad? Any more of those dizzy spells?"

Disgust curled her father's lips. "No more dizzy spells. Those doctors may have finally gotten something right with that new medication they put me on."

They talked of inconsequential things after that. When the topic veered too close to Matt, she tried to steer them in another direction. It helped when Charli came out of the house.

At sixteen, she carried herself as if she had seen everything. Her sleek, dark-blond hair was knotted haphazardly on top of her head, and her regular glasses were replaced by a pair of bright red frames. Even though it was a special day, she had her standard jeans and t-shirt on, but she was still damn cute.

Gina stood up from her chair and Charli squealed when she saw her. "Mom said you were here, but I didn't see your car." She wrapped her arms around Gina's waist and squeezed.

Gina was just as glad to see her little sister and held her tight. It had been several months since they'd been able to get together. Charli was one of the few people in her life who didn't dote over her as if she were sick all the time. She was born a few years after Gina had kicked the illness and had no memory of all the fuss and worry. Mary Beth, their older sister, was constantly mothering Gina, because she *did* remember.

She pulled back and motioned to Matt. "Charli, this is my friend Matt. He drove me today."

Charli's hazel eyes widened as Matt stood from the chair, but she shook his hand like it was no big deal. "Hi, Matt."

"Charli. Happy birthday."

"Cool tat." Charli beamed and turned back to Gina. "You've been busy," she murmured.

Embarrassment warmed her face. She and Charli spoke all the time, but she hadn't felt comfortable telling her about Matt. As mature as the girl seemed, she was still only sixteen, and certain things were beyond her scope of knowledge. At least Gina hoped they were. She didn't want to think of her little sister doing the nasty.

A group of girls gathered behind Charli, and they tugged her away, giggling.

Relatives and friends started to filter in, and Gina was busy greeting people she hadn't seen in a long time. She tried to keep Matt company, but it wasn't possible all the time. Surprisingly, though, he seemed to fit in fairly well. He played football with some of her younger male cousins and helped her dad carry firewood for the fire pit. At one point she even saw him transferring food out to the banquet table for her mother. Everything was good until the final guest came around the corner.

Chapter Ten

Gina knew before he was even introduced that this was the infamous doctor her mother had tried to set her up with. He was definitely good-looking, blond-haired and blue-eyed, but way too aware of his looks. Gucci loafers sank into the grass, and his knife-sharp khakis looked out of place amongst the jeans everybody else was wearing. He was carrying a brightly tissued gift bag and a container of store-bought baked beans. Why hadn't Mom uninvited him? She glared at her mother as she rose to greet him.

Linda had the good grace to look a little embarrassed, but she plowed on. "Grayson, over here. Everybody, I'd like to introduce you to Dr. Grayson Cooper. He just moved here from Florida."

Some of the crowd waved hello, but the response was unenthusiastic. The teenagers twittered and stayed huddled in their little group.

"And this is my daughter, Gina."

Smiling, Gina waved her casted arm as an excuse not to shake his hand, but she didn't move from beside Matt. Tightening her hand around his, she waited for the awkward situation to disappear.

Of course, it didn't.

"Gina, would you mind showing Grayson where to put things, please?"

She glared daggers but still responded to that tone in her mother's voice that said she wouldn't take any sass. With an apologetic glance at Matt, she rose to her feet. "This way Dr. Cooper."

"Grayson, please."

Gina smiled as politely as she could and directed him across the patio to the banquet table reserved for the food. "You can put your beans here, and the gift for Charli can go on that table."

Grayson juggled the two and tried to shift hands, but somehow bumbled the move. The beans dropped to the table and the thin plastic split up the side of the container. Bean juice splashed across the table and onto Grayson's khakis. The gift bag dropped to the ground and Gina heard the sound of breaking glass from inside.

He stared at the mess incredulously and Gina's reserve melted. "Oh, no. Here."

Gina scrambled for napkins to blot the mess up and handed a fistful to the doctor. She heard snickers from the group of girls and tossed them a murderous look. It was bad enough to walk into a group of people you didn't know, let alone have them laugh at you. She felt bad for the poor man. Grabbing the tub of beans, she tossed the whole thing into the trash can, then swiped again with the napkins. Her mother arrived to help, and she told Gina to take Grayson into the house to clean up.

Gina knew her mother was still trying to manage her, and it was seriously beginning to piss her off. Now was not the time to bitch, though.

"This way, Grayson."

She led him into the house and down the hallway to the bathroom just off the laundry room. The bean splash had managed to cover most of the front of his nice pants, and she had a sneaking suspicion he would need to put something else on.

"I don't know if those pants are going to be okay or not. I can get you a pair of my father's to put on for now, if you don't mind. We can wash the khakis and hopefully the stain won't set in."

Grayson's attractive face was twisted with aggravation. "I can't believe I did that. I haven't been that clumsy in years."

Gina laughed. "Must be nice. I'm clumsy all the time." She held up her wrist.

"Yes, that's what your mother said." He looked down at his pants in resignation. "I believe I'm going to have to accept your generous offer of a pair of pants. I don't believe I can comfortably drive home in this."

"Let's get your pants changed, we'll get your dress pants in the wash and you can come out and enjoy the party. What's your waist size?"

Luckily, he was the same size as her father. Gina crossed to the laundry room and tugged a pair of her father's jeans out of a stack. She handed them off, and accepted the dirties when he passed them through the crack of the door. She pre-treated them and tossed them in the washer.

If anything, Grayson looked even more uncomfortable when he stepped out of the bathroom. "I don't normally wear denim," he explained.

"Well, maybe you should. You look good in them." And he did. The legs were a little long, maybe, but they definitely fit him everywhere else.

"Thank you, Gina. You are as nice as your mother said you were." He smiled, and Gina felt like crap because she needed to clear the air.

"Uh, Grayson, thank you, but I need to tell you. My

mother invited you, but I already have a date. I'm sorry. I know this is kind of awkward for you, and I apologize for that."

His pretty blue eyes darkened with disappointment, and his smile became a little forced. "I wondered. I saw you holding the big man's hand when you stood up. He glared at me when you escorted me into the house."

Gina nodded. "Yes. We haven't been dating long, but it's pretty intense. I'm sorry. You seem like a very nice man."

He shrugged lightly and seemed determined to close the subject. He held the door open for her to precede him out to the fire-ring, then took a vacant chair a couple spaces down from her.

Gina sat in her own chair and placed her hand back over Matt's, but he didn't respond to her touch. She squeezed a bit, to get his attention, and he turned to look at her. "Are you okay?" she asked.

"I'm fine." His glance flicked to Grayson. "Should you go sit with him?"

"No. He's an adult. He'll find somebody to talk to. Mom can deal with him; she invited him. I'm with the person I want to be with."

One side of his mouth tipped up and he relaxed deeper in the chair. "So am I," he told her quietly, and squeezed her hand.

Gina felt her heart literally skip a beat. That was the biggest admission he'd ever made to her, and tears burned her eyes. She leaned her head against his broad shoulder to hide her emotion. He raised his arm and she burrowed into his chest. *I love you* was on the tip of her tongue, but she clamped her mouth shut. *Not yet.*

The conversation ebbed and flowed as the afternoon wore on. Dad got up and lit the barbeque, and Mom headed indoors to gather the utensils and meat. They were their usual selves, kissing and hugging each other as if each small absence hurt. Gina had grown up watching them love each other, but it appeared to fascinate Matt. Several times she caught him surveying their by-play with a quizzical expression.

"They're something, aren't they?" she whispered to him at one point.

Silvery-green eyes flared with heat when he looked at her and nodded.

"They met years ago when my dad did a tour in the Air Force. Mom was a waitress off-base from where he was stationed, and she says they fell in love within hours. They married a few weeks later."

"And they're always like this?" He motioned a hand at them as they huddled together near the barbeque, flipping meat. Her mom's right hand was in her father's back pocket.

"Always. Actually, my grand-parents on my mother's side were the same way. They died several years ago, just a few hours apart. They had done everything together throughout their lives. It was only fitting that they died the same way."

He hummed thoughtfully in his chest, and she left it at that.

They ate barbequed burgers and hot dogs, complemented by the casseroles people had brought in to contribute to the meal. Grayson made his apologies about the ruined beans, but Linda waved him off. They had plenty. Gina was very proud of her family full of wonderful cooks. Matt seemed to appreciate them as well, judging by the way he piled the food on his plate. Gina finished her own plate and then went back for dessert.

After dinner, Charli started to open her gifts. She was thoughtful and appreciative of everything she received and stacked the gifts carefully to the side of the table. Matt tensed when she got to their gift bag. Gina had gotten her a laptop backpack and a gift card. Charli was appreciative, but she positively melted when she pulled out the hand-carved, oak jewelry chest. "Oh, wow!"

She flipped the lid and pulled out the drawers, exploring, and when she was done she crossed the crowd to give Matt a huge hug. "Thank you so much. It's beautiful. I can tell you took a lot of time with it."

If it weren't for the darkening evening, Matt's face would have been red. "You're very welcome," he rumbled.

Gina was surprised at Charli's affection because she was usually more reserved. Maybe she, too, could see how badly Matt wanted to fit in.

The only gift that topped the chest was the car. Charli grinned when she unwrapped the tiny box with the keychain inside. Dad drove the car around the side of the house just then, and every teenager at the party screamed. Charli lost her natural reserve and jumped up and down like the young woman she was, then suddenly felt the need to go for a drive.

The party wound down after that. When his pants were dry, Grayson made his goodbyes to Linda, promising that he would get Charli a new, unshattered, present. The few people that were left gathered around the fire pit. Gina scooted her chair close enough to Matt's so he could wrap his arm around her. They sat that way until everybody had gone home and the fire was all but out.

Gina eventually tugged Matt into the house and up to her old room. Both of their bags were on the floor, so her mother must have gotten the message she was *with* Matt. Sitting on the edge of the full bed, he looked around her room curiously. Gina also sat down and tried to see it through his eyes. She probably looked like a spoiled girl with all the knick-knacks and baubles lying around. He motioned to the line of medallions and medals on one bookshelf. "What are those for?"

"The bigger ones are from Honor Roll, and the smaller ones from spelling bees. I used to be really into those." She rested a finger on the shelf above. "These things are from family vacations. The Grand Canyon, Disney World, Smoky Mountains." She touched each little memento as she pointed them out. "In between rounds of chemo or whatever medicine I was on at the time, my parents would make it a point to take us places. It was something to look forward to when I was going through treatment."

She motioned to the shelf on the bottom, full of spiral-bound notebooks. "And those are my dreams. Every want, need, thought, fantasy I had is in those books." She chose one at random, and flipped through. She stopped at a dog-eared page and started to read. "I want a prince to come to my room and bring all of his desert horses with him."

She shrugged self-consciously. With what she knew of his childhood, it was hard to be happy about her memories. "Did you get to do anything as a child?"

The ball cap tipped down as he looked at his feet. "Well, George took me to a couple of county fairs when I was smaller. Rick never had the money."

"Oh, I love fairs. The smells, and the lights, and of course the food."

Matt grinned at her. "Exactly. Once I knew what they were, I badgered George to take me every year."

Gina sat on the edge of the bed and crooked a knee to face him. "So, what do you like the best? The rides? Or the animals?"

"Oh, definitely the food. I would make myself sick on fair food when we went. I still go even now. Every year, religiously. Hell, it's where I. . ." He stopped suddenly, clamped his jaw and looked away.

Gina was fascinated by the sudden halt, and his reaction. "What? Where you what?"

Matt looked at her for several heartbeats of time. "It's where I first saw you."

"Really?" she whispered. Her heart pounded against her breastbone, and her eyes started to tear.

"Four years ago last September."

Her mouth dropped open. He had seen her four years ago? And remembered her? "Seriously?"

Matt nodded once and crossed his arms over his heavy chest. "You were standing with your friend Madison at the end of the horse barn, and you had called out a hello to somebody. Your hair was blowing in the breeze and you had on a pretty blue shirt that matched your eyes. For just one second, you looked at me. Then you turned away."

Gina was floored. "Did you speak to me or anything?"

He shook his head. "No. You were with friends and I didn't want to interrupt."

She swallowed heavily. What was going unsaid was the fact that he *did* remember her from years ago, meaning she had affected him somehow. "I wish you had, Matt. I was pretty lonely back then. I had decided to stay in Shelbyville after school, rather than head back home."

"Maybe if I had known that, I would have." He smiled at her gently, but she had a feeling he wouldn't have said a word.

Gina didn't know what to think. She certainly couldn't remember what shirt she had been wearing that night. It hadn't been memorable to her. It had been to Matt, though. Her heart warmed at the thought.

"So, when did you decide to bring George in? A couple months after that, right?"

"Yes."

"Did you know I worked there when you brought him in?"

He hesitated. "Yes."

Gina's eyes widened. Again, she was knocked off balance. Had he orchestrated taking George to see Dr. Hamilton so that he could see her again? She asked him, and his eyes flared with guilt.

"Yes. Although he *was* one of the doctors suggested to us after the transplant."

"So, why didn't you ever talk to me or ask me out? You just stood in the hall or sat in the waiting room and didn't say anything."

Matt ran his hands through his hair in agitation, dislodging the ball cap and sending his hair into spikes. The hat fell to the bed, then the floor, but he didn't seem to notice. "I couldn't. You're beautiful and friendly and everything I'm not. I should be shot for even being with you, because I don't want my bad reputation to rub off on you."

"Wait a minute." Gina waved her hand. "You don't have a bad reputation, your dad did."

His shoulders shifted in a shrug. "Calvin. That's all you have to say and people cringe."

Gina scrunched her face in aggravation. "Actually, it's not. They talk about your carpentry, a lot, actually, but I had never heard anything about your dad until you talked about him."

Matt didn't look like he believed her, but he didn't say anything more. He just clamped his lips and shook his head in disagreement.

"So, you've been watching me, kind of, for four years?"

He nodded once, expression guarded. "Yep."

"So, that day I ran into you. . ."

"I had finally decided to say something to you. About your hair. Turned out great, huh? Bet you wished I'd have left you alone."

Gina sighed at the bitterness she heard. "Actually, no. What I told my parents still stands. I think running into you was the best thing that's happened to me in a long time."

She rested her hand on his chest and tugged his chin toward her for a kiss. Reluctant at first, he was hard to move, but he gave in with a groan and cupped her head in his hands. Gina leaned into him, and when he guided her down onto the bed she was more than ready. If she could get him past the doubts, perhaps they would actually have a chance to create a life for themselves.

They made love that night slowly, and he cradled her afterward almost poignantly. It was like there was an ephemeral something in the air, and they were hesitant to speak of it because they didn't want it to drift away. Gina didn't want to go to sleep, because she was afraid this perfection was going to disappear. They both had doubts and fears, she knew that, but she also knew in her heart they could find some kind of common ground.

She woke in the morning wrapped in his strong arms, with his breath puffing in her hair from behind. Goose bumps raised the hair on her arms when she felt the stubble on his jaw brush against her. When she shifted, he tightened his arms around her. "Not just yet," he rumbled in her ear.

Gina was more than happy to stay where she was, but her body wouldn't let her relax. "I have to go," she whispered.

Sighing deeply, he relaxed his arms from around her. Gina padded to the bathroom and did her business. She brushed her teeth and finger combed her hair, then headed back to her room. Matt was sitting up on the side of the bed, rubbing his hands over his head. Gina paused at the doorway just to look at him and etch in her mind how content she felt. There were lines on his face where he must have lain on a folded piece of fabric, and his eyes were blurry with sleep, but when he saw her at the door, he smiled. Just for her.

She crossed the room to press a kiss to his lips. "I love you, Matt Calvin."

Stiffening, he pushed her away. There was a harsh frown on his face. "What?"

"I know I promised not to pressure you, but I had to tell you I love you."

Gina expected to feel fearful of his reaction, but instead she was totally content. Why not tell him?

Matt shook his head and left the bed to gather his clothes. Avoiding her eyes, he hopped on one leg, dragging his jeans up around his hips. He snatched his shirt on the way out the door.

Gina watched him leave, but she wasn't concerned that he hadn't responded. It would be shocking, hearing 'I love you' from a woman. Hell, it might be the only time he'd ever heard it. Her heart broke a little at the thought, because she knew it was probably true. It would take a while for him to assimilate her words, but if he had been watching her for four years, three little words weren't going to chase him off now. At least, she hoped not.

Chapter Eleven

Matt didn't know what to do. Dragging his t-shirt on as he jogged down the stairs, he walked down the hallway to the kitchen and stopped. Gina's mother stood at the stove, turning something in a skillet. She smiled when she saw him in the doorway, and he was struck by how much Gina looked like her. Curly hair, rounded cheek bones. Gina would look exactly like her in twenty years. His stomach turned in fear, and he fought not to bolt out the door.

Linda must have seen something in his eyes because she pointed at the exterior door. "Go out in the garage."

Matt shoved through the door and powered across the yard blindly. The door of the garage stood ajar and inside Eric sanded something on the workbench.

The smells of the shop immediately welcomed him, and he looked for something to do. Eric seemed to know what he needed. He thrust a plank of oak into his hands, and Matt turned to the double-side planer table in the corner. Feeding the board into the machine, he smoothed off a miniscule amount of wood. Flipping it over, he fed it back through the machine. Over and over again, he repeated the process, smoothing until it was uniform. Eric handed him another board, and he did the same thing to it, leveling the rough spots and making the surface usable. For the better part of thirty minutes he and Eric worked without saying a word.

Matt finally felt calm enough to look Gina's dad in the eye. "I don't understand your daughter."

Eric chuckled and smoothed his hand over the piece of wood Matt just finished. "Why are you telling me? Her mother's just as impossible."

Matt huffed and shook his head. "How do you. . ." He motioned with his hands, searching for words. He didn't know Eric well, but if anybody would understand, hopefully it would be him. "I've never been in any kind of long-term relationship, so I don't know what's expected or required. Is there some kind of manual to go by or something, or do you just flounder around and make a fool of yourself?"

Eric leaned against the workbench. "Definitely the latter. Women are fascinating, quicksilver creatures. Just when you think you know what makes them tick, they throw you a huge curveball. I've been married probably longer than you've been around, but I'm still barely keeping my head above water." He shrugged. "It's what makes us love them though."

Matt frowned. "I don't know if I can give her what she needs."

"What has she asked for?"

Frustrated, he shook his head. "Nothing specifically, but she needs more emotionally than I can give her. I'm not. . .equipped to be in a relationship. I have no idea how one even works."

Eric's keen eyes smiled at him.

"It works like any relationship, with give and take by both parties. Compromise. You need to be caring of the other person's well-being and accepting of their mistakes. But I'll tell ya," he said with a grin, "when it works right, you can't ask for anything more. There is definitely an art to love."

Matt was awash in emotions. On the one hand, he was honored that Gina had told him she loved him. In his wildest imagination, he'd never expected that. When he spoke to her in the doctor's office, he thought perhaps they could talk to each other occasionally about things other than George. Hell, it had only been a little over a week since he'd knocked her down and broken her wrist. His mind just couldn't fathom how quickly they'd connected. It had to be too fast. Maybe she was misunderstanding the gratitude she felt for him. Hell, maybe she told all the guys she went out with she loved them.

That depressed the hell out of him. He didn't want to be just another number in her long line of men.

"So, how long was it before you knew you loved your wife?" Matt asked.

Eric looked down at the plain gold band on his left hand, then held it up for Matt to see. "I knew within hours that I loved Linda, and I bought the wedding bands a couple of days later. I couldn't believe it when she agreed to go out with me, then accepted my marriage proposal. There were guys panting after her like crazy, but she took a chance on me." He shrugged philosophically. "You can't choose who grabs your heart."

Those words settled into Matt's mind and stuck there. He was exactly right.

Matt felt more relaxed than when he had stormed in. "Thanks, Eric. I didn't mean to rush in here and scare you or anything. I just needed. . ."

The older man waved him off. "No worries. Anytime, Matt."

Eric shifted and brought Matt's attention to one of the projects he was working on, and Matt was glad of the distraction. For the better part of an hour they talked shop, compared machines and methods, until Gina suddenly burst through the door. Her hair was wild and her face was pale.

"Gabe's in trouble. We have to go."

Tension gripped Matt's stomach. "What's going on?"

Tears filled her eyes as he reached out to grip her shoulders. "He called my cell phone from my house and left a message. Says he's hiding from Chuck because he went off the deep end and started destroying the house. We have to go."

Matt turned and shook Eric's hand, then herded Gina out of the garage. Linda met them at the truck with their bags. She hugged Gina and pressed a kiss to her cheek. "Call me," she whispered. Then she turned a tugged him down for a kiss on his cheek. Matt was stunned. "Take care of my little girl," she told him

Matt nodded and urged Gina into the truck, settling her in the middle. He climbed in beside her, made sure they were both belted in and started the truck. "She'll be fine," he promised before he shut the door and took off.

They didn't talk much on the way home. Gina called her friend at child protective services, but reached her voicemail. She debated calling Shelbyville PD. There was a chance if they did find Gabe the police would just turn him back over to Chuck. It had happened before. If there was no identifiable trauma on the boy, he had to go back to his legal guardian. It was logged as an unruly child call. It was ridiculous that the child got the blame.

Tears came to her eyes as she thought about him hiding under her stairs. He'd let himself into the house with the key hidden outside, then called her from her kitchen phone. She'd told him where to hide, and the fact that he hadn't blustered and said he was fine told her how scared he was. He took the receiver with him and she told him if he heard anything to call 911.

She glanced at Matt. His jaw was tight, brows furrowed fiercely. He had both hands on the wheel, and his foot was heavy on the gas pedal. She prayed they didn't get pulled over.

Time seemed to drag as the miles zipped away. And it seemed the closer they got, the longer it took. The last few blocks to her house took forever, and when they finally pulled into her drive a little after ten, she jumped out of the truck and ran to her steps before Matt had even stopped the vehicle. The house next door was quiet, but there was stuff scattered all over the lawn. Chuck was nowhere to be seen, though his car was parked sideways in the driveway.

Gina shoved her key in the lock and ran inside. Terror stopped her in her tracks when she found Chuck standing inside her hallway, digging at the panel where Gabe was hiding under the stairs. "No," she screamed.

Chuck grinned fiercely when he saw her and lunged. His bloodshot eyes were wild. "I'm so damn tired of you, bitch."

Before she could even turn away, he had grabbed her by the hair and shoved her face first against the wall. Pain blazed through her cheekbone. He didn't get a chance to do anything else though, because Matt blasted through the doorway. Chuck took a swing at the bigger man and missed, and Matt was on him. The first punch shattered Chuck's nose. Blood gushed. The older man turned back for more, so Matt cracked him in the jaw. Gina heard the bone break from across the room and watched in satisfaction as Chuck dropped to the floor like a bag of rocks. He lay there, unmoving.

Gina fumbled her phone out of her pocket with

shaking hands and called 911, telling them she needed a squad car and an ambulance at her address. Her cheek blazed with pain, and she actually hoped there was bruising so that she could press charges against Chuck.

She stumbled to the hidden door and tapped on it gently.

"Gabe, you can come out, honey."

The door was unlocked from the inside and shoved open. Then she was holding him tight against her. As he broke into sobs, it was all she could do to stay on her feet, so she sat down on the floor and cradled him to her. "It's okay, buddy. It's okay," she whispered.

She looked over Gabe's head and saw Matt just standing at the front door. His bloody fists were clenched, and he glared down at the unmoving older man. Gina thought she should maybe get up and check on the man, but Gabe was her priority right then. After several minutes, his tears began to ease and he pulled back. The sounds of sirens built until they suddenly stopped outside her house. Gina shifted to look down at the boy. A dark purple bruise spread across the left side of his face, and she cursed. "He did that to you? Why didn't you tell me, Gabe? I'd have had the cops here sooner."

He shook his blond head. "I wanted to wait for you."

Matt went out the door to meet the policemen. Gina heard yelling and a sudden scuffle. With fear in her throat, she rushed to the door, tugging Gabe behind her.

Matt was lying face down on the porch, hands cuffed behind his back. One policeman had his knee on Matt's neck to hold him down.

"No," she yelled. "You have the wrong man. Leave him alone!"

A young cop held her back as she tried to get to Matt. She grabbed the man's arm and tugged him toward the house. She pointed at Chuck sprawled on her hardwood floor. "He's the one that broke in here after the boy. He went for me and slammed me into the wall." She pointed at her face and prayed it was red enough for him to see. "Matt saved us. Chuck kept coming at us, but Matt stopped him. You have to let him go."

But it took thirty minutes and a gazillion repetitive questions before they finally felt comfortable releasing him. Matt outweighed the largest of the cops by about fifty pounds, so she could kind of understand the hesitation. They snapped digital pictures of Gabe's face, then her own. They also found where he had broken in through the kitchen door.

Matt's eyes burned with anger and humiliation, and she wanted to go to him, but Gabe was her priority. The ambulance arrived and checked him over. They told her he needed x-rays to confirm that nothing was actually broken.

A woman from Children's Services arrived and took a report but refused to allow Gabe to stay with Gina. The woman told her how to go about filing for temporary custody but was implacable when it came to taking the boy. "You are not a relative. You are a neighbor. That's it. You need to go through the proper channels to be granted custody."

Gabe was stoic. "It's okay, Gina. I kind of knew this was going to happen eventually. I'll be fine." He hugged her hard one last time, then followed the woman to the car.

Gina burst into tears for the first time as the car disappeared down the block. She didn't know what would happen to him, and it broke her heart. Matt unbent enough to cradle her in his arms and let her cry.

The police left and the ambulance hauled Chuck away. He had roused and started to spout threats, which backed up their story even more, but it was hard to feel victorious as her life fell apart around her. Even though Matt held her, there was a distance in him that was absolutely terrifying. More than anything else she'd gone through that morning.

Using her cell phone, she heard him call her parents and let them know everything was all right, and that she would call later to fill them in on the details. Then he guided her up the steps and into her house. In the kitchen he filled a cloth with ice cubes and held it to her face. Then he apparently caught sight of his still bloody hands, because he cursed and moved to scrub them under the faucet.

"I'm sorry, Gina," he muttered. "I shouldn't have been touching you with that nastiness on my hands."

She stepped close enough to run her hand down his back, but he pulled away. He snatched a handful of paper towels off the roll, pulled a cleaning bottle and trash bag out from beneath the cupboard and headed back to the front. "Matt, don't worry about that. I'll get it."

But he didn't appear to hear her. Maybe he was just ignoring her.

He wiped up the small pool of blood Chuck had left behind, bound the trash bag and put it in the can outside the kitchen door. Gina followed along behind, aware that he was going to do what he thought he needed to do before he would relax. Drained, she sat at the kitchen tabled and watched as he put the supplies away. Then he stood at the kitchen sink and looked out the back window.

There was so much brittle emotion on his face. She was afraid to start a conversation, because she didn't want to bring anything to a boil, but she was afraid that if she didn't, she would lose Matt.

"Thank you for saving me. I never in a million years expected him to be standing on the other side of that door."

Matt snorted, and his head bowed. At some point he'd lost his hat, and the dark brown curls were mussed.

"I didn't do anything, Gina. Just pounded the shit out of some guy that deserved it. I guess the Calvin genes came in handy for once."

"Yes, they did," she agreed. "I wish I could have done it myself. You stopped when you needed to, though. Your dad didn't."

He shook his head, still not looking at her. "I didn't stop because I wanted to."

"Well, regardless, you did, and I thank you for it."

Bile rose in Matt's throat as he heard her words. When he'd seen Chuck with his hands on Gina, he had literally seen red. He'd kicked Chuck's ass, and she just didn't understand how easy it had been. For years he'd lived his life carefully, removed from the rest of the world because he knew what kind of vengeful monster lived inside him. That monster had LOVED breaking the older man's nose and jaw. It had appealed to the animal in him to protect his woman and child, and if the same threat was presented, he'd do it again a million times over.

But what was to keep his anger from going wild and hurting the very ones he vowed to protect? He was hooked on Gina bad, but what if she pissed him off at some point? Would he lose control of his anger like he had tonight and go off on her? Or worse, on the boy?

Redness on his wrists caught his attention. They'd cuffed him because he looked like a criminal. Could he blame them? The damn tattoo wrapping around his forearm certainly didn't proclaim him a lawyer or a doctor. But then, he'd kind of screwed himself in having the ink put on in the first place.

Nausea turned his stomach at what he had to do.

Gina was pale, and her fine brows were furrowed over her eyes. The redness on her cheek wasn't fading, and he knew it would bruise within the next few hours and be sore as hell. Her right wrist was cradled to her stomach.

Every mark on her was directly or indirectly because of his actions.

"Gina, I need to go."

Disappointment shadowed her face, and she looked down at her feet without saying anything. When she looked back up, her eyes swam with tears. "Okay Matt. I understand. I guess I'll see you tomorrow."

He shook his head sharply. "I don't think so. The banister is done, and I've gone to your cook-out. I've done everything I said I would."

Her jaw slackened as she realized what he was telling her. "You're breaking up with me?"

Frowning fiercely, he crossed his arms over his chest, fighting despair. "We were never together. I told you I couldn't give you what you wanted. I've had fun with you, but that's it."

"So the fact that I love you doesn't mean anything?"

For a terrible minute he faltered, wanting desperately to cave. How could he tell her something so precious, something he'd never had before, didn't mean anything? He couldn't. "I think you might be confused right now. Your emotions are pretty upset with Gabe being gone and everything."

Blue fire glared up at him. "That doesn't mean I don't know what's in my heart. I told you I loved you this morning, before all this crap happened."

She waved her good hand at the foyer where the battle had taken place.

Matt fought not to be swayed. "You did. But when you have a chance to think about things, you'll realize it was the best decision that I left. I'm not the right man for you."

Gina shook her head and stared at him through dazed eyes. One tear slipped down her cheek, but she swiped it away. "I think you're wrong Matt Calvin. You have some crazy thought in your head that I would be better off without you, but that's a load of bull."

He shrugged and dropped his arms. "I'm not the man for you, Gina."

Then, before he lost it completely, he turned and walked out the door.

Gina's eyes burned with tears, and her head throbbed. She'd just had two very special men ripped from her life within the space of an hour. Her emotions were zigzagging from low to even lower. What the hell had she done to be punished this way?

Grabbing a paper-towel from the rack, she blew her nose and took several deep breaths. It didn't do any good to break down now. The situation with Matt needed to take the back burner. She needed to find out what could be done about Gabe.

Apparently, nothing.

Patrice called several hours later, but the news was not good. With the new manager she had at the Department, everything needed to be done by the letter. Gina would need to petition the court for custody the next day. Assuming she actually wanted Gabe to stay with her.

Gina sat back in her chair to digest the words her friend had spoken. Of course she wanted Gabe, but would she be the best alternative to take the child on?

Flashes of curling up on the couch and watching TV with him and stuffing his pockets with food bombarded her. Would she do it again? Absolutely. Did she think she could be a good influence on the child? Again, absolutely. Did she want a child and all the responsibility they entailed?

She thought about that one for a total of about three seconds before deciding the answer was unequivocally yes. It would be a change for her lifestyle, but it would be for the better, for both of them.

Patrice promised to meet her at the courthouse the next day to file the papers. Gina called Dr. Hamilton to let him know what was going on, and that she would need the morning off. She told him about the incident that morning and he readily agreed, cautioning her that she would need to secure child care for the evenings she needed to work late. Gina promised him she would tackle the task the next morning.

Then, emotionally drained, she dragged herself up the stairs to take a hot bath. And allow herself to cry.

Chapter Twelve

Matt didn't see Gina for a solid week, and when he did catch a glimpse of her it was by chance. He'd thrown a few groceries into a cart when he saw her at the opposite end of the aisle he was in. She was scanning juice boxes, totally oblivious that he watched her. Standing completely still, he traced his eyes over her. She looked good, of course, though there were dark circles beneath her eyes.

He wanted to walk up and tell her how very much he missed her. The truck upholstery still smelled like her, and the night he'd broken up with her, he'd found a blue hair scrunchy in his bed. He slipped his left hand into his pocket to reassure himself that it was still there, then shook his head at the sentimentality. He needed to pitch the damn thing in the trash. Instead he flexed it around his fingers and held it tight. Gina had been a brilliant detour in his mundane life, and if this was all he had left of her, they could pry it out of his cold, dead hand.

George had heard through one of his cronies that Chuck was unable to post bond, so he would be in jail until he went to court. He had three aggravated assault charges, child abuse charges and a raft of other things he had to account for, so hopefully he would be away for a good, long time.

Matt was glad that the boy wouldn't have to deal with him. He also found himself worrying, though, too. Orphanages were not nice places.

For the heck of it he'd called Children's Services to see if he was okay. They wouldn't release information to Matt, of course, because he wasn't a relative. He asked what the process was for filing for adoption, then shook his head at his own foolishness. There was no way on earth he could take in a young child like that, but he found himself taking notes anyway.

If he knew Gina at all, she had already applied for custody. He'd seen how much the boy meant to her, and vice versa. The two of them would be together eventually, he had no doubt.

He and Gina, on the other hand, were done.

Leaving the cart in the aisle, he turned and walked out of the store. The chain across town had a better selection anyway. Or at least that's what he told himself.

Gina thought she saw Matt's big dually leaving the parking lot when she looked out the big plate glass windows, and her heart thudded painfully. She missed him, desperately, and it wasn't easing up. He'd only technically been in her life for a week, but it had been the best week of her life, broken wrist aside. Even though he was gruff and reclusive, he'd tugged at her heart with his humility and doubts. But those doubts had overwhelmed any chance of a relationship they might have had.

In spite of what he had done to Chuck, Gina knew Matt was a gentle man struggling with demons from his past. The altercation had just brought all those demons howling to the forefront of his mind.

She tried to tell herself that he had never had a healthy, romantic relationship, so he didn't know how to proceed. And the thought of being vulnerable to another person was difficult. She knew. In spite of telling him she loved him, he walked away. Destroying her.

Her eyes burned with tears and she swiped them away angrily. She was tired of crying over him and feeling so whipped. Besides, she had a new son to take care of.

Two weeks later, Gina saw George's name on the patient roster for later in the day. Matt would drive him in and she could finally talk to him for a minute. About Gabe, and other general things. She could thank him for the locksmith he had sent over to fix her back door after Chuck had broken in.

From behind the reception desk, she watched as the big dually pulled into the parking lot, and Matt circled around the hood to help George step down. Resting her hand on the window, she tried to see Matt's expression, but his head was tipped down, and the ball cap shaded his face as he spoke to the elderly gentleman.

Gina hustled into the back when they disappeared from view and debated sending one of the other girls to check on the old man. That was cowardly, though, and she didn't want to be like that. So, when a space opened up in the exam area, she went out to the reception and called George's name.

For the briefest second she glanced at Matt and was stunned at how lean his face looked, even covered by the light beard. The old man stepped in front of her and smiled, taking her good arm as they walked down the hallway. The entire time she could feel Matt's hard eyes following her, tracing down her back, and in spite of where they were and how they had ended, she felt desire curl through her belly.

George was his same old ornery self, teasing her as she took his vitals, but when she prepared to leave he gripped her hand. "Sit down a minute, girly."

Swallowing, she sat in the chair beside his. "What do you need, George?"

Rheumy blue eyes squinted at her in humor. "I don't need anything. That boy out there does, though."

Her eyes suddenly burned with tears. "Is he okay?" she whispered. "He looks. . ."

"Like he's had his heart broken," George finished. "Now, I don't know what happened between the two of you, but he did everything he could not to come in here with me, and he's been snappin' my head off like crazy when I talk about you. What's going on?"

A tear rolled down her cheek, and she brushed it away.

"He didn't want to stay with me. I told him I loved him, but he got into that fight with Chuck and it all fell apart. It was like he thought he was going to just snap and hurt me one day, and he's not like that. It made him sick when we ran into each other and I broke my wrist. He would never intentionally hurt me."

George nodded and swiped his hand over the few gray hairs on his head.

"We know that, but he doesn't. That boy got his ass kicked almost every day for years on end. Watched his momma get beat up a few of those years. He grew up in violence, and he thinks that if something sets him off, he'll go back to what he knows. That's a lot of learning to change in just a couple of weeks."

Gina nodded. George was absolutely right. Things had moved very fast between them, and it probably had overwhelmed him. Maybe if she just bided her time and tried to be positive, they could build something stronger that would last.

She leaned over and gave the old man a hug. "Thanks, George. I'll try to be patient with him."

"How's that boy Matt talked about?"

"Oh, he's wonderful!" she gushed. "The judge granted me temporary custody, and I can eventually petition for adoption. We're going to his old house tonight and moving boxes of his stuff over. He's changed so much already."

George grinned and patted her good arm. "I think you're the best thing to ever happen to that boy."

Her eyes watered at the vote of confidence. "Thanks, George."

Wiping her eyes and taking a deep breath, she stepped out of the room, placing the chart in the holder by the door. She paused long enough to glance at Matt and give him a small smile. "Hi, Matt."

"Gina."

"Thank you for sending the locksmith over to fix the door. I wasn't in a good frame of mind to think of it."

He shrugged, arms folded tight to his chest. The glower on his face was positively scary and reserved. Exactly what he wanted, she thought.

"No problem."

Gina really tried not to be hurt by his abrupt attitude, but the pain must have shown on her face. For a split second, his frown softened, and he looked about to say something. She held her breath, but one of the nurses came down the hallway and shattered their privacy. Matt clamped his jaw, shuttered his gaze and stared over her head.

"Well, it was nice talking to you," she whispered, wounded all over again. Gathering her shredded confidence, she turned for the break room. She asked one of the other nurses to assist with George and waited until she knew for a fact they were gone.

"She's moving."

Matt almost wrecked the truck as he whipped his head to George. "What?"

"Packing tonight, she said."

"Gina? What about her job? And the boy?"

The old man shrugged and looked out the windshield.

Matt clamped his hands on the wheel and fought not to throw up. She hadn't said anything to him at the office. *Well, of course not. You were a total asshole to her.* But if he meant anything to her, shouldn't she have at least mentioned it?

Matt pulled up in his driveway and walked George across to his own house, still tossing the question around in his mind. Letting himself into his garage, he snatched up a long piece of rough plank wood and went to the planer, running it through the machine. What did he expect her to do? Wait around for him until he thought he might be okay to be with her? Before he'd walked into the office earlier, he'd worried that he would hear about whoever she was dating this week. He certainly didn't expect to be broadsided by her leaving.

The thought of never seeing her again brought damnable tears to his eyes. She was the first honestly good thing he'd ever allowed into his life.

Doubt nagged at him. Maybe George had heard her incorrectly. Maybe she was helping a friend pack or something.

Indecision whittled at his mind. He could drive over there and talk to her and put all these questions to rest. But what right did he have to even question her? If she wanted to move away, he couldn't do anything about it.

He'd given up that right when he'd turned his back, literally, on her love.

For a couple of hours he wavered back and forth. A nasty, inch long splinter in his hand forced him away from the workshop and gave him the perfect excuse to go to her. Hopping into the truck and heading to her house, he debated what he would say. If she was moving, maybe he could. . .his mind shut down. The thought of her leaving hollowed out his gut. For four years she'd been a vital part of his life, whether she knew it or not. He simply couldn't imagine her not being there.

The stack of mismatched cardboard boxes stacked on her porch told him he would have to find out what it would be like without her.

Parking in Gina's driveway, he turned off the truck and just sat there, unable to believe she was leaving him. After everything she'd told him, and done for him, she was leaving. He shook his head as pain tore through him. Then anger. Every word she'd spoken had to have been a line. The entire time he'd been with her, she'd been playing him. That was the only explanation. If she did love him, surely she'd stay as close as she could, right? And wait for him to admit he cared for her?

Not even understanding what he was doing, he slammed out of the truck and jogged across the sidewalk. He leapt the stairs like they weren't even there and pounded his fist against her front door. Gina answered almost immediately. Her expression turned guarded when she saw him and he hated that he had dimmed her spirit that way. "Why didn't you tell me you were moving?" he demanded. "In the office, why didn't you tell me?"

Confusion creased her brow and her mouth fell open. "What?"

He motioned to the boxes angrily. "Why didn't you tell me you were leaving? Thirteen days ago, you told me you loved me, and now you can't wait to get away from me. Why the hell did you tell me you loved me? Was it a game to you, showing me what I could have and then tearing it away?"

The confusion cleared and anger took its place. She folded her arms across her breasts. "I didn't tear it away. You were the one who left me, remember? I told you I loved you and you walked away. During one of the most traumatic nights of my life, I might add."

But he wasn't listening to reason.

"If you change your mind that easily, maybe it's best that you do leave."

She reared back as if he had slapped her. Matt felt like the lowest kind of snake. Tears filled her blue eyes, but she swiped them away angrily. She stared at him for a long moment, then stepped back and shut the door quietly in his face.

"You're just plain stupid!"

Matt turned from the door reluctantly. Gabe stood at the base of the porch steps, arms wrapped around a cardboard box. Anger twisted his young face. "Why did you tell her that? She's always nice to you and stands up for you even when you aren't around. If she told you she loves you, then she means it."

The boy stomped up the stairs and dropped the box next to the rest on the porch. "She's not the one moving. I am. The court said I can live with her, and she's going to adopt me. We've been moving my stuff over from Chuck's house."

Matt felt the world shift on its axis. She wasn't leaving? But George had said. . .what needed to be said to get him over here. And now he'd made her cry. Because of his own insecurity.

The one person he cherished most in the world and he kept hurting her. He dropped down to the top step of the porch and put his head in his hands, scrubbing his eyes furiously.

What a fucking idiot.

A gentle hand on his shoulder drew his attention.

"Gina doesn't stay mad very long. If you apologize to her, I bet she'll forgive you for what you said."

Matt wasn't so sure. All he'd done ever done was hurt her. How could she still love him?

Gabe stood beside him, hand still on his shoulder.

"I don't know, Gabe. I was pretty mean. I've never been in a situation like this. Not sure what to think. Or do."

Nodding his head, the boy settled on the step beside him. "Neither have I, but if I can be anywhere in the world, it would be with Gina. I promised her I would keep my room clean and everything if she would take me in, but she said I only needed to love her."

Matt's stomach turned. Was this desperate, frantic feeling actually love? Or obsession? He didn't have the slightest idea. It wasn't something he'd ever dealt with before. It was like he was standing on a cliff and either way he jumped promised pain beyond what he could imagine.

"You need to go tell her you're sorry," Gabe told him, arms folded.

"I know."

But did he have the guts to see the condemnation in her eyes? He wavered for several minutes before he finally got frustrated with himself. *Get it over with.*

The front door was unlocked, so he walked through. She probably wouldn't have voluntarily let him in, but he chose to remember her last directive, when he had been allowed to enter as he pleased.

Gina wasn't in the living room or the kitchen. Matt ran his hands over the re-built banister and climbed the steps to the second floor. Gina was in her bedroom, sitting in the chair on the far side of the room. She stared out the window, but he didn't think she actually saw anything. Her face was blotchy with tears, but Matt still thought she was the most beautiful thing he'd ever seen.

"If you're just going to be nasty, you can head right back down those stairs."

"I'm not going to be nasty," he sighed. "I'm going to apologize."

She glanced at him from beneath her curly hair and crossed her arms over her t-shirt. He walked close enough to kneel in front of her but didn't touch her. "I'm floundering in deep water here, Gina. Everything about this situation is new to me and it scares the shit out of me. I don't know what to think from one minute to the next.

"Gabe told me he was the one moving over here. I'm sorry I jumped to conclusions."

She continued to stare out the window and avoid his gaze.

Matt began to panic.

"Gina, I don't want to lose you, but I'm not sure how to keep you. Do you know what I mean? I don't know what to do to make you happy."

Finally, she glanced at him, tears filling her eyes again. "You just have to be with me, Matt. You may not understand it, but just being close to you, and talking to you, and making love to you makes me extremely happy. You are a wonderful man, whether you see it or not."

He looked down at his boot, but the damn thing was blurry. He swiped at his eyes, but it didn't clear up.

Gina's heart broke at the confusion she saw in Matt's eyes. She leaned forward and wrapped her arms around his head, knocking his ball cap to the floor. She pressed gentle kisses from the crown of his head all the way down the side of his neck.

"I understand why you left. You were defensive about what you did to Chuck and you expected me to jump all over you. So you removed yourself from the situation before you were hurt. But I'll tell you a secret."

She leaned down enough to look in his eyes. "If I could have done that to Chuck, I would have. You protecting us doesn't mean you have a monster inside of you that's going to lash out and hurt me. It means you're human."

Matt shook his head. "You don't understand how much I enjoyed it, though. It was the best feeling to let my anger out on him."

Gina nodded. "I'm sure it was. And I'm sure you probably envisioned Chuck as your dad and imagined beating the crap out of him like he did you all those years."

A stunned look settled on his face and Gina wondered if he'd ever talked these things out with a counselor. Most assuredly not.

"Matt, I love you. Those aren't just words. It's a commitment that I will support you in whatever you want to do, or be, or whatever. If you want to paint your house neon green and line the sidewalk with carpet, I'll be right there beside you. If you want to run for state senator, I'll be beside you. Love doesn't stop just because the other person has hang-ups, or issues, or reservations. We can go as slow as you want to go. If you want to be friends right now, I'll try to be good with that. If you want to move into my house and start planning a future together, I'm good with that too.

Although you're kind of getting a ready-made family with Gabe moving in." She grinned at him and rested her hand on his face. "I'll take anything you're willing to give."

Oh, so gently, she pressed her lips to his, afraid he would pull away. But he didn't. Instead he wrapped his arms around her and lifted her up from the chair, holding her high off the floor. Gina tried to keep her breath as he squeezed her tight and buried his lips against her neck.

"I think I love you," he whispered.

Her heart stalled in her chest, then started to race. Tears flooded her eyes and rolled down her cheeks and she tightened her own arms around his neck. She knew that was probably the first time he'd ever said those words, so she branded them on her mind. And heart.

"Is he moving in too?"

They both laughed and pulled apart to look at Gabe standing in the doorway.

"Well," she hedged, "not right now. Hopefully he'll be around a lot, though."

Gabe nodded like it was a done deal and continued on to his room.

Matt set her on her feet and cupped her face. "If you're sure you want to take a chance on me, I guarantee you I will be around. And I'll do everything I can to deserve your love."

He wrapped his heavy arms around her, and Gina knew it was where she was meant to be.

Epilogue

Five months later. . .

Matt felt like a bull in a china shop. A dirty bull, at that. He should have at least changed out of his work clothes before he walked through those glass doors, but he'd wanted to be early.

He glanced around. The guy in the suit at the far end of the room stared at him hard. Matt tugged the bill of his ball cap down further over his face and hunched into his coat, then realized that that probably just made him look even more criminal. Hell.

Deliberately, he turned to the acres of glass cases that surrounded him. Where to start? This area seemed to be chains and little dangly things. He moved on down. Watches. Looking around, he finally spotted a case of rings on the far side of the room.

As he passed the front door of the store, the bell attached to the handle rang as Monroe walked in, looking relaxed and happy in ragged jeans, t-shirt and jacket.

Matt moved to shake his hand, relieved that his best buddy had actually shown up.

"I thought you'd forgotten."

Monroe grinned and slapped him on the back.

"Nah, I just couldn't resist a few more minutes in bed. Gotta take it when I can get it, you know?"

Matt nodded, but he couldn't imagine being on call the way Monroe had to be. This year's fire season had been fierce and he hadn't been in town very much at all, even though it was almost winter time. It seemed like as soon as one fire was battled down, his team were called to another.

Matt didn't know how Monroe did it, being on the run all the time.

The door bell rang again and Gina's friend Madison came in the door, looking exactly as a person should in a place like this. Trendy and put together, her dark hair tossed by the wind. Much more so than the two of them standing in the middle of the floor.

Out of the corner of his eye he noticed Monroe straighten and he laughed softly to himself. Madison didn't put up with crap and Monroe was full of it. Could be interesting.

"Anderson Monroe this is Madison Cleary, Gina's best friend. Madison, this is my buddy Monroe."

The two of them shook hands and exchanged smiles but Madison pulled her hand away quickly. For a split-second it looked like Monroe didn't want to let her go, but he did.

"Nice to meet you, Madison."

She tipped her head. "And you as well, Mr. Monroe."

"Nah, just Monroe."

But she'd already turned toward Matt. "Have you looked yet?"

Matt shook his head and followed her as she went to the ring section. Of course she'd known exactly where it was.

Matt watched Monroe watch Madison from behind. She had exactly the look that appealed to his friend. Long, dark hair, pale eyes, trim shape. She was a nice woman though. He didn't want to jeopardize her friendship with Gina.

"Monroe, I don't think she's your type," he whispered.

Monroe didn't even spare him a glance. "Of course, she is. Every woman is my type."

He moved forward to stand beside her at the glass case, but she shifted subtly away.

Matt shook his head. Sometimes his friend refused to see the obvious.

"Have you looked at any other stores yet, Matt?"

He shook his head as he stepped to Madison's opposite side. "Not very much. A couple of places. I thought you might be able to give me some insight."

She nodded and peered into the cases. When the salesclerk came around she requested a couple of trays be pulled out.

They looked for several minutes but nothing appealed to him in the engagement section. Monroe pointed out big gems that would be too much for Gina. Madison's suggestions got closer to what she liked, but nothing just leapt out at him.

Until a shine of blue in the next section caught his attention.

When he leaned down to look more closely, he knew he'd found the one. The round sapphire was good sized but not too big. More importantly, it reminded Matt of Gina's eyes. "Let me see this one." He stabbed a finger at the glass.

The manager stepped over and pulled the ring from the case for him. Matt felt awkward as he took the tiny thing in his hand. He'd never handled a piece of jewelry like this and he was afraid to drop it. "This is a sapphire, right?"

The manager smiled and nodded. "It is. A one carat total weight natural round stone with another half carat of diamonds flanking it. The ring is fourteen karat white gold."

Matt turned the ring and caught sight of the price tag. Wow. That was a lot of furniture money. But she was worth it. How could he not get it? It was the exact shade of her eyes.

Madison grinned at him and nodded her dark head. "That's perfect for her. She'll love it. She's a size six."

He handed the ring back to the manager. "How soon can I get it sized?"

"Wait, you're buying it?" Monroe looked shocked.

Matt frowned at him. "Why did you think we came in here?"

His buddy shrugged and glanced away. "I just didn't think you were that close."

They settled the bill and the manager disappeared into the back with the ring, promising to be out in a little while. He turned to Madison.

"Thanks for coming. I really appreciate it."

"It was my pleasure. When are you going to ask her?"

Matt swallowed heavily, fear crawling up his spine. "I have dinner reservations Friday. Maybe then."

She reached forward, gave him a quick hug and pulled away. "I'm sure you'll do fine. Gina will be overjoyed. She's nuts about you. You know that."

He nodded, though he didn't know anything of the kind. It seemed like they got along great together, but it had only been about six months. How did a person know they were with the one they were supposed to be with the rest of their lives? He loved Gina. He did know that. But would it be enough to last for the next fifty years?

Monroe snorted, leaning against the glass case. "I can't believe you're actually doing it. I can't believe you want to stay with the same woman for thirty or forty years."

The echo of a variation of the fears floating in his head made him pause.

"Nonsense," Madison admonished. "If you find the right person the years will be easy. Believe me."

A sad look crossed her face. Gina hadn't told him a lot about her friend, only that she was a jaded romantic at heart and a wonderful nurse. Madison blinked and the sadness disappeared.

"You guys have fun. I have to get to an appointment. Don't doubt what you feel Matt. Gina will love it."

She tossed Monroe a cool smile and sailed out of the store.

"Man, she's cute, but that girl's trouble."

He glanced at his friend in surprise. "Why do you say that? I thought 'every woman was your type'?"

"Not that kind." He shuddered as he watched her walk across the street out front. "She's got 'commitment' written all over her. Dangerous."

"Just because you're a commitment-phobe you'd pass her over? She could be really good for you and fun. But how would you know if you don't go out with her?"

Monroe turned to stare at him and Matt realized how much he'd changed since he met Gina. Not too long ago, he'd been a commitment-phobe as well, but his tune was completely different now.

The manager came back with the ring, then, and handed it to Matt. It was so damn tiny. For curiosity's sake he slipped it on his pinky, but it wedged after the first knuckle.

He prayed Madison had been right about the size.

Monroe split when they left the store and Matt wondered if his friend had even heard his words. He'd seemed put out with him.

As Matt walked down the street to his truck, he wondered what kind of woman it would take to make Monroe fall as hard as he himself had.

Gina glanced at the wall clock in frustration, chewing absently on a thumbnail. Matt was late. Dinner simmered on the stove ready to dish up as soon as he got home. Gabe had gone to a friend's house after school and would call her in a couple of hours for a pick-up. She smiled at the thought of the look on his face when he saw what she'd gotten them.

She glanced at the corner of the room and was attacked with doubts yet again. Maybe they weren't ready for something this big. Things had been going very smoothly in the household and she didn't want to upset it unnecessarily.

Gabe had settled in as if he'd always been here, without even a whisper of concern for his incarcerated uncle. The boy's injuries had healed quickly, but occasionally she still caught him glancing at the house next door fearfully as if he was afraid his uncle would come after him again. Chuck hadn't been able to pay the rent while in jail so a new family had moved in. They seemed really nice and had a couple of younger kids Gabe could play with.

She grabbed the washcloth off the sink and wiped the counter down again, well aware she'd just done it.

Gravel crunched outside the house as Matt's truck pulled into the driveway. Gina was suddenly attacked by nerves.

She shouldn't have done it.

Even though it had sounded like a good idea in her head, it probably wasn't.

The front door opened and closed and she forced herself to walk out to meet Matt in the hallway, running a hand over her hair in nervousness. When she saw his familiar shape, her anxiety eased a bit.

He grinned when he saw her. "Something smells good." Leaning down, he pressed a kiss to her lips.

Gina welcomed his touch, amazed yet again that she'd been the one to open his shell. When they were alone he reached out to her all the time. In public he was a little more reserved, but she'd learned to appreciate those touches all the more now.

She leaned into him, inhaling the laundry softener smell of his t-shirt and deodorant. He wrapped his massive arms around her, as she'd known he would. It had quickly become her favorite place in the world, wrapped in his embrace.

She held him a little longer tonight to take courage.

He seemed to sense that something was wrong.

"Are you okay?"

Gina felt him kiss the top of her head. Tears came to her eyes and her throat tightened with emotion. He knew without her even saying anything that something was wrong. She pulled away, dashing the tears from her cheeks with her hands.

"I'm fine. I just did something today that I hope you'll be okay with."

A frown darkened his eyes with concern. "Ok." His arms fell to his sides.

Gina cursed herself inside. He thought something was really wrong.

"It's nothing major. I mean, it is, but not big, big. Hell."

She turned back to the kitchen.

"Wait here."

She quickly crossed to the corner of the room to retrieve the item.

Matt's mouth fell open in shock when she walked down the hallway to him. He didn't say anything for several long seconds. Gina began to panic as the drowsy puppy woke up and started wiggling in her arms.

"I made the mistake of stopping at the animal shelter today and he looked at me like I was there just for him. I've been thinking, well, Gabe would probably love to have a puppy. And then I thought a little more and I wondered if you had ever had a puppy when you were growing up?"

Matt shook his head.

Gina ruffled the fur on the puppy's neck and tried not to let Matt see how sad that made her.

"Every child needs a pet growing up. I'm sorry you didn't have that. But I want to make it up to you now."

He looked up at her, surprised. "This is for me?"

She nodded her head and stepped forward, close enough to transfer the wiggling animal to his arms. Matt didn't seem to know what to do with him, but his big hands wrapped around the pup, holding him securely. The dog immediately began licking up one side of his neck and chin. The attendants at the shelter were unsure of the animal's lineage, but assumed because of the buff colored coat and his bulky size that he was part Labrador retriever. Only a few months old, he was the last of a litter that had been dropped off.

"I'm sorry I didn't talk to you about it. I mean, we're still settling in and all and getting used to each other. But I wanted to do something for you that would mean something."

She crossed her arms over her stomach when he still didn't say anything, afraid that she'd gone too far.

"We can take him back if it's too much."

Matt flashed her a look. "No."

Wow. That was pretty definitive.

The dog managed to turn in his arms and plant a paw on each shoulder as he administered the tongue-lashing. Gina thought Matt was getting frustrated trying to get away until he chuckled and set the pup to the ground, then sat down on the floor beside him. The dog thought this was great and bounced around in excitement, going from corner to corner of the entryway, then circling back to gnaw on Matt's big hands.

A broad smile split Matt's face. She started to relax.

The pup found the hammer loop on the side of his jeans and attacked it with a vengeance, tossing his head and trying to rip it off. Laughing, Matt leaned back against the door jamb and just watched.

Finally, he lifted his gaze to hers. "You know, I always wanted a dog when I was a kid, you were right about that. But Rick hated dogs. It just never seemed like the right time to get one. And I remember thinking it wouldn't have been fair to the dog."

Gina cringed, wishing she could go back and change how he'd grown up. But then, it was a catch-22. If she had, he wouldn't be the man he was now.

"But I think now is the right time," he continued. "I mean, I'm here all the time now. I think I've kept my house just to have an out in case things didn't work, which I've half expected because this is still so new. I never expected to need you as much as I do, and want to spend time with you the way I do."

Tears filled her eyes at the heartfelt words. She felt exactly the same way.

"I love you," she whispered.

He nodded his head.

"I know that. And believe it. Nobody else would have ever done something like this for me."

He stared at her hard for several long seconds before levering himself up onto his knees in front of her, completely ignoring the puppy. He swiped his hat off his head and dropped it to the floor.

Gina's heart began to thud as he moved closer. She started to lean in to meet him for the kiss, but he held up a hand to stop her.

"Just a minute."

He slipped his hand into his hip pocket and pulled out a little black velvet box.

Gina felt her eyes widen. She slapped a hand over her mouth to contain a gasp.

"Now, I had planned to do this Friday when we went out to dinner." He paused to clear his throat. "But I can't imagine a time more perfect than right now."

Tears rolled down her cheeks and over her fingers.

Matt rested his hand on top of the box and Gina was humbled to see it tremble.

"Gina Carruthers, I know I'm probably not what you ever expected ending up with, but you are more than I ever could have imagined. I'm so damn in love with you it hurts. I can't imagine not being with you. I promise to love you as well as I know how."

The tears flowed even faster, but there was nothing she could do about it. Her heart was bursting with love.

When he lifted the lid she completely broke down. A ring with a blue sapphire stone in the center sat nestled inside. He pulled the ring from the box, dwarfing it in his massive hands.

"Would you do me the absolute honor of being my wife?"

Nodding, crying, she waited long enough for him to slip the ring onto her shaking finger before surging into his arms. She held him as tightly as she could, overwhelmed with emotion.

"I love you more than I can ever tell you. Of course I'll marry you."

They knelt there in the hallway wrapped in each other's arms and were content.

With another kiss, Matt pulled back.

"If you don't like the ring, we can take it back. I only picked it because it was the same color as your eyes."

Gina shook her head. "No. I love it. How could I not?"

Matt smiled and swung her into his arms, then pushed to his feet.

"I thought you would. I want to see you stretched out on the bed only wearing that ring. How long do we have before Gabe calls?"

Excitement slammed through her at the thought of consummating their engagement.

"Not for at least an hour. But we need to put the puppy away first."

Matt looked down for the puppy, but the little dog was nowhere to be seen. Their romantic escape turned into a game of hide and seek as they looked for the puppy. And Matt's favorite hat.

But it was okay, because they were together.

# # #

From J. M. Madden

I sincerely thank you for reading *A Needful Heart*, and would greatly appreciate it if you would help others enjoy this book as well. You can:

LEND it- To your friends and family.

RECOMMEND it- to your friends on social media, discussion boards, etc.

REVIEW it- at the outlet you purchased it from.

Also, if you would like to follow me on social media, check me out here:

WEB: www.JMMadden.com

FACEBOOK: J.m. Madden

TWITTER: @authorjmmadden

Excerpt from

THE EMBATTLED ROAD

June 2007

Duncan could not wait to get the fuck out of this sand pit. He had grit in his junk, his armpits, the creases of his eyes. It didn't do any good to try to rub it away because all you did was scratch yourself.

Fucking desert.

Jungle fighting would be welcome right now, and that said a lot. He hated the jungle.

Three more months before he reached the end of his tour and could go home. His last tour. He'd already decided to go on drill instructor duty when he was done, so he could train recruits at Parris Island in relative comfort instead of here. He'd served his time. Perhaps he and Melanie could actually build a life together.

The Humvee rattled over a rock, bouncing him in the seat.

"Monroe, you gotta hit every damn rock on the road?" Bates groused. "My ass is killin' me."

The driver grinned and glanced behind him at the other two Marines. Bates always complained. "Dude, you've been here long enough to know the damn rocks breed like crazy. Scrape 'em off and they're right back with a new layer. I'm following the tracks exactly."

The men snorted in the back and Duncan looked out the window. The monochrome, hilly landscape stretched for miles, leading to the mountains in the distance. Rocky outcrops dotted the land, interspersed with scrub grass clumps, perfect ambush points they had to pass to get to the northern base, where they were due to relieve the current MP force rotating out. The convoy had been traveling for hours. It was slow going through this rough terrain. Driving in Iraq wasn't like driving in Colorado. You had to be aware of everything and follow in the path of the truck in front of you. Too many men had died already by IEDs this year, and more died every day.

Beauchamp had been the most recent. Blown to hell by a young Iraqi on a motorcycle that pulled alongside his window while he was talking to a group of kids. Three of the kids had been blown away as well, but insurgents didn't care about them. They were supposedly blessed by Allah for dying a glorious death. He wondered if the mothers felt the same way as they gathered up pieces of their children.

The radio squawked to life with men yelling. His ears were hit with a reverberation of sound and he knew immediately that an IED had been triggered. Duncan gripped his weapon, ready to jump to the ground as he searched for the source of the explosion.

Monroe slammed on the brakes, sending the Humvee skidding in the loose gravel. Duncan glanced in the side mirror. The vehicles behind them had disappeared in a cloud of smoke and fire. Burning debris rained down in chunks on their vehicle. Black smoke swirled upward. Duncan saw the vehicles were still there, but heavily damaged, all shoved akilter. The men's screams reached his ears before they were drowned out by rifle fire.

"Out of the vehicle! Bates and Clark, cover fire! We've got men down!"

He threw himself out of the Humvee and shouldered his M16. There was a copse of rocks several hundred yards to the west. The attack seemed to be coming from there so he fired in that direction. Smoke obscured his vision as he took cover behind the truck, but he could still hear men screaming. "Monroe, get on the horn and make sure we have air support coming!"

Crouching, Duncan ran across the open expanse of

ground between his vehicle and the one behind him in the caravan, the M16 barking in his arms. Bates and Clark laid down cover fire as he ran. The first Marine he reached was already gone, a gaping hole in his sternum. Duncan circled the truck, which sat at an odd angle, flipped with the roof to his side. The front passenger's side wheel was in a hole, but the ass end poked in the air. He tried to follow the sound of screaming while staying under cover.

At the back of the truck, he found another young Marine trying to crabwalk around the vehicle. The distinctive chatter of the enemy's AK47s echoed through the air, and the answering response from the Marines. Ignoring the heat of the smoldering truck, he surged to grab the kid beneath the armpits and drag him around the vehicle. Bullets struck the dirt in front of him and he jumped, rolling with the kid out of the line of danger. Monroe was there, then, laying down cover fire as Duncan dragged the Marine out of reach of the bullets.

The passenger side door of the Humvee fell open just above them and two men tumbled out to the sand. One hustled to the front of the vehicle, raised his weapon and started to fire. The second fell to the ground and didn't move.

Duncan glanced down at the kid he'd just helped. His tag said Fallon. He gasped for air but Duncan didn't see any obvious blood or breaks. "Hey Fallon, looks like you skinned by with this one. You're fine, you just need to breathe. Just breathe. I'm going to check on your buddy."

Fallon blinked and nodded his head. He still had his helmet on.

The Marine who had fallen to the ground did not. Duncan scrambled across the sand, ever conscious of how close the little puffs of dust around him reached. Some were within inches of his feet. The insurgents had planned this ambush perfectly. Before he rolled the kid over, he felt for a pulse. There, but faint. Again, he didn't see any obvious blood but in situations like these what you couldn't see was more dangerous. The impact of the percussion to the body and then the body against the vehicle could kill a Marine in minutes. Not an easy death. He called for a Corpsman, but all he saw was swirling smoke.

Pulling the kid over enough to look at his face, Duncan leaned in. *Shit.* Parker. Newest of the bunch. He'd only been here two weeks. Poor kid had a hell of a dent in his head that Duncan hadn't seen at first.

A bullet pinged off the undercarriage inches from his face and he knew he needed to move him whether he wanted to or not. Slinging the rifle around to his back, he grabbed him by the pits and pulled. Parker didn't rouse at all. Bad sign.

The Corpsman dropped down beside him as he lowered Parker to the ground, twenty feet from the overturned Humvee. He motioned to the young Marine's head. "Head wound!"

Scrambling back to the truck, he pulled his weapon forward and took position behind Monroe, firing toward the rocks. The gunfire slowed and he wondered if the enemy had retreated.

Eventually the firing dwindled away. Duncan stayed put. Sometimes the enemy stopped shooting and waited till the Marines relaxed, then set in on them again. This time, though, they seemed to be gone. Or dead. Several bodies littered the outcrop.

He clapped Monroe on the back, impressed that the young grunt had done exactly what needed done.

The medic shook his head when Duncan returned to

him. "I don't know if he's going to make it or not First Sergeant. He's got serious swelling on the brain. I've called in a 9-Line Medevac but I've got other wounded to eval."

In other words, there was nothing more he could do for him.

Duncan nodded and waved the man away. Monroe helped Fallon over to sit with Parker. Fallon still wheezed and held his gut, but he'd probably be fine. Duncan followed Doc to the next vehicle in the convoy, obviously the epicenter of the blast. Bodies lay strewn behind the burning carcass of the Humvee. The transports were armored, but only to a certain extent.

Obviously, this one had been deliberately targeted, fired upon repeatedly after it had hit the IED. Did they think he had been in it? The driver's side was ripped open like the lid off a can, with its guts strewn everywhere. The men in the fire team were all men he knew and had spoken to hours ago. Now, they were all gone. The gruesome sight was enough to turn his normally cast-iron stomach. It had been his responsibility to get the men in these squads to the camp safely.

His throat tightened as he went man to man, cataloging names when he could see them. Six dead, total, from two different teams. Six families he'd have to call when he got to base. Sorrow threatened to drop him to his knees, but he had to shove it aside.

The third Humvee affected by the blast had little to no damage and the men were fine, though banged up. One had a bullet hole through his leg but was conscious and calm as the Doc bandaged him up.

Duncan sent out a squad to secure their position. A few minutes later he heard the distinctive thwop-thwop-thwop of the Medevac. Shielding his eyes from the sun, he watched the chopper roll in.

It was a couple hundred yards away when a surface-to-air rocket blasted out of the hills from the west and struck the side of the massive two-rotor machine, sending it floundering in the air. Rifle fire sounded, three shot bursts, but it was lost in the whine of the overtaxed engines as the pilot tried to recover the craft.

Too close. The thought registered as his feet began moving. He tried to get the men up before the chopper came down right on top of them.

Even as he started shoving Marines out of the way, he knew it was too late. The monstrous machine hit the ground behind him and blew. For a heartbeat of time, everything stopped- sound, motion, thought. Then the blast struck him in the back, flinging him into the air. It seemed like he flew forever before landing with a sickening crunch on top of one of his men. Heat seared his body from shoulders to toes.

His burning world went dark.

Duncan jerked awake, then realized all he did was open his eyes. Reality smacked him in the face as he focused on the beige tile floor. Yep. Still at Walter Reed. Landstuhl Hospital's floor had been pale blue with darker flecks in it. He remembered that much.

Somebody had turned the page of the automotive magazine for him, but he was still strung up like a marionette, arms stretched out to his sides, in the medical contraption immobilizing his spine and protecting his burns. The mattress beneath him was hard. After three weeks in the same position, you'd think he'd remember. But no. Every time he woke up, he wondered why God hadn't just killed him and gotten it over with. At least then the pain would end.

One of the nurses squeaked her way into the room.

Pink rubber Crocs stopped beside his bed. What was her name? Lacey? Or Lainy? Something like that. He glanced into the edge of the mirror not covered by the magazine. She smiled at him, that professional nurse smile meant to conceal how very desperate his situation actually was.

"How do you feel today, First Sergeant?"

He rocked his head as much as he could and closed his eyes. If she was going to ask stupid questions like that he wasn't going to answer her. She circled the bed and he felt her tug at the sheet over his burnt back. "How is your pain right now?"

He sighed. She wouldn't leave until he answered her. "About a seven."

She hummed under her breath and moved to the IV stand, adjusting something there. Within seconds he felt a blessed wash of numbing heat roll through his body. Seemed like the only thing that made him happy anymore was morphine. He closed his eyes and tried to sleep his life away.

August 2007

"That fucking hurt!"

The grey haired doctor at the foot of his bed grinned at him. "Good."

Duncan reeled against the mattress, in spite of the pain the movement caused his raw back. It had *hurt*. "Do it again," he demanded.

Richards ran the weirdly shaped roller up his foot and for the first time in two months Duncan felt something. "It's about fucking time. Why did it take so long?"

The doctor shrugged. "Well, in addition to the spinal

shock you had the burns and the cracked vertebra. Your pelvis was broken in two places. It took time for all that to heal. Now the nerves are fixing themselves. I think a couple more months and you should be up and moving."

"Months?"

"Yes, at least. Because I want you to take it easy. We can't rush this, or it could set you back right where you started. You'll end up in the chair permanently if we're not careful of your recovery."

Duncan let the information sink in, shocked. He would be fine, it would just take a while. He could stare at the walls a little longer.

His heart raced at the first glimmer of good happening to him in months. A huge chunk of his company—those valiant men—were gone and his career fried, literally. Uncertainty yawned before him like an abyss. But finally, that one little tickle had changed his life.

That following Saturday, anticipation thrummed through his body as he watched the clock. Sixteen thirty-four. Melanie would be here any minute. He'd debated calling her to tell her the news but decided he wanted to see the happiness on her face when he told her in person. In spite of the doctor's assurances that she could handle whatever happened, she'd been slowly withdrawing. Maybe this could also be her galvanizing spark.

As if in answer to his thoughts, the hospital room door swished open and Melanie walked in, looking beautiful as always in the tan coat that matched her hair so perfectly. Her pale cheeks were flushed and her blue eyes glittered. She crossed to kiss him like she normally did but moved away from his side, instead choosing to stand at the end of the bed, hands folded in front of her.

She kept her jacket on.

His gut twinged in warning.

"Melanie, are you okay? How was your drive from Columbus?"

"Fine, Duncan. A little busy but not too bad. You're looking good."

"Thank you," he murmured. He'd shaved the stubble from his face and gotten his hair cut this morning, expecting her.

Narrowing his eyes, he cocked his head. Obviously she had something on her mind to talk about. Some instinct made him hold his own news close and wait as she fidgeted. Finally, she looked up at him with tears welling in her eyes. "Duncan, I can't do this anymore. I can't be here for you anymore."

Chills rippled over his skin. "You mean here at the hospital? That's fine. If it's too much of a drive you don't have to do it."

She shook her head, biting her bottom lip. "No, I don't think I can be here for you." She waved a hand at the medical equipment around the bed. "At all. With all of this."

Duncan stared at her, hard, until she shifted uncomfortably. She dropped her eyes to her white-knuckled hands. "I know you'll get better, eventually, but I need to move forward with my life." Straightening, she stepped to the side of his bed and held out the engagement ring he'd given her a year ago. Dazed, he took the ring, folding it into his palm.

She folded her hands against her stomach, drawing Duncan's gaze. White-hot anger exploded when he realized what the swell beneath her hand meant. She'd worn the jacket to try to conceal it. "Ahh, it all makes sense now. So, who's the lucky guy? Or do you even know?"

Melanie sucked in a breath. "Don't be like that," she implored. "What did you expect me to do? Go without companionship for nine months while you were gone who knows where?"

He looked at her incredulously. "Yes, exactly, just like I did. And are you serious? I was in Iraq fighting in a God damn war!"

She broke into harsh sobs, but he didn't—couldn't—soften. She looked to be a few months along, so, just before he got injured. Hell, even if he hadn't gotten injured he'd have come home to find her knocked up by some other guy. Betrayal turned his stomach.

Something had nagged at him about the relationship anyway. She'd been remote since he'd gotten back, not very communicative. She'd moved to her parent's house in Ohio. Hell, she'd only been up to Maryland to see him a few times since he got back in the States, and only called a few times besides that.

Melanie was needy and spoiled. He'd known that a long time ago. Honestly, in his heart of hearts, if he was honest with himself, he'd kind of been expecting this.

He looked down at his motionless legs. It was probably a hell of a downer for the party girl to think she was going to have to take care of him the rest of her life.

The fact that feeling had begun to return to his legs didn't matter. It wouldn't change the outcome tonight, so he kept the information to himself.

His *ex*-fiancée continued to weep beside the bed. Her audacity spiked his fury.

"Ok, Melanie, you can stop with the water works."

She looked up at him from tear-drenched eyes that did nothing for him. She'd chosen her path.

"I'm sorry, Duncan. I wish things had turned out differently."

He wasn't interested in her platitudes. "Yeah, well, drive safe back to Ohio. Ship my stuff to my parents in Colorado."

Her eyes widened at the dismissal, and she opened her mouth as if to argue. Instead, she snapped her jaw shut, turned on her heel and disappeared from his life.

The amount of relief he felt that she was gone surprised him. They'd been a little rocky to begin with, before he ever left for Iraq, but he didn't think she'd betray him with such a flourish. He was a little regretful that he didn't have anybody to share his news with other than his parents, who were on the other end of the country.

Lacey walked in just then, as if she'd heard his thoughts. She gave him a cautious smile. "I saw your honey leave. She didn't look happy."

He snorted. "She's not my honey anymore. Guess she got tired of waiting for me. She's pregnant."

The nurse winced. "Ouch. Nice. Let me guess, she was lonely and needed companionship?"

Duncan looked at her, surprised. "How did you know?"

Lacey shook her dark head. "Sad to say, but it happens a good bit in here. You guys are long term, and a lot of people just can't deal with the way their lives have to change." She shrugged. "I've been doing this several years, and the ones that hang around the first few months post-injury will likely be around for a long time."

He mulled that over as she fiddled with his IV. Some of the guys had family at the hospital day and night. Others didn't have anybody. One Marine down the hall hadn't had any family visit. Ever.

His parents had just left for home in Colorado. They'd been here for most of his recovery, until he'd told them to get back to their lives. They'd been reluctant at first, unwilling to leave him alone, but he'd persuaded them, promising that he'd relocate back there.

It was the first time his father had left the family print shop for any length of time. Sam, his brother, was running it while they were gone.

He had to be honest with himself. The Marines had no use for a grunt in a wheelchair. Even a career man like himself. The thought of trying to find a job while restrained this way absolutely nauseated him, but no other option was available. His father had reassured him that there would always be a job available at the shop, but that would be the same as taking welfare.

It made him that much more determined to get out of the chair.

Lacey paused beside his bed, an earnest look on her young face. Her pretty eyes were soft with understanding. "You need to know that when they walk out like that, it's not the patient's fault. It's a failing in them, not you guys. I've been a nurse here for six years, and it always happens the same way. But the Marine always conquers and adapts."

Duncan snorted at the way she dropped her voice and puffed out her chest for that last part.

"Well," he admitted. "I'll let you in on a secret. I'm not that upset. I think I kind of knew it was coming."

Lacey grinned and nodded her head. "I thought not. Besides," she said as she turned to leave, "you've got much bigger things to think about."

She wiggled his blanket-covered toes before walking out the door.

A week after he started getting sensation in his feet, they moved him out of the single unit room into a double occupancy. The threat of infection had passed, for the most part, and they needed the room for more wounded rolling in.

His new roommate was Gunnery Sergeant John Palmer, incomplete spinal cord injury, or SCI, paralyzed from the hips down and angry at the world. It took Duncan a week just to get a 'fuck you' out of him. He eventually realized this was the guy that had no family, and it made Duncan all the more determined to connect with him, in spite of his surly attitude.

Duncan watched two young nurses just out of school leave in tears because they tried to talk to the paralyzed Marine and had been ripped to shreds. The only nurse not outwardly affected by his nastiness was Lacey. She grinned when he cussed her out and shook her dark head. "If you weren't so cute, Gunnery Sergeant, I'd smack that sour look off your face."

"Fuck you," he snapped.

She grinned that much more and sailed out of the room.

Duncan felt slightly offended on the sweet nurse's behalf.

"Dude, they feed you. You better cut them some slack."

"Fuck you," he snarled, with no regard to rank.

Duncan didn't try to correct him because he understood where the man came from. A week ago he'd thought he would be in the chair permanently, and it hadn't been a good feeling. The tiny, living, feeling area that had stretched up to his ankles had reignited all his desperate hopes for a normal life.

Available at major ebook retailers

About The Author

Terminally addicted to romances, thanks to finding her aunt's stash of 'Harlequin Presents' years ago during a sleepover, Jennifer loves any and all good love stories. Most particularly her own. She has two beautiful children and a husband who always keeps her on her toes.

Jennifer was a Deputy Sheriff in Ohio for nine years, until hubby moved the clan to Kentucky. When not chasing the family around, she's at the computer reading and writing, trying to perfect her craft. She occasionally takes breaks to feed her animal horde, and is trying to control her office-supply addiction, but both tasks are uphill battles. Happily, she is unemployed right now, so it's given her a chance to seriously jump into writing full-time. She has several projects in the works and loves to hear from readers.

Other Books by J.M.

The Awakening Society: Book 1

Tempt Me- Book 2 of the Awakening Society

Wet Dream
(Part of the 1NIGHTSTAND Series)

Urban Moon (anthology)

Second Time Around

Love on the Line

The Embattled Road
Prequel to THE LOST AND FOUND Series

Her Best Mistake

(a bonus novella)

by

Donna McDonald

Story description

Ever climb into bed with the wrong guy? No?

In "Her Best Mistake", Lisa Dennison ends up in bed with the wrong man.

Or maybe she doesn't.

Finn Roberts certainly doesn't think it was a mistake.

Chapter 1

Finn Roberts tried to stand, but quickly found his legs wouldn't hold him up. Whatever intelligence allowed him to finish two masters and one doctoral degree before the age of thirty obviously did not extend itself to helping him make good decisions when it came to his wicked brother, Eric.

"What the hell was in those drinks?" Finn demanded, grabbing the table to keep from pitching forward and falling on his face. Dizziness engulfed him and his head spun. Thirty-six hours of flying had taken its own toll. Alcohol had only worsened the resulting jet-lag.

Eric laughed, stood, and put an arm around Finn to hold him up.

"Look at you, Finn. Two girlie drinks and your ass is all but on the floor. God, I've missed you. I wish you'd quit digging in the dirt and come home to Boston."

"Digging in the dirt?" Still feeling ill, Finn had to work to put the proper amount of outrage into his voice to keep up with the insult game about their chosen careers. "Well, at least it's better than gambling for a living."

"What can I say?" Eric admitted. "All those people

with money to invest and I just love helping them with it. It keeps me in BMWs and Italian shoes. What are you doing with all those college degrees of yours, pretty boy? T-shirts and sandals don't exactly scream *success,* Dr. Roberts."

Eric laughed as he guided a grumbling Finn out of the bar.

"The dig site is in a very remote location. There's nowhere in the middle of the desert to wear a damn suit. I told you I hadn't had alcohol in two years, yet you have me doing shots within minutes of my plane landing. How do I let you talk me into acting so insanely? You've been doing this to me all our lives. Lord, I think I'm going to be sick. I just hope I hit your expensive Italian shoes when I spew."

"Don't you dare. I like these shoes," Eric said as he laughed harder, halting just outside the lounge. "Okay. Stop walking a minute. Get your breath."

Finn stopped, closed his eyes, and took a few deep, steadying breaths. When he opened his eyes again, Eric was still there holding him up, eyes full of both love and mischief.

And that's how he always did it, Finn decided. His brother wore him down with a wicked smile and love in his eyes.

"Remember I'm bigger than you. If I fall, I'm taking you with me," Finn warned.

"Come on, Dr. Roberts. Let's get your inebriated ass to the room so you can sleep this off. My condo is still a renovation construction zone, so I went all out and booked you a suite here at the Copley under my name. I'm sure it won't have the ambiance of your desert tent, but it comes with a few perks I think you will appreciate. In the morning, I'll come by and take you to breakfast if you're up to it. If not, we'll make it lunch."

"Where are you spending the night?" Finn demanded.

"You're such a worrier, Finn. I have plans to sleep elsewhere," Eric explained, favoring his serious sibling with a knowing grin. "Besides, there's only one bed in the suite anyway. I'm not pulling out the sofa, even for you."

Laughing at Finn's careful steps as they staggered across the lobby, Eric patted his chest as they stopped at the front desk.

"Hold up, bro," Eric said to Finn on a laugh. "Hey, Cindy. Got my room ready?"

"Hey yourself, Eric Roberts," Cindy said with a welcoming smile as she lifted her gaze from the computer to stare at the pair of handsome males leaning on the check-in counter.

Twins. Now that gave a woman wicked ideas.

Both were tall with reddish-brown hair and mile-wile shoulders.

Her interested gaze took them in as she bit back a sigh. She needed her job too badly to hit on hotel guests, which was really, really too bad.

"You never said you were a twin," Cindy teased, swallowing her disappointment as she made the men a key card.

"Twin? This guy? You're kidding, right? This is just some drunk I picked up in the hotel bar. But since I'm feeling sorry for him, I'm going to let him sleep it off in my room," Eric stated, snorting over Finn's low 'duplicitous bastard' comment. No other male he knew could swear as poetically as his Harvard professor brother.

Cindy giggled before sliding a room key through the scanner. She handed it over to Eric, laughing softly. "Here you go."

"Give me two more and something to write on," Eric requested.

"Okay," Cindy said, sliding two more key cards. Really, they were only supposed to give out two total, but this was Eric Roberts. He was a regular at the hotel. Not that he was ever lacking for company when he came around, but a girl could always dream.

"Why do you need three keys?" Finn demanded, cringing on the inside. *Oh, shit. Surely he didn't.*

Eric grinned and patted Finn's chest. "Not now. Thank me later, bro."

He turned back to Cindy behind the desk. "There's going to be a beautiful brunette walk in here later and ask for a key to my room. I want you to give it to her for me, along with this note, okay?"

Finn watched as Eric passed the note he'd written, a key card, and a twenty to Cindy.

"No problem at all," she promised, winking at his grin.

Finn rolled his eyes as he let Eric resume dragging him across the lobby. Once in the elevator, he leaned back against the wall, hoping it would stop his head from spinning long enough to make his case.

"Eric, tell me you did not fix me up with one of your booty calls. I was jet lagged when I got here, and now I'm drunk too. Even if I was interested—which I am not—I'll be of no use to any woman until I acclimate."

Eric turned and put his hands on Finn's shoulders. "I love you Finn, and I know you. You're still living like a monk out there in that desert you call a job. Alicia is fun and uncomplicated. You'll like her. She doesn't mind being the one in charge, so it won't matter if you're not a hundred percent."

"Damn it, Eric—"

"Don't worry, Professor, I didn't use your name.

Pretend to be me for once and see how a real man lives," Eric ordered.

"You're disgusting, and yet I know women fall all over you. I don't get it. Call and stop her from coming, Eric," Finn demanded.

Eric sighed dramatically, shaking his head no. The elevator finally stopped at the top floor. He put an arm around Finn again as they exited into the hall.

"Please, Eric," Finn begged, not caring that he sounded pathetic. "Call off your friend. I really don't want to deal with one of your fix-ups today. I need to shower and then sleep; otherwise, I'm going to be seriously sick. I'm really, really tired."

Finn watched Eric studying his face, which he knew had to be showing the wear and tear of his long flight, plus all the work he had done on the plane.

"Okay." Eric conceded. "Maybe this weekend before you leave, eh?"

Finn sighed but nodded, trying to look as disappointed about not scoring as his brother would expect him to be.

He knew Eric well, and knew that he had to at least pretend to go along with next week in order to get out of today.

Chapter 2

Her cell phone battery failed for the hundredth time and Lisa chastised herself for not letting her assistant order her a new one. Trying to make sure she hadn't missed him, she resorted to just looking in the hotel restaurant and bar, even though she didn't see Eric Roberts waiting as he promised.

She and Eric had met a few months ago during a conference at the Copley. They had clicked about business matters that day and gone to dinner once since. She hadn't even been surprised when he'd called and invited her to meet him there for a drink today. He'd said something about his brother maybe joining them, but she didn't remember the details.

Since the Copley was within walking distance of her office, she'd agreed hastily without really thinking about whether it was a good idea or not.

Eric Roberts was handsome, charming, and mostly good company when he wasn't distracted with his phone. Either his business was demanding, or he was one of those people who had more of an online social life than a face-to-face one.

After their one date, Lisa hadn't learned enough to

judge his true character, but she also hadn't learned anything that made her not care either.

In the last week, she had gone over and over why their date had not exactly left her pining to see him again. She probably should have said no to drinks, but since she was already here at the Copley, she might as well make the best of it and put out an effort to find him. It was the least she could do since her phone wasn't working. For all she knew, Eric could be trying to reach her right now. She frowned and sighed in frustration.

After ten minutes of checking everywhere she could think to check in the hotel, Lisa decided she'd had enough. On the off chance Eric had had an emergency and left unexpectedly, she went to the front desk to check for any messages for her.

"Hi, my name is Lisa Dennison," she said, smiling at the desk clerk who smiled back. "I'm supposed to be meeting Eric Roberts here for a drink, but I can't find him. Did he maybe leave a message for me at the desk?"

Cindy looked at the tall, mostly red-haired woman, laughing that Eric had called her a brunette. What did the man see in this one, she wondered? She was obviously older than Eric, but also much older than the typical dates he brought to the hotel. Even though the woman wasn't bad looking, she also wasn't the model type either. The woman looked like every other businesswoman in Boston.

"Yes. Eric left a note for you and a room key." Cindy said brightly, handing them both over with a friendly smile.

Lisa looked at the room key in her hand with confusion, and then back at the clerk, who just shrugged her shoulders. *Unbelievable.* This was only their second date and supposed to be just a quick drink in the bar, maybe meet his brother. *A hotel room key? Really?*

Whatever happened to patience? Eric was attractive, but damn it, she wasn't ready to jump into bed with him yet. Or at least that's what she'd been telling herself since she saw him last. Hell, maybe she had been putting out a 'desperate woman' vibe without knowing it, but she hadn't meant to come across that way. She hadn't really been dating much when Eric asked her out.

Looking down at the key in her hand again, she figured this sideways play to get her in bed was probably what she deserved for dating a younger man. She was too old for these games, Lisa decided as she reluctantly unfolded the note. Eric had the very nice, very legible handwriting a person would expect an investment banker to have, and obviously he had the masculine sensibilities of every other male his age.

My brother Finn, the great Harvard anthropologist, just got in from Egypt. I had a few too many drinks celebrating his return and decided I desperately needed to sleep it off. Didn't want to miss our date so I stayed here. Looking forward to being woken up by you. ~ Eric

Well, it wasn't a completely indecent proposition, Lisa thought, frowning over the note. Maybe she could just pop up to the room and wake him up. Maybe it would even be fun.

Yeah, and maybe when he kisses me this time I'll feel something wonderful instead of nothing. Lisa sighed over her inner bitching, trying to remember the last time a man had truly excited her with a kiss. That was why she'd said yes to Eric Roberts in the first place. She simply couldn't remember the last time she was interested at all.

Maybe she was getting old. What other reason made any sense?

A hot younger man was wanting to sleep with her, and here she was standing in the hotel lobby debating his blatant invitation to take things to the next level. The whole reticence thing she was doing was her most pressing problem. She was freaking forty years old and already losing interest in men and sex.

Well, no. Hell, no. She wasn't going to let that happen.

Lisa marched over to the elevators and fiercely punched the button. Once inside, she chewed her bottom lip as the elevator climbed to the top floor.

Use it or lose it, her OBGYN had told her. What a lovely gift that had been for her fortieth birthday. "You heard the woman. Get in that hotel room and wake the man. *Use it or lose it, Dennison*," Lisa chanted out loud, as she walked down the hotel hallway.

At his room door, she tapped softly. When there was no answer, Lisa took a deep breath and slid the key into the lock, making herself push the handle when the security light changed to green.

Inside was luxury. An executive suite. *Very nice*, she thought, smiling as she stepped quietly through the door. In the sitting area that greeted her, there was a battered leather gym bag sitting on the coffee table, with several luggage tags hanging off it. Obviously that belonged to Eric's brother, Lisa thought, worried a little now that she might be walking in on the two of them.

But then why would Eric invite her to his room if his brother was staying here? Surely he wasn't thinking of sharing her, was he?

That certainly wasn't her style, and if it was Eric's, she would let him pitch his case and then leave with dignity.

Taking a deep breath, Lisa moved quietly into the single massive bedroom, barely able to appreciate the polished woods and gleaming surfaces all around her. Instead her gaze was locked on the biggest, most luxurious bed she had ever seen and the miles of naked male flesh in the middle of it.

If his complete nudity wasn't a blatant sexual proposition, then she was definitely off her dating game. But at least there was only him, Lisa noted, so the brother must be safely elsewhere. Breathing out a sigh of relief that her wide imaginings hadn't been the reality she walked into, she let her now considering gaze wander over the one naked male again.

She chewed her lip a moment wondering what Eric had done with his poor jetlagged brother, and then chastised herself for worrying about something that wasn't her problem or concern. He was probably just in the another room, she decided, since the bag was still in the sitting area.

Frowning at her mind wanderings, Lisa pulled her attention back to the matter at hand. Her sole concern should be whether or not she was going to wake up the sleeping man who had asked her to do so. She had to admit that he looked damn good without his clothes.

Lisa smiled despite her irritation at his nerve in stripping off to wait for her. He was lying facedown with muscular legs spread wide, feet hanging off the end of the bed. She'd had the impression Eric was tall the other night but hadn't really processed him as all that much taller than her.

A guy had to be really tall not to fit a king-sized bed. Right?

But any woman would have to be dead from the waist down not be intrigued with all those muscles and long expanses of tanned skin, she thought, firmly pushing the distasteful thought of Eric going to a tanning bed from her mind. It wasn't like lots of men didn't visit tanning beds regularly to chase their natural New England paleness away.

Suddenly a giggle welled up at her silly thoughts over a man with an ass to die for, tanned or not. A normal woman would be using her cell phone and taking a picture of what was very likely was the most perfect male ass she'd ever seen. If her phone had been working properly, Lisa might have talked herself into clicking a shot for a souvenir. It would have been something to smile about later at least.

Damn, she needed to buy a new phone and stop putting it off.

Snorting as quietly as she could, Lisa took in a nervous breath, stopping to sniff the air. What was that smell, she wondered? Her stomach rolled and flipped while her heart began to flutter. Sniffing the air again like a dog, Lisa almost laughed out loud at herself, but *what was that?*

She walked to the bed, leaned over him, and sniffed hard. Smiling because it *was* him, she ended up feeling like an idiot because dear god, the man smelled incredible.

What was he wearing?

He smelled like sandy beaches and something else she couldn't quite figure out.

Leaning over him now, Lisa smiled down at his perfect ass and breathed him inside her, moisture gathering in almost forgotten places. It made her sigh at how good it was to know her body was still working the way it was supposed to in such a situation.

After her divorce, things had changed a lot for her. Now it looked like the freaking gynecologist had scared her for nothing, though she had to admit that two years was a really long time to have had no desire for intimacy at all.

She rarely even pleasured herself because she simply hadn't felt the need.

It was a relief now to know that her libido had merely been sleeping and not in the process of dying.

Who knew a great smelling, naked man was all that was needed to change that?

Lisa sat down gingerly on the edge of the mattress, trying not to wake the sleeping male because she still wasn't sure she wanted to. But indulging the rampant desire flooding her senses, she leaned a little closer and sniffed again. Yes, that was definitely him smelling so good, and it was definitely getting her all jazzed up.

Now why hadn't she noticed his masculinity last weekend?

Her reaction exasperated her.

She tried to recall their dinner date, how Eric had looked, what he had worn. Maybe he had been wearing some sort of woodsy cologne that evening, she could barely remember now. She certainly didn't remember him smelling like this.

What she remembered was him texting in between conversation bits with her. When the food came, he finally paid attention to it, and had been more attentive to her after that.

But this smell, Lisa decided, this she should have remembered clearly, especially since it was definitely revving her engine.

Up this close, she could also smell a little alcohol on him. Since that meant he was being truthful in his note to her, she gave him credibility points.

It also explained why he was so completely unaware of her presence.

Sighing, Lisa stood and walked to the giant window to look out at the city. She thought of all the other women out there just like her, some not even dating anyone.

Again, just like her.

Boston was a large city, and it wasn't always easy to meet guys you were interested in that were interested back, especially enough to cause this quandary she was facing.

Certainly she loved the city because it had always been home, also because it was busy and important and endlessly interesting. The Copley Plaza Hotel was both a landmark and a fixture, as well as one of her favorite places to have a drink now and again. She had even stayed in the hotel a time or two, but never in a suite. And definitely never with a man she was dating.

Lisa looked back at the bed. Sure enough, her belly tightened in desire as she let her eyes take in the male landscape splayed out for her viewing pleasure. It had been so long since she had felt real arousal that she was actually scared of her feelings, which was disturbing on many levels because it wasn't really like her to be afraid.

Once, she would had been brave with men she wanted. Once, she would have looked at his perfect ass, stripped with enthusiasm, and crawled into that big bed to take a bite. It made her smile just thinking about it. After her divorce though, her sexuality seemed to wither. It felt damn good to feel sexually attracted to someone again, even if it was for someone she barely knew.

Lisa looked at the man in the bed and thought hard.

Really, what did she have to lose if she decided to take him for a test run? Sure, they had little in common. That and other things, like the age difference, made it impossible for her to think they might have a real future together.

Then she chided herself for her serious thoughts because the arousal had her feeling lighter than she had in several years.

She took a deep breath and smelled him again. Once

more she ran her gaze over his back muscles and the back of his legs. She wondered how the other side of him looked. Eric certainly had been hiding a great body under those suits. Her thoughts about the front of him had moisture gathering again, which really was her body making its own decision about what to do.

"Oh, what the hell," Lisa said softly. She was not a prude, and the man had issued the invitation. It wasn't like she was just using him without his permission.

It took about thirty seconds for her to drop her clothes into a nearby chair.

She walked completely naked to the bed, already anticipating his pleasure as she woke him up.

God that felt good. If it was only a dream, Finn decided that he definitely did not want to wake up. Her hands were cool, but her mouth was hot as it explored his back, his shoulders, his. . .hey, did she just bite his ass?

He pried open one tired eye and saw a mass of reddish-brown hair hanging over his hip.

Rolling to his side, Finn saw smooth white skin dotted with freckles. Then he saw her breasts about three seconds before her hand clamped around him and stroked.

Lord, that felt wonderful too.

Finn blinked several times, trying to clear his head enough to think about things. His eyes drifted closed again as he let her raise his interest to the point of a painfully hard erection. It had been so long—

No, she had to be stopped. But. . . damn, she was good at what she was doing.

Finn looked into soft brown eyes that smiled and crinkled at the corners.

"Hi" she said.

"Hi," he said back, thinking she was definitely a fantasy woman. "Can I kiss you? I would really like to while you do that."

She snickered at him and then laughed, obviously thinking it strange that he would ask so politely to kiss her when she had her hand busy stroking his erection.

"I really wish you would," she said, crawling up the bed to give him access to her mouth.

His lips skimmed hers once, then a second time. He kept his eyes open and on hers. Why was it so different today, Lisa wondered? A little shiver danced along her arms in response to his heated gaze.

On the third pass of his talented mouth, Finn ran the tip of his tongue across her bottom lip. When she stopped stroking him to enjoy the moment, Finn smiled, knowing what she felt. Again, he ran his tongue along her lips, this time pushing the tip of it into her mouth just a little. She moaned and closed her eyes.

Why did she not remember how good this could be, Lisa wondered?

When his mouth crushed hers hard and his eager tongue tangled with hers, she stopped thinking about the past to focus on the present. She had to remove her busy hands from the interesting parts to brace them on his shoulders as he took more and more control away from her.

Lisa gasped when he rolled until she was under him. The full force of his weight rested on her, and wow—did he feel good.

Thank God I found my nerve, Lisa decided.

When Finn broke the kiss, he pulled back, his erection pressed against her navel. She shivered, and then he shivered, pressing down on her more.

He was about to follow his urges for both their sakes, but then he remembered what had to be asked.

"I want this more than I want to breathe right now, but I have no protection," he said regretfully. "Did you bring anything?"

He sighed along with her as she sighed loudly and shook her head sadly from side to side.

"Damn," he said slowly.

Crossing his fingers that Eric had for once really took care of *everything*, Finn rolled and pulled her over on top of him in one smooth motion as she laughed. Wrapping one arm around her to keep her from leaving, he leaned over and pulled out a drawer of the side table. In it was a strip of condoms. *Bless you, brother.* Finn pulled them out and handed them to her, needing to let her make the choice.

Lisa took the packets, turning them over in her fingers. She tore one off and tossed the others on the table. She felt him shift his hardness and her in the process. He was very strong, she acknowledged with a thrill. Who would ever have thought that of an investment banker?

"Is that your way of saying this is okay? I need to hear it," Finn entreated, running his hands down the curve of her back to her hip, stopping there to cup her bottom and pull her more tightly against him.

Instead of answering his question, Lisa tore the condom open with her teeth and slid down him. She ran her hand along his length, and then repeated the action with her tongue. He bucked, but she held him in place with one hand while she sheathed him in the condom with the other. No sooner had she done this, then he rolled them again, this time pinning her under him with intent.

She moaned and scooted herself into a position that raised her knees alongside his hips and tilted her pelvis to receive him. His heart hammered against her.

Thinking that this was a surprising heaven to discover, Lisa wondered why she had waited two years.

It was all Finn could do not to drive himself into her when she raised her knees. He could feel her arousal, knew that she wanted him. It was so tempting to take all he wanted, how he wanted, every way he wanted. Good lord, it had been a long time. He had to hang on to his control, he thought, reminding himself that she deserved to be pleasured too.

Finn raised up on his elbows, looked down into her face. She was absolutely gorgeous. This was a woman, not a young girl with stars in her eyes, but instead a woman with both heat and demand in her. She was squirming under him, impatiently waiting for him to be in her. Her heart was beating fiercely against his chest.

His mind took a detour, suddenly wishing they had more time. He wished that he'd met her across a crowded room, had asked to go out with her, and had talked her into this. His body had other plans though, so he pressed a little forward, stopping at her moan. He was finally at that point where he knew this was going to happen and that he was going to let it. Maybe he should just pretend he was Eric for once and be grateful. She ran her hands up his back, across his shoulders, making him feel more masculine than he ever remembered feeling in his life.

"What are you wearing?" she asked, her voice husky, her body clenching. "You smell like sandy beaches. It's amazing."

"Hotel shower gel, I think," Finn told her, but he was guessing. "Are you sure. . ."

The question died as she raised her hips and gripped his to pull him into her.

"Sorry," she actually blushed. "I wanted. . .it's been a while since I. . ."

"Sssh..." he said, pressing his lips softly to hers. Her eagerness for him was thrilling to say the least. "It's been a while for me too."

Finn withdrew slightly, and then pressed forward again. He did this several times, each time feeling her body's slight resistance to him give a little more. With each stroke, he grew harder and more anxious to have her completely, which complicated the process even more.

She moaned, arching her hips to give him all the access she could.

"God, I want you, all of you. Please. . ." she begged.

Finn answered that simple demand by driving forward hard and all the way. She cried out in relief, and then wrapped herself around him. She followed his rhythm, matching him stroke for stroke.

It wasn't elegant or practiced. Instead, it was primal with every stroke only seeking the next one.

He felt himself nearing the edge when his rational mind finally clicked off. Then he didn't care who she was, or why she was there. He was only grateful, profoundly grateful that she held him, wanted him, seemed to need him back.

He devoured her mouth again, finding her tongue, absorbing her scream as she climaxed around him. His body shook like an earthquake while he pounded himself into her. He didn't stop moving until every last shudder had passed for them both.

Then they held each other as close as they could, hearts thudding from the exertion.

After a while, when the shock had faded some, Finn rolled them to their sides again keeping their bodies connected. He smiled and smoothed her hair back from her face, kissing her eyes, her cheeks, her chin.

"Thank you," he told her. "That was amazing."

Lisa shivered with pleasant aftershocks and kissed his closed eyes. Then she smiled as he put his face into the side of her neck and fell dead asleep. She inhaled him deeply, gratefully, equally amazed—both with herself and with him.

In no hurry to end the blissful connection, Lisa enjoyed his warm body next to hers and waited until she was fairly sure he was not going to wake again before gently disengaging her body from his. The moment it was done, all she wanted was to wake him again and start all over until he was back inside her.

Great, now her body was completely awake after two years of nothing, but the man who woke it was fast asleep. Grinning at her giddiness, Lisa closed her eyes, reliving every second of his persistent lovemaking which had ended her dry spell in such a fantastic way. He had been gentle, taking his time, loving her thoroughly. Then he'd been lost in her, pounding away to pleasure both of them as much as possible.

Damn it, Lisa thought. It was just supposed to be simple sex. It started out like sex. Biting him on the rear and stroking him to make sure he was interested, well that was certainly sex. But somewhere in those minutes after they'd found the condom, it simply became something else. It had felt so unexpectedly *nice.* He had been the perfect blend of consideration and aggressive need, she decided. In fact, he'd been nearly perfect at all of it.

Swearing at her sentimental female musings when her unexpected lover was already snoring, Lisa pulled far enough away to look at his peaceful face. Talk about romanticizing a quick tumble for relief. Sheesh—she was being as unsophisticated about sleeping with someone as a woman could get. What was the matter with her? Great sex was just that—nothing more.

The man now slept like someone who hadn't slept in days, but she still looked longingly at his sleeping form as she slid from the bed.

Good for him for sleeping, Lisa thought, walking to her clothes. At least he was sated. She must have done something right. After great sex, men slept soundly and deeply. She remembered that.

She quietly picked up her clothes and dressed, fighting the urge to giggle about the twinges she felt in places that hadn't ached in a very long time.

She had an early meeting the next day and really couldn't wait for him to wake up again, but wow, it was shocking how much she really wanted to. Maybe dating someone so much younger had been a good idea after all.

In the sitting area, she stopped by a large desk. Seeing a pad of paper and elegant pen next to it, she decided to leave him a note. Maybe he would smile when he read it as much as she was smiling now.

The next day when Finn finally woke up, it was nearly lunchtime. He immediately looked at the empty bed, disappointed to find no one beside him. Must have been a dream after all, he thought. But wow, it had sure seemed real.

Then he felt something on his body and found the condom still attached even after all the thrashing he had done in his sleep. It had been a pretty snug fit—just like she had been. *Okay—enough of that,* Finn decided as he climbed out of bed, his body starting to twitch at he thought of her. *So it hadn't been a dream. So what now?*

Nothing probably, Finn decided, grateful he'd exercised enough common sense in the heat of the moment to at least use protection. God knew, he was disgusted with himself in just about every other way.

He couldn't remember her name at all, wasn't even sure he'd asked her for it. As tired as he had been, Finn figured he had passed out from exhaustion and never even said goodbye. Evidently, he had just fucked her and fallen dead asleep as soon as it was over, pretty much acting like Eric even though it wasn't Finn's usual style.

Guess there was no use asking Eric for her name and number today. By now, the woman had probably concluded he was a world-class jerk. Or at least she probably thought Eric had been one. Finn snorted, remembering the note Eric had crafted to lure her to the room in the first place.

Okay—maybe the woman thinking he was his evil twin wasn't such a bad thing after all, Finn concluded, amused at the idea of worsening Eric's reputation.

But remembering her welcoming smile, her yielding body, and the sheer desire in every kiss, he sighed at the magnitude of his loss as he headed to the bathroom.

When he came out, it was to find Eric waiting in the sitting area, answering email on his phone.

"Don't you do anything but work?" Finn asked, surly to see Eric so calm and unconcerned.

"Hey, Finn. You certainly look better today. I came by this morning, but you were still out cold. I left and decided to check back at lunch. I heard the shower when I came through the door a few minutes ago and knew you had finally come back to life."

"I do feel better today. Amazing what a good night's sleep can do for a man," Finn said, running a hand through his damp hair, but thinking it hadn't the been just the shower that had revived him.

"Let's grab some lunch. If you have some time, I'd love to take you by to meet my new girlfriend. Her office is just a few blocks away," Eric said.

For once, Finn was relieved Eric was so absorbed in his email and text messaging. No embarrassing questions about last night were forthcoming. He had already decided that if Eric didn't say anything, then he wasn't going to either.

"What girlfriend?" Finn asked, as he got a clean t-shirt out of his leather bag and pulled it over his head. "I thought you kept everything free and easy, no commitments."

"Turning thirty shifted my thinking. We had our first real date last weekend and it went very well. Lisa is a graphic artist who works for several design companies, has her own business, and is somewhere between 5-10 years older than me. She's also just about the nicest woman I have ever met. I'm thinking about marrying her."

"After one dinner date you decided to marry the woman? That's kind of quick, don't you think?" Finn asked, the questions rolling off his tongue in shock.

Eric was a take-what-he-wanted type of guy which more often than not ending up meaning taking advantage of the woman he was dating.

His brother definitely wouldn't marry a woman just to sleep with her, but Finn also hoped Eric wasn't planning to marry someone he didn't love in his quest for the perfect business wife.

Even after his lousy marriage, Finn still hoped to do better next time around.

"Once you meet Lisa, I think you'll understand why I'm acting so fast," Eric assured his skeptical brother, sending a final text before putting the phone in his pocket. "I feel that way even though Lisa didn't show up for our second date last night, which could have been my fault because I changed our meeting location after I tucked you in. I guess her cell was off because I tried for a couple of hours and couldn't reach her."

Finn snorted in disbelief. "Your new girlfriend stood you up? Doesn't sound so perfect to me. Why didn't you sleep at her place last night?"

"Lisa did not stand me up." Eric denied.

"You just said she did," Finn declared.

"No, I said Lisa didn't show up for drinks. That's how I know something was wrong. I've known her for several months. She's not that kind of person."

It didn't escape Finn's notice that Eric never revealed where he'd spent the night, even though it was obvious that it wasn't with his perfect girlfriend. Finn watched Eric whip out his phone again and start typing like a fiend. When his brother finally lifted his head from his electronics, it was to frown at Finn. "Don't you have some real clothes?"

Finn looked down at his t-shirt, jeans, and sandals.

"I have a jacket I can throw on over these if you're offended by my lack of a suit. This is all I have. There's not much use for dress clothes in the desert. I have a polo and one pair of khakis with me, which I plan to wear for my speaking engagement tomorrow at Harvard. Your fancy girlfriend will just have deal with my lack of fashion sense."

Chapter 3

At Finn's insistence, they ate at a restaurant near the hotel and then walked a few blocks more to the building where Eric's girlfriend worked. The outside was chrome and steel, but inside the office was all muted blues and grays. Finn thought it would be a very soothing place to work in every day.

A very polished woman smiled and stood as a barrier between them and the rest of the office. "Hello. Can I help you?"

"We're looking for Lisa. Is she in?" Eric asked.

Finn watched the woman look back and forth between them, obviously not nearly as impressed with their semi-identical twin faces as Cindy the desk clerk at the hotel had been. Her serious demeanor made him grin. Maybe Eric had met his match.

"Do you have an appointment?" Finn heard the woman ask, directing the impersonal, but very polite question to Eric.

Finn looked at his feet, trying not to laugh at his brother striking out so hard. Must not be much of a girlfriend, Finn thought, if the woman's assistant didn't even know who Eric was.

"No—no appointment today, but will you just tell Lisa that Eric is here? I think she'll want to see me. We have a date this evening," Eric lied, smiling at the woman, who huffed but reluctantly went back into the offices somewhere. He hoped it was to deliver the message.

Finn crossed his arms, staring at his brother after the woman left them alone.

"What? Little white lies are a gift," Eric defended. "See? I hear Lisa coming now."

There was a clicking of heels on tile and blur of more blue. "Eric, I wasn't expecting you. . ." Lisa's voice died off as she noticed there were two of him. She looked back and forth between the nearly identical men.

"Hi, Lisa, I thought I'd come by and introduce you to my brother, Finn." Eric smiled and waved a hand in Finn's direction.

Lisa smiled warmly at both men. "Twins, eh?" she asked, making conversation by stating the obvious, while inside she was marveling at how much they looked alike.

Then she noticed "Finn" was staring at her with open admiration, his eyes traveling from her toes to her hair, and back to her toes again, totally checking her out as if his brother wasn't just standing right next to him.

Well how rude, she thought, offering him a tight smile.

Eric punched his brother in the shoulder, pushing him forward. "Don't they say hello in Egypt, Dr. Roberts? This is the woman of my dreams. Shake hands with her and pretend to be civilized."

Lisa laughed nervously at the teasing sibling rivalry and walked closer, extending her hand to Finn. He stuck out his hand automatically, still staring way too boldly at her, still not really saying anything. *What an odd man,*

Lisa thought. Her hand slid into his, and then she sniffed. Realization widened her gaze. *Oh, my god. Oh, no. What have I done?*

"You smell like sandy beaches," she said in near whisper, her hand actually quivering as she shook one of the hands that had lifted her hips to hold her up to him while he gave her a rocking orgasm she was still daydreaming about... "I mean, it's good to meet you. . .uh, Finn." *Oh, my god. Oh, my god. I slept with the wrong man.*

"Sandy beaches? It's my shower gel, I think," Finn said softly, his gaze never leaving hers, his hand automatically moving up and down. He thought of her hand on him last night, stroking him with confidence, making him. . .

"Lisa, it's good to meet. . ." Finn began roughly, then stopped, not sure what else to say—what to do. She looked so shocked.

Laughing at the awkward social moment, Eric put his hand on Finn's back to rescue his brother from embarrassing any of them further. He laughed when Lisa and Finn actually jumped away from each other at the same time. Finn nearly knocked him down backing away from the woman.

"Sorry. My social skills are rusty," Finn said, excusing his nervousness.

"I'll say," Eric said on a laugh, pushing Finn's slightly larger body away from his. He looked at Lisa and smiled as he shook his head. "My semi-identical twin can't hold his liquor or manage to talk to a beautiful woman intelligently, despite all his education. Sometimes I'm not sure he's really my brother, much less my twin."

She bit her lip as she moved her gaze back and forth between the two men. *Think Lisa.*

She looked at Eric. Nothing. It was just like the

dinner date.

She looked at Finn and moisture gathered just like it had last night. Shocking, but still not good. Definitely, not good.

Get the hell out of here for now, her brain yelled.

Lisa decided that was a good idea.

"Eric, I hate to be rude, but I was in the middle of. . . something. Can I call you later?"

Her eyes darted to Eric then to Finn, who promptly looked away.

"Sure," Eric said while at the same time answering a text on his phone. "Oh, and sorry we missed each other last night."

Lisa's eyes went wide with shock.

Finn's heart nearly stopped while he waited to see what Lisa would say.

"My phone is still not acting right. Besides, something unexpected came up that I had to take care of. . ." she began, then blushed at how those words could be construed by Finn.

Lisa watched Finn smile wickedly at her confession, boldly doing so at her without any remorse that she could see. She fought back a sigh, not wanting to have to explain her frustration to Eric.

Finn pretended to have a sudden interest in Lisa's shoes as he considered how to handle their mutual revelation.

Something came up, she had told his brother.

Well, with her help something had certainly come up. Her excuse was an honest one and as close to the truth as the sexy-as-hell woman could get without blurting out what had happened.

He admired that Lisa could think of anything to say given what they had discovered, because he was fucking speechless to know he'd slept with the woman his brother had talked about wanting to marry.

He remembered Lisa's love bite on his backside, her hand stroking him until he'd kissed her deeply and distracted her. He hardened instantly thinking about it again, like he had every time he had thought about it all morning.

Finn knew his thoughts were reflected on his face when Lisa flushed another shade darker while holding his gaze. He watched her fighting hard not to look at his crotch for evidence of his reaction to her words. He smiled again when she fled without further goodbyes.

As they hit the street outside, Eric looked at Finn with a serious face. "Do you think Lisa is upset or something? She was acting really strange. Maybe I should have called before we came by. I've never dated anyone as nice as her before."

Finn watched Eric messing with his cell phone and knew that his brother had totally missed the nuance of what had just happened. He was both glad and mad about it.

"You're the expert on women," Finn said, unable to keep the sarcasm from his tone. "I could never tell what my ex-wife was thinking in or out of bed. I'm pretty sure that's why Megan divorced me."

"No, Megan divorced you because she was into sleeping with lots of other men, and you expected fidelity. Fortunately, I love you more than her and chose not to be one of them."

Finn watched Eric tuck his phone into his pocket for the hundredth time in the last hour. *Great,* he thought. The one time Eric decided to be honorable had to be with a woman Finn hadn't cared about during the last couple years of his marriage. He also hadn't slept with Megan himself after he had found out she was a habitual cheater.

"I know I usually bed women quickly, but I'm not sleeping with Lisa yet. She doesn't move that fast. She put that out there for me on the first date. I respect that about her. We're in the dinner and kissing phase, but that's all," Eric explained.

"Good to see you finally learned to treat a woman respectfully," Finn observed dryly, feeling like a hypocrite.

"Well, don't get crazy on me. I have lots of women I can call for a good time, and I still do when I want. Where do you think I spent last night? It's just my instincts tell me Lisa is going to be worth waiting for. She may even be *the one*," Eric said.

Great, Finn thought, *let's just pile the guilt higher*. Eric's perfect girlfriend had gone to the next phase of their relationship with him and not Eric. The only thing that eased his guilt at all was hearing that while he had been with Lisa last night, Eric had been cheating on the woman he thought was above such things.

But why had Lisa Dennison climbed into bed with him?

The only conclusion that made sense was that Eric had no idea who the woman actually was or what she wanted out of a relationship.

"Lisa is certainly more interesting than your usual female," Finn said, meaning it sincerely.

"I'm sure she could even keep up with your brain, Dr. Roberts, but hands off bro—I met her first," Eric said on a laugh.

Finn sighed and kept on walking.

Back at the hotel and out of his brother's company, Finn dropped down on the small sofa in the sitting area of his suite.

Looking around at the opulence Eric had generously

provided, Finn pondered just how badly he had wronged his brother, even if it had been accidentally.

As he stared at the incredible luxury surrounding him, Finn saw the note left neatly on the desk. Rising to walk over to read it, Finn shook his head at the feminine handwriting, mostly hidden by the two elegant pens lying across the hotel tablet. That she had bothered was charming enough, but it was Lisa's words that had him sighing.

Once again he found himself wishing like hell that things could have been different.

Sorry to leave while you are sleeping. If I stay, I would have to wake you up again, and you really seem to need to sleep tonight. Being with you was the best surprise I've had in a very long time. You were wonderful in every way. Thank you. ~ Lisa

Finn re-read the note many times. Then he folded it carefully, tucked it into the side pocket of his duffle bag, and zipped it closed.

The grateful words were his.

Lisa might not be, but last night was.

Though tired and partially drunk when he'd been with her, Finn still remembered all the important parts. He remembered how aroused she had been and how she had kept holding herself back from rushing, even though she had wanted to rush.

Then when she had finally given in to the need to rush, she had stopped to wait for him.

And he remembered exactly how many strokes it had taken to get inside Lisa Dennison all the way, including the last hard slide home she had begged him for.

It was damn unfair that the most amazing sex of his life was with his brother's dream girl.

Shit. How had it happened?

He was not that kind of guy, much less a shitty brother. It made his head hurt something fierce even thinking about what he had done to Eric. . . and to Lisa.

Kicking off his sandals, Finn stretched out on the sofa, focusing on his breathing and on blanking his mind. He would think about it all later, he decided. The pain in his head immediately eased with that decision, and seconds after he felt himself drifting into sleep again.

Chapter 4

Lisa tapped on the door of the suite. When there was no answer, she almost turned to leave but then reminded herself she was not that kind of person. She had made a mistake and now she had to try to make it right.

Taking the key card from her wallet, the key card that she was happy now she had neglected to turn back in, she slid it through the lock and stepped into the suite.

You just want to see him again, a voice inside her insisted. *You want to see if he's naked and waiting for you.*

The first thing she saw inside the room was the object of her thoughts. He was stretched out on the sofa, feet hanging over while sound asleep, but unfortunately not naked. Lisa sighed with regret as she closed the door softly behind her.

Then she smelled him again.

That damn shower gel or whatever it was. Her toes curled and arousal hit instantly. Moisture gathered and this time her nipples pressed against the rough lace of bra. She looked down at her breasts in disgust.

Hello, girls. Where the hell have you been hiding for the last few years?

She dropped silently, and dejectedly, into a chair across from the man she now realized was Finn Roberts.

She watched him sleep while she tried to decide what to do.

Finn looked like Eric in many ways, but now she could see there were some significant differences. They were semi-identical twins, Eric had said. Finn was a lot taller, probably three inches.

Then there was the way he stood, the way he spoke, the way he looked at her. The way he was looking at her now. *Shit. Busted.*

Lisa sighed as his curious gaze met her guilty one.

Maybe, Finn thought, he should be shocked at her boldness in coming into his room uninvited, but instead he was just happy as hell Lisa Dennison had returned. The illogical thought had him smiling.

"Hi," Finn said, surprised at both the excitement and the happiness in his voice.

"Hi," Lisa replied reluctantly, mad that all the butterflies in her stomach lifted into flight at his smiling hello.

They stayed like that for a few minutes, looking at each other in shock. Lisa shook her head again, mostly because she was still at a loss for the right words to explain what had happened.

"So should I apologize?" Finn finally asked, figuring one of them needed to say something.

"I don't know. Have you done something you regret?" Lisa asked, trying to make a joke and failing.

"Well, last night I made love to an incredibly beautiful woman who it turns out is my brother's girlfriend. I guess I *should* be sorry for that, but seeing you sitting across from me and wanting you all over again, I can't seem to work up the proper guilt," Finn explained.

Well, that was certainly putting the truth out there, Lisa decided, feeling her heartbeat double. The inner voice inside her was doing a happy dance. She ordered it to calm down and grow up.

"One dinner and a chaste kiss goodnight last weekend didn't make me Eric's girlfriend," Lisa declared, sounding more defensive than she'd meant to be.

She sighed in irritation at herself for her rationalization of her mistake, realizing the same could be said about what she'd done with Finn. Crawling all over him in bed didn't necessarily mean anything either.

But then what did sleeping with any man have to mean anyway?

Nothing, Lisa told herself fiercely. It could mean nothing but the need to scratch an old itch. It could be just one of those casual, temporary things. People did that all the time.

Yet no matter how casual she told herself it had been, Lisa still couldn't tear her eyes away as Finn sat up, all his muscles fluidly moving at once. He was certainly graceful for a tall man. And incredibly strong, she remembered, sighing for a different reason as she watched him move around. She shook her head just to make herself stop looking at him.

"I admit that I did think you were Eric at first. You look so much alike, or at least you did to me yesterday. Not so much right now," she corrected.

She ran a hand through her hair, and then looked at Finn to see his reaction to what she had said. He was staring at her with an intense gaze that made her feel like she was being doubted.

Out poured her thoughts without her permission.

"Okay fine. You want honest. Well honestly, after you put your hands on me, I didn't care who you were because I hadn't felt that way, been able to feel that way, in a really, really long time. Shit—maybe I should be the one apologizing to you," Lisa said unhappily, crossing her arms. "Are you happy now?"

Finn thought the woman facing him now might just be the most honest woman he'd ever met. He could like her, he decided swiftly. And since she had told him a hard truth, he told her one in return.

"I've been divorced for two years, and you're the first woman I've been with since my ex-wife," he said flatly, enjoying the shock that came into her face. Her reaction almost made the last two years of abstaining worth it.

Lisa stared. Words dried up in her throat.

She shook her head because she truly had trouble believing that this incredibly sexy guy had gone two years without female companionship.

How could she believe such a thing when he made her wet and aroused just by looking at her with that gaze that seemed to strip her naked?

She cleared her throat to speak, chagrined when no words came out. She tried again, finally managing a squeaky, nervous explanation of her own situation.

"I've been divorced for several years myself, a little longer than you. I haven't really felt any interest in sex for a while."

Then appalled at herself for telling him all her secrets, Lisa leaned back and closed her eyes.

"What I mean is that I have dated, but I haven't. . .been with anyone. . .either. I'm sure that was really clear to you last night."

She blushed at her confession.

Why was she admitting more to Finn Roberts than she had told her freaking OBGYN doctor?

Shut up, Lisa. Just stop talking.

"I tried to go as slow as I could. Did I hurt you?' Finn asked quietly. He didn't think he did or she wouldn't be here, but he wanted to see if she would answer him. He wanted to see if she would answer intimate questions just as honestly.

"Hurt me?" Lisa said, hearing her voice squeaking again as she confronted the serious concern that was reflected in his face. "You're serious, aren't you? Okay—no. No, you didn't hurt me. You were. . .," she stopped to consider her words.

What? How could she describe the experience of being with him without gushing about how amazing it had been?

"You were just the right amount of careful," Lisa finally said, her need to reassure him winning out over her urge to protect her pride.

"Well, you certainly didn't make that easy for me," Finn said with a grin, his voice low and rough from the desire she stirred in him. "You kept moving under me, urging me on. I almost unleashed the beast several times."

"Unleashed the beast?" she repeated, laughing at the strange term. "That's a new one. What do you mean?"

Finn looked at her pointedly. Could this incredibly hot female truly not know how it could be between a man and woman?

"It's not something you can explain. It's one of those experiential things. Maybe I could show you sometime," he challenged.

She crossed her arms and looked at him, wondering at his sudden change of tone. Was he coming on to her?

Yes, the voice inside her yelled.

"You know, you could be saying the ugliest things to me right now and I'd never know the difference, would I? I bet that sexy voice of yours works well for you in the classroom, Dr. Roberts."

Finn smiled at her snarky, defensive response, and shrugged as if it didn't matter, but it did. He liked that she challenged him back. He liked that she was demanding in bed. He liked that she had come to him to admit her part in what happened. So far there wasn't a single thing about the woman he didn't like.

Lisa thought Finn looked like every woman's fantasy right then, a man who any minute might just drag her off to bed. She got a sudden image of her riding him until they both screamed, shocked at the direction of her thoughts.

Coming out of her musing, she blinked rapidly, hoping she hadn't said anything in her stupor.

When Finn saw her pink face glowing, and the light in her eyes as she looked at him, it tightened every muscle he knew about and some he'd forgotten he even owned.

"I have to just tell you something that's probably rude as hell, but you certainly blush a lot for a woman your age. How long were you married?" he asked.

"A *woman my age?* Gee, thanks," Lisa said on a harsh laugh, deflated that Finn had been thinking about how old she was while she'd been having hot sex thoughts about him. "I guess that sums up what you think of me, doesn't it? I was married ten years, not that it's any of your business."

"It was meant as a compliment," Finn insisted on a hard laugh. "You can't be much over forty—if that. And forty is not old, just past the age where women blush about sex—usually. It makes me want to show you what you've been missing all the time you were holding out these last few years. I think I would really like to do that."

Lisa swallowed at his words and couldn't think of a reply that wouldn't get her into more trouble with him.

To give them both a little time to absorb the conversation, Finn got up, went to a small refrigerator, and pulled out two bottles of water. He brought one over to her.

Lisa frowned at having to look all the way up to see his eyes, which took her gaze past intriguing parts of Finn she really didn't need to see that up close and personal right then. She took the bottle of water simply because it gave her something normal to do while Finn stood there staring down at her.

"I still want you," he said flatly. "If you give me the slightest indication that you're interested back, I'd be more than happy to show you my beast."

Lisa had no idea what he meant, but his tone alone had moisture gathering again, accompanied by an overwhelming desire to say yes to whatever he was offering.

"Look, I did date your brother—once," she told him, staring at the floor, at the ceiling, anywhere she could look besides him. "It somehow doesn't seem right to date you too—even if I find you interesting."

"Why didn't you sleep with Eric? I mean, before you thought you were last night?" Finn asked. He already knew the answer, but he wanted to hear her say it. He needed to hear Lisa confirm out loud what his body already knew and what Eric had said. His heart hammered in his chest until he was sure she could hear it too.

"I don't sleep around—normally," Lisa answered, staring at the floor. "I didn't want to sleep with Eric—still don't want to."

He paced a little ways away hoping she might look at him.

Finn wanted to see her face, feel her gaze holding his when he pried the answer out of her.

"Okay. Then why did you make a different decision last night?" Finn asked, trying to ignore her blush, trying not to read into it what he wanted to believe before it was confirmed.

Lisa shrugged and shifted in her chair. "I seriously don't know."

"No, I think you do, because something overrode your instinct to stay away from my brother and made you climb into bed with me. Help me understand how in my jet-lagged sleep, I could have so totally taken advantage of your mistake. I am not that kind of guy, or at least not usually," Finn said, tossing his empty bottle into the trash.

Lisa looked at him. He was dead serious about that alright. It was in his face, the set of his jaw, and the tenseness of his posture.

"Finn, I don't know you well enough to think you are any particular kind of guy. And I never said you took advantage of any situation. I have already admitted that I was the one that crawled into bed with you, not the other way around. Shit, this is awkward to explain," Lisa swore, leaning forward to put her head down on her knees.

Finn watched with great interest but little sympathy. For some reason, Lisa's continued discomfort made him insanely happy. It had to mean she had wanted him.

"So on a whim, you just decided to climb into bed with a naked man that you had only dated once and didn't really want to have sex with?" he asked.

Lisa raised her head, glaring at him.

"Wow, you make that sound really awful. The front

desk clerk gave me a note from Eric and a key, both she insisted were meant for me. One minute I'm staring out the window looking at the Boston skyline, and the next minute I'm crawling up your naked body and biting your ass. I honest to God don't know why. Sue me, I guess the smell of you made me horny enough to do what I did. Don't you think if I had a logical explanation, I'd share it with you?"

A grinning Finn looked down at the floor, trying hard not to laugh at her admission. He was going to make sure he took the hotel's shower gel when he left. In fact, he was ordering a case of it.

"Stop gloating," Lisa demanded. "If I have to believe *you're not that kind of guy*, then you damn well have to believe I don't do things like that either. When I saw you and Eric today, I still didn't have the urge to do anything with him. Yet when I look at you, I can't explain my interest in you either."

Finn watched her take a giant gulp of water, continuing to glare at him, which only ratcheted up his arousal another fifty notches or so.

Frustrated with the conversation and the situation, Lisa found herself just blurting it all out.

"Look—after the first few minutes, it wasn't just the way you smelled. It was the way you acted with me. It was how careful you were, how sweet you were, how you rolled us over in bed looking for condoms. You were every fantasy come true for a short while, and I just wanted to keep on feeling that way for as long as I could. That's not a damn crime."

She dropped her gaze, unable to look at him a single moment more.

Finn walked to the chair where Lisa sat, decision made long before he got there. He didn't ask permission, just pulled her all the way up into his arms which had been aching to hold her again. He lifted her hips and guided her legs around him before she could really protest. Then he spun them both, dropping back into the chair with her straddling his lap.

Lisa started to complain, but his eyes were soft, regretful, and full of heat for her. The finger across her lips to keep her from speaking wasn't even necessary, but desire chose to arc across even that small touch.

"Ssssh...don't say anything for a minute," Finn begged softly, running his thumb along her bottom lip because he just had to stroke her somewhere. "I have to hold you to confess the rest."

"The rest?" Lisa squeaked.

Finn nodded gravely and took a deep breath. "Eric's my brother and I love him, but he can be a damn pain in the ass. He acts and doesn't bother with the details. I don't know how he is so successful when he spreads confusion wherever he goes."

Lisa heard love in Finn's voice, but also an understanding of who Eric really was. She laughed without humor.

"I wouldn't know much about Eric," she said flatly. "I never got to know him that well."

Finn leaned his head back and met her gaze, frowning. "The key at the front desk wasn't for you. The hotel clerk made a mistake too. Eric was setting me up with a booty call friend. I was supposed to pretend to be him. He frequently tries that sort of thing when I visit, especially since my divorce. But I swear I have *never* taken advantage of it. Never. . . but. . .shit. . .that's who I thought you were last night."

Lisa blinked, her brain slow to take it in. *Booty call?* She thought Finn was his brother, and Finn thought she'd been a booty call friend of Eric's?

Finn sighed.

"Look, I begged Eric to call it off. Now I think he probably did because no one came but you. Eric didn't say anything to me about it today, and I didn't ask. The truth is you crawled into bed with me, put your hands on me, and I came back to life. It had been a damn long for time me too, and after a certain point I didn't really care who you were either. I just wanted it not to end. You can't imagine how wonderful it was to know you wanted me."

The brutal truth from a brutally honest man, Lisa thought, not completely sure how she felt about Eric having booty call women in the first place.

Why the hell had he been dating her then?

She turned her face away, unable to look directly at Finn anymore.

As her silence stretched on, Finn squirmed a little under her in the chair. At least Lisa wasn't bolting for the door. Not that he'd let her leave, but he took her silence as a good sign. It meant she was still thinking about what he had said.

"Look," Finn said finally, "I'm telling you the truth because I want you to believe that I didn't intend anything to happen. When you touched me, I acted because in that moment I wanted you badly. Even today, after knowing what I know, I still want you. Being sorry would mean having to forget it happened, and I don't want to go back to being dead."

"So, let me get this straight. . .you only slept with me because you thought I was a booty call?" Lisa asked, licking her dry lips.

Finn looked like he wanted to die rather than answer her question, but he held her gaze and nodded his head yes.

Tomorrow she might be outraged at the idea that he had just this once—even if unknowingly—given in to the temptation to take advantage of a booty call.

At the moment, she was just disgusted that Eric would arrange such a deceitful liaison, and the action only validated the instinct that had made her so careful with him.

It was just hard to be sincerely outraged about Eric's behavior or Finn's confession when the heat of her was pressing down on evidence of Finn's continued interest in her. God, the man beneath her was real, Lisa thought, suddenly thinking he might just be the best mistake she had ever made.

"*Now* do you want me to apologize?" Finn asked again.

Instead of answering right away, Lisa turned her face back to his and looked at him. She looked in his eyes. She tried to see Eric there, but couldn't. There was just Finn.

And she was interested.

"Apologize for the booty call thing or sleeping with your brother's girlfriend?" she demanded, willing to risk teasing him again.

"We've already decided I'm not sorry for the girlfriend thing. It's not my fault Eric didn't score with you," Finn informed her, keeping his tone as firm as the rest of him.

Lisa couldn't help laughing at Finn's logic, so she did and it had her shifting closer and bearing down on him more. He pushed himself up a little to better fit himself between her thighs.

To her, Finn looked completely unrepentant, totally male, and totally irresistible.

He tightened his hold on her hips as she stared at him, and it seemed like he was waiting for something to show him the next logical step.

She was right there with him, searching for it too.

Lisa decided that it was impossible not to like the man.

"You don't strike me as being as calm about all this as you're pretending to be," she said dryly.

"I'm not. Having been married, I have the good sense to realize the booty call thing may be more offensive under the circumstances," Finn explained.

Wanting to comfort her, maybe even reassure her, Finn ran his hands up Lisa's arms and back down her sides before letting them rest at her waist. She sighed and relaxed under his strokes, making him want to hug her.

"I swear on a stack of bibles that you weren't just a convenient warm body. I've had plenty of opportunities for those and said no. I said yes to you because you made me want you so badly that saying no wasn't a possibility," Finn said.

"So now I guess you want me to thank you for telling me the truth?" Lisa demanded, her laughing eyes softening her sarcastic tone.

Finn smiled, his lids lowering as he pushed himself against her weight, lifting her with each upwards thrust until she moaned and pushed on him to hold him still.

"Okay. I admit that not many men would have said anything. Personally, I don't think I would have said anything myself if our positions were reversed. So I guess I don't think you're a bad guy, maybe just a pent-up desperate one. . .which makes me feel better in some sick, twisted way," Lisa told him.

Finn laughed, letting his body relax under hers, or as much as it was able to in his current condition.

"Okay. I'm not bad and you're not bad. So what do you want me to do now? I could let you go and swear never to say a word to Eric, but I'll be damned if I come to the wedding."

"As I've said several times, it was just one date with your brother. I hardly think Eric has marriage in mind. I doubt that our sleeping together will have an impact on a relationship that wasn't really happening," Lisa said.

A lot she knows, Finn thought, smiling at her. Roberts men set their minds on something and that pretty much was it. Eric had that more than he did—or so he had thought before Lisa Dennison had crawled into bed with him.

Closing his eyes, Finn raised his hips under hers, seeking Lisa's heated response again, raising her up in the chair and inviting her to ride the next wave of arousal with him.

Giving in to her instincts, Lisa moved her hand down to the waist of Finn's jeans, popping the snap before shifting her shocked gaze to Finn's as he opened his eyes in surprise. She saw a mirror of her desire in his serious, gray-blue gaze.

"Tell me what you want," Finn invited, wanting to hear her say it was to be with him. He needed to hear her admit she wanted him again now that she knew who he was.

Lisa toyed with the button on his jeans. Finally, she lifted her eyes to meet his. "I want to know more about your beast, Dr. Roberts."

That was admission enough for him, Finn decided. He stood with Lisa wrapped around him and starting walking with her while she tightened her hold.

By the time they got to the bed, he almost had her naked from the waist up. He fell on the bed with her, making her absorb his weight.

He kissed her everywhere he could, while pushing her into the mattress and holding her there. If he was hurting her with his aggressiveness, she made no protest.

He yanked her slacks down as far as he could before invading her, pushing two eager fingers into the source of her heat. It told him everything he needed to know at the moment.

"Finn..." She called out his name, arching against his hand. She looked at him with surprise. "Please. . ."

A few strokes later and Finn watched her face as she cried out in release. His control snapped.

All he wanted was to make her do it again and again.

Pulling his fingers out, he licked her eager wetness from them as she calmed. She shivered watching him, the first flickers of fear in her face warring with the desire still in her gaze.

Finn's last rational thought was wondering how the woman had managed to stay so inexperienced. Then he realized that she wouldn't be after tonight. He rose over her, let out a large sigh, and stared hard at the woman he wanted to make his.

"What are you planning to do?" Lisa asked, incredibly aroused but still a little afraid about what his possessive gaze meant.

His voice was dark and husky as he threw her words back at her. "This is the last chance you have to change your mind about being with a pent-up, desperate man like me. I'm about three seconds away from it being too late already."

But even as he said the words, Finn knew it was just word play. Now that he knew Lisa wanted him, he had no intention of letting her walk out of his life yet. Maybe he wasn't as nice as he told her he was because she was going to remember tonight for the rest of her life.

He rose off her and grabbed a condom from the nightstand where she'd tossed the remaining two last night.

He unceremoniously yanked off the rest of her

clothing and all of his, not caring where it went so long as it was out of the way.

"Come over here to the edge of the bed," he ordered.

Lisa just looked at him, not sure what to do. No man had ever looked at her like Finn was looking at her now. She was still aroused, still waiting for him to join their bodies and fill the emptiness.

"Now," he said harshly. He dropped to his knees and dragged her hips to the edge of the bed, spreading her thighs urgently with his hands. Then he pushed his tongue as far as he could inside her while she screamed his name over and over.

"Finn. Stop, Finn. Wait. . .please. . ." Lisa begged, all but sobbing as he used his tongue and fingers, driving her up and over again to another violent climax.

Damn right, it's Finn, he thought, maddened now by the taste of her release—twice. He held her at the edge of the bed, his body bent to his task of making love to her with his tongue, laughing wickedly as she throbbed and throbbed against his mouth.

Finn replaced his tongue with two fingers, as he sucked her center until he felt her legs shaking. He craved her release again, was really close to climax himself from just watching her and listening to her beg him to stop and then to not stop.

Too bad for you, Eric, Finn thought, everything in him bent on claiming possession. *This one is mine.*

Just before she shattered a third time, Finn pulled her the rest of way off the bed impaling her on his aching erection, forcing her hips around his as he knelt there with her wrapped around him. She screamed his name as she rode the waves of another quaking climax, gripping his shoulders to hold her body in place on him.

"Lisa!"

He yelled her name as he finally exploded inside her,

one hand holding her hips while the other was tangled in her hair.

She sobbed with her final release, tears streaming down her face while she kissed his chin, his neck, and pressed her pounding heart against his heaving chest.

He soothed her with his hands, kissing her face, murmuring praises and compliments, holding her close as he lowered them both to the floor, already regretting the harshness of his actions.

Too soon, Finn thought, filled with regret. *Way too soon for this.*

Finn held Lisa without speaking, then finally closed his eyes, wishing he had been more gentle with her this second time. But it was too late to wish.

For an hour, Lisa watched Finn sleep, letting herself imagine how it would be to wake him again. Would he be an animal like before? Or had what they had done soothed the beast? The pent-up, desperate statement had been another brutal truth evidently.

She waited until Finn's breathing became slow and deep, until she felt she could untangle herself without disturbing him. They had ended up on the floor among the remnants of their clothes and fallen asleep wrapped around each other.

Wow, Lisa thought. She stood on wobbly legs and stared down at her weakened limbs. She would no doubt have some bruises tomorrow. Finn hadn't stopped or even slowed down no matter what she had said. Thank God, but still. . .she wasn't even sure he even heard her talking to him.

And how many climaxes had she had before he finished with her?

She was pretty sure it had been three big ones, but

two was more than she had ever known before.

Finn had definitely unleashed the beast in both of them, Lisa decided, shivering at the thought of being wanted that way, being taken that way.

Then she wondered how often it could happen and if Finn would ever want her that way again. She was inundated with his smell, his feel, his taste, and her taste on him.

Wow, Finn, Lisa thought with her heart tight in her chest. Years of nothing and now all this passion when she hadn't even been looking for it.

Feeling guilty, but also feeling the need for some privacy to think about things, Lisa sighed and dressed quietly like before.

And then just as quietly, she let herself out of the suite again.

After Lisa had gone, Finn finally opened his eyes and dared to look around. She had gotten really emotional during the last climax but had never cried a tear during the long minutes he'd held her afterwards. Nor had she spoken a single word of complaint.

But regret had owned him, so he had intentionally taken the coward's path and faked sleep. He hadn't wanted to risk making her more upset than she might already be with him.

Finn had shocked himself and now didn't know what to do about it. He had never been that rough with a woman, not even his ex-wife while they were married. But then he'd never been so mindless to have the total attention of one the way he wanted to with Lisa Dennison. He felt the need to banish even thoughts of other men from her, especially thoughts of his brother.

But where had any of that come from? That dark feeling of feeling possessive about a woman who was never meant to be his anyway?

Damn it.

He already wanted her again, wanted to pretend the last hour had never happened.

If he ever got another chance, he would linger over every touch, every curve, and discover every possible way Lisa could achieve release.

Crazy to make her his, he'd gone over the careful line of new lovers, which was probably worse than telling her about the damn booty call.

Would she now hate all men because of him? Never be able to trust another one to touch her?

The idea pleased him so much Finn was disgusted with himself again.

He was scum and worse than Eric, especially where Lisa was concerned.

Shit, Finn thought. Years of no women at all and now he was completely obsessed with another one.

Chapter 5

The next day at work, Lisa moved slowly, walking and sitting carefully. She saw the moment her assistant Martha noticed and winced at the worry in the older woman's expression.

"Are you okay? You're going to have to tone down those aerobic workouts some if they have you limping around all the next day," Martha said.

"It's a new exercise program," Lisa said, trying to make the white lie sound as good as possible. "I just overdid it a bit."

Actually, when she thought about it, she had barely participated at all. Finn had carried her to bed, undressed her, dragged her to the edge of the mattress, and literally forced her to climax over and over before making her ride him for his own relief. Her legs still quivered over it today. He had surprised her with his aggressive demands. No one had been like that with her before.

And she really had to stop reliving it over and over, Lisa decided, her underwear already suffering for her lustful thoughts. She'd walked around aroused since she'd gotten her first whiff of Finn.

The front door buzzer rang and Martha zoomed off to see who it was. She came back moments later loaded with an enormous vase of flowers.

"Well, look at you," Martha told her. "Looks like that young man really does have a serious thing for you." She pulled the card and read the signature. "Who's UB? I thought his name was Eric."

Lisa frowned. *UB?* No—he couldn't have signed that card UB. What had he told the florists? She shook her head and laughed as she thought about it.

Martha continued to look at the card. "This card doesn't make sense. Maybe the courier delivered it to the wrong person."

Lisa rose reluctantly from her chair and came around to take both the flowers and the card from Martha. She read the card several times, her heart fluttering, an idiotic smile on her face. She had to go sit back down to really take it in.

I have as many apologies for you as there are petals on these flowers. I know I keep saying this, but I really am not the kind of guy who gets carried away, especially like last night. Please don't hate all men because of me. Come back one more time. I'm leaving Sunday and I don't want it to end like this. ~ UB

PS: Speech at Harvard 3pm today if you want to come by.

She laughed at Finn's dramatics. What did he think? That he'd broken her or something?

The note was priceless. *'Speech at Harvard'* was preceded by *'Please don't hate all men because of me'*.

First she was a booty call. Now today he was worried he'd gone too far with her. The man was a total wreck, as bad as she was.

Maybe she and Finn were more like twins than he and his brother were.

Small surprise she had crawled into bed with him a second time. No surprise at all that she wanted to again, especially after her three giant orgasms with him yesterday.

The only question that remained for her was how rational to be about all of her sexual interest in him, which Lisa took about five seconds to decide just wasn't worth losing brain cells over.

"Martha, reschedule appointments for the afternoon. Move them to later in the week, will you? I have to go to a lecture at Harvard at three."

"Shouldn't be hard. All we have this afternoon is a conference call. Are you taking classes again? Why aren't they on the calendar?" Martha demanded.

Lisa met Martha's gaze. Her assistant had been with her for five years and ran the office like it was a military post.

"No classes, just going to a lecture," Lisa said firmly, smiling at her confused assistant.

"Okay," Martha said, face wrinkling in concern.

Lisa rose gingerly from the chair to walk around the desk. "Do we have any aspirin?"

"I may have something in my purse. Do you need to go get checked out? You seem like you're hurting all over today."

Lisa saw Martha looking at her with great sympathy. It suddenly struck her as incredibly funny, so she dissolved into laughter.

"I know it's been a while since you've seen me with a sex hang over, but I swear I'm going to live," Lisa assured her. "I'm not dying. I just got laid really, really well last night. My body is just way out of practice, and he was. . .outside anything I'd known before."

She watched Martha blink twice. Probably unable to believe she had said *'laid,'* Lisa thought, grinning wickedly at the idea of the witty Martha being scandalized.

"I'm confused," Martha admitted finally.

"It wasn't an exercise video, okay?" Lisa exclaimed finally, blurting out the truth as she was tucking Finn's apology into the side pocket of her purse.

"Hold the rest of that explanation for a minute. Let me get you the medicine first."

Lisa watched Martha scurry away. The woman probably needed time to assimilate the information. Lord knows she did. *UB?* What had possessed him to sign the card that way? His nerve made her laugh.

While she waited on Martha, Lisa dug through the contents of her purse for a pair of long, dangling earrings she had dropped in there a couple weeks ago.

At the time she'd thought the bundle of silver circles were too much to wear to the office. Today they suited her mood.

Humming, she fastened them to her ears, smiling at the jingling sound they made when she moved around.

Martha came back, stopped, and stared at the sight of her boss humming. She was definitely going to have a little talk with Harlan tonight. She hadn't hummed in a great while. "Okay. Explain now."

"We got a little carried away last night. Today, I feel like I've been hit by a truck, but happier than I've been in a very long time. So now I have to go tell the idiot I slept with that he didn't hurt me and that I like it rough sometimes."

Martha lowered her voice to a whisper.

"Yeah, that happens to me once in while with Harlan. We call it '*the Viking and the Maiden*' at our house."

She stopped, remembering the apology on the card, which had her looking at Lisa Dennison with new eyes.

"He referred to what we did as *unleashing the beast*."

Lisa supplied in a whisper back. "Hence *UB*."

"Was it the one in the t-shirt or the one in the suit?" Martha demanded, mentally crossing her fingers.

"Guess," Lisa teased, following Martha slowly to the door, taking the pills from her assistant's hand and tossing them back with a cup of water from the cooler near the front desk.

"I'd put my money on the t-shirt guy," Martha finally said. "He wasn't as polished as the other one but looked like he'd be a lot more fun in the sack. The polished one probably can't pay attention long enough to get a woman there. He seemed to have more interest in his phone than in impressing you."

"Martha!" Lisa exclaimed, pretending shock as she walked out the door.

She laughed about it for entire her walk to the subway, remembering Finn's preciseness in getting them both there—her several times.

When she got to the building where Finn was speaking, Lisa saw it was packed to capacity. She moved around the edges looking for an empty seat because she wasn't going to be able to stand the whole time in her current condition.

Then she saw him. Finn was wearing a blue polo and khaki slacks. One hand held a bunch of index cards, and he was using the other to emphasize something he was saying to a man standing next to him.

Just as Lisa was wondering if she should go up and say hello, Finn lifted his head and saw her. Everything in her leapt to attention as he smiled.

Silly girl, Lisa chided, but a part her of was so excited she could barely restrain herself from giggling.

She smiled back, especially when Finn stopped talking and walked away from the man, laughing when he stopped and turned back, probably remembering to be polite. She heard him excuse himself before he started walking towards her again.

She met him halfway, a soft smile on her face.

"Hi," she said.

"Hi," he said back.

"Thanks for the flowers," Lisa said.

"Did you come all this way just to say that?" Finn asked, smiling.

"No, I came to tell you that you didn't hurt me. Well, you did hurt me a little," Lisa admitted, remembering how he felt about honesty. "But the end result was worth it."

When Finn flushed, looking guilty and remorseful, Lisa only smiled at his discomfort.

They needed lot more privacy for this discussion, Finn decided, taking Lisa's arm to lead her out into the hall. He pulled his hand away as she flinched. Then he saw a ring of blue bruises around her arms peeking out of her sleeve.

His fingerprints, Finn thought, where he had gripped her yesterday, held her to him as he. . .fuck—he'd hurt her.

A muscle started ticking in his clenched jaw.

He wanted to swear in the hallowed halls of Harvard. If it had been anyone else that had done that to her, he'd have killed the guy. He would have literally torn the man apart with his bare hands.

"Lisa. . ." Finn began, but she cut him off.

"If you apologize, I'm leaving and you will never see me again," she warned.

"I have never bruised a woman in my life until you," he said, keeping his words to a whisper in her ear.

"How much time before this starts?" Lisa demanded instead of responding to his comment the way she wanted.

Finn checked the clock at the end of the hall. "Ten minutes or so."

"Then it will have to do. We need to clear this up." Lisa grabbed Finn by the hand and pulled him into the hallway and down a corridor until she found an empty classroom. She opened the door and dragged Finn inside with her. Once in, she pushed him back against it.

"Kiss me," she demanded. "And I want it all. Don't you dare hold back. I haven't been able to think of anything else but your mouth on mine all day."

He slid his hand into her hair and tugged her head back, careful not to grab her hard with his hands. He kissed her lips, at first just playing with her mouth, but finally giving in to stroke her tongue with his until they were both on fire.

This was just how it was between them, Finn thought, too new to be tamed by inappropriate circumstances. He wrestled with his conscience, trying to be okay and to believe she still wanted him.

He hoped like hell Lisa wasn't bluffing about how she felt.

Freed of Finn's mouth, Lisa pulled away and looked at him.

Her breathing was unsteady. Her hair was tangled. She knew she probably looked like a woman who'd just climbed out of bed, but she didn't care.

Finn was giving her a look that promised all sorts of rewards for getting horizontal with him. She was never going to be able to hear a word of his lecture because of it.

"Are we good?" she demanded, stepping back from him, trying to get herself under control.

"Yes," Finn said roughly. "Are you coming to see me tonight? Mind you there is only one acceptable answer."

Lisa nodded. She felt the exact same way.

"Is Eric here?" she asked, realizing it had just occurred to her to check.

"No," Finn said. "Eric hates these things. He wining and dining a rich client today."

Despite the conversation circling back to his brother, Finn didn't argue or grill Lisa for more revelations about her feelings. Instead, he just pulled her to him for a fierce hug. Then he wove their fingers together and walked her back down the hall to the auditorium.

Lisa was amazed. Somehow even in the crowd, Finn found her an empty seat and for the next hour she listened and watched as Finn held the attention of a packed auditorium full of people.

When it was done, he answered questions for another fifteen minutes.

Finally, he held up a hand and told them he had to leave. She stood and waited for him to walk to her.

"Very impressive, Dr. Roberts. I had no idea how smart you were. If I had known, I might never have gotten the nerve to. . ." Finn cut off what she was saying by clamping his mouth on hers in a kiss that said that he had been waiting too long to do it.

People stopped talking to look at him, and then at her, undoubtedly because they were in public at one of the most prestigious universities in the U.S. Finn Roberts just got accolades from his field for his work. And he had just kissed her senseless in full view of the world like he could care less who saw.

Feeling Finn's eyes so hot on her, Lisa was shocked at how much she wanted him. She had never had a relationship where being with a man felt so necessary.

"Let's get out of here and find someplace private," she suggested, her voice husky. "I don't want to wait until tonight. I want to be alone with you now."

Finn didn't say anything in agreement, just pulled her along with him to the gates of the campus where he picked the first cab he saw. He gave the driver the name of the hotel.

As they moved through Cambridge into Boston's Back Bay, Finn held her hand in his lap, with her knuckles grazing his thigh. At the hotel, they ducked into the first elevator and punched the button for the top floor.

When they got to the room, he opened the door with his card. This time it was Finn who backed her up against the door as he secured the deadbolt to keep out the world, as well as his brother. Then he was tugging her hair back again, stroking her tongue with his tongue again, holding nothing back at all.

When the fire threatened to consume them, Finn lifted Lisa into his arms and carried her to the bedroom. It was a long time before either of them said anything else.

A couple hours later, Lisa decided Finn seemed calmer, but he was still kissing her bruises, laving them with his tongue and making her shiver. Yet under all the passion, there was something more, and it concerned her. Her nerves were stretched, but Lisa still felt compelled to ask.

"Finn," she whispered in the short space between them, "what's wrong? Don't be worried about last night. I'm fine. Swear to God, and hope to die." She crossed her chest with an X hoping he'd laugh.

He didn't.

"I'm falling in love with you," he said firmly.

Lisa was stunned by his pronouncement, and it showed.

"You barely know me," she said, trying to sound logical, already building a case against it.

Finn gave her a "don't-be-stupid" look that Lisa imagined he used on students who couldn't keep up with his thought processes.

"I don't want you making love with anyone else. I feel like you're mine. That means I have to tell my brother that he *can't* have you, and I don't know how to do that because Eric has always been the evil twin," Finn said, rolling to his back and staring up at the ceiling.

Lisa watched him for a moment, considering her words before she spoke.

"You know, you Roberts guys are way too intense. One date and a passionless kiss goodnight, and suddenly Eric thinks I'm the woman of his dreams. Now two days of extremely passionate, mind-blowing, maybe even life-changing sex, and you're in love with me? Think about this. The idea is heart stopping and romantic, but probably not love, Finn."

Lisa ran a hand down his chest and across his stomach. He felt so fine under her hands.

The necessary words weren't as easy to say to this man as she had thought they were going to be.

"You know, I may not have your brains, but I know there's a good chance this is a momentary infatuation that's going to pass. I'm not that damn naïve about sexual relationships. I dated for a lot of years before I married," she said.

When Finn retained the mutinous set to his jaw and didn't answer, it was Lisa's turn to roll to her back and stare at the ceiling.

But then she remembered that this was the intellectual brother, the one that logic should appeal to most.

"Despite the fact that it seems you've reduced me to your willing sex slave, I'm normally a practical woman.

It's only been three days since I crawled into bed with you. You're going back to Egypt in two more. Your feelings will likely change once you go back to your real life, Finn. Any number of things could happen."

Lisa let her statement trail off wistfully, a part of her hoping that Finn would be willing to pretend with her just a bit longer. She didn't want to lose him until he left. But she also didn't want him ruining his relationship with his brother over her.

"Professor Roberts, I didn't expect you to change your life just because you had the most phenomenal sex of your life with me," she teased. "I didn't know I was that kind of woman until I met you." *Please agree with me,* Lisa silently begged. *Don't make us have to end this now.*

Finn turned to her at last, looking at her open face, her lust filled eyes.

"I spent a lot of time married to a woman who I later learned was never honest with me or anyone. As I came to terms with that, I realized that most people keep the truth inside, thinking that not saying it out loud is somehow better than risking the truth. I made myself a promise to be completely honest. It kept me out of bed with women for a long time. I've been told I'm honest to the point of brutal."

"You're saying this to try and make me believe you, aren't you?" Lisa asked.

"Yes," Finn said baldly. "I wouldn't tell you if I wasn't sure. I'm falling in love with you, Lisa. Plus, I like you and want to get to know you more. Right now, I'm so in lust that I would probably do anything short of killing someone to keep you in bed with me. I have to tell Eric because I don't want to keep feeling like you're his girlfriend."

"Finn," she squeaked. "You barely know me. Eric

barely knows me. How could this have happened in three damn days?"

He covered her body with his, his erection pressing against her navel again. She ran her hands down his back while he kissed her neck.

It wasn't rational enough to be explained, Finn decided. So instead, he just showed Lisa once again exactly how it was.

Chapter 6

Finn looped his duffle over his shoulder, smiling tightly as the cheerful airline counter attendant handed him the boarding passes for his flight. He turned and looked at his brother, who was putting his phone in his pocket. He couldn't count the number of times he'd almost told Eric about Lisa, but then in his head he'd hear her pleading for him not to ruin his visit.

"Going to miss you, bro," Eric said. "Quit sifting sand and come the hell home in three months. Don't renew that damn contract."

"Eric, look—we need to talk about something. I've been trying to tell you for a couple of days now," Finn said, searching Eric's smirking face for any clue the man might already know.

"Too late for wishing, dude. You should have let me call Alicia back to reschedule when I offered," Eric declared. "When you come home for good, I'll set you up again."

"Fucking hell..." Finn said roughly, running a hand through his hair. "I don't want you to fix me up. I'm trying to say that I love you, but. . ."

"Finn—chill. That's an order," Eric said, mock

punching his uber serious brother in the arm. "One day you're going to find someone great, maybe even as great as Lisa. If things work out, I may need a best man by the time you get home."

"No. Listen Eric. . ." Finn began.

"Bro, it's okay. She didn't think you were lame. I asked Lisa what she thought of you," Eric said.

"Asked her. . .? When did you see her last?" Finn demanded.

"Before you came into town, but we've talked on the phone a couple of times since you've been here. She's had something going on lately. I'm going to drop by her office today, take some flowers, maybe even lunch. The woman works too hard and doesn't know how to play at all. I'm going to have a great time teaching her," Eric said.

"Lisa may be too old for kids, you know," Finn said stiffly, trying not to respond to Eric's comments about trying to charm the woman he wanted. "What do you like about her so much?"

Eric shrugged. "Can't explain it. She makes me smile when I see her. Ever had a woman like that?"

"No," Finn said roughly, realizing finally that he wasn't going to be able to tell Eric the truth in the last five minutes before he got on the plane and ran away. He was a bullshit coward for saying nothing, but he couldn't just coldly yank Eric's dream of Lisa away. He hoped like hell Lisa had more nerve than he did, or she'd end up married to Eric before Finn could come back and stop it from happening.

Resigned, Finn leaned forward and hugged his brother, hoping he wasn't going to lose the genuine affection between them over this. "I love you even if you are a womanizing jerk. Be good to Lisa no matter what happens, okay?"

"She said you were too serious and intense for your own good. Still want to be her biggest fan? You need a social life, Dr. Roberts," Eric said on a laugh.

Finn pulled away from Eric's friendly embrace.

"Tell me about it," Finn said sarcastically. "When you see Mom and Dad, tell them I said hi and that I haven't made up my mind about renewing for another two years. I've got a lot to think about." *Like never seeing Lisa again*, Finn thought. *Like making sure she and Eric got their chance.* Maybe if he just stayed away, he and Lisa would both forget.

He gave his brother a wave and headed through security, knowing that forgetting Lisa wasn't even a real possibility. She might forget him, but he was never going to forget her.

Lisa sat at her office desk, staring off into space, thinking about the night before. Finn had refused to hurry, refused to do anything but spend their last hours stroking her to blissful state after blissful state. And during it, he had kept saying he loved her over and over.

How could his ex-wife have ever cheated on a man that amazing in bed?

Never once in her marriage had her ex-husband shown her even a fraction of that kind of dedicated attention. She was going to remember Finn's slow deliberate lovemaking for the rest of her life. It had been like horizontal dancing. He had hummed in pleasure the whole time, and she had cried like some silly teenage girl with no control over her emotions.

The last time, she had sniffed back tears like the romance heroines she liked to read about, repeating his name over and over the whole time he had moved inside her. That kind of man was supposed to be just a fantasy. How the hell was she supposed to get him out of her mind?

Now he was gone, back to Egypt and his dig, back to the contract he had to fulfill. And she was supposed to go back to normal with no more than fond memories of a lusty week of—damn it—the best sex she had ever had.

When Martha came in and caught her lost in daydreams for the third time that morning, her assistant put her hands on her hips and shook her head. "The building plans are not going to draw themselves, you know."

"He's gone, Martha. He left today, and here I sit like an idiot missing him already. I thought you were supposed to get wiser as you got older," Lisa said, complaining.

"That's a myth. I hate to be bringing you more bad news, but I couldn't stop him from coming over," Martha said, watching her boss's face light up with hope.

"Finn's coming over?" Lisa asked, wondering if he had changed his mind about going back.

"Not the t-shirt honey. The suit with the phone," Martha declared. "He's on his way over with a picnic lunch surprise for you. He was determined. Short of telling him the truth, there wasn't much I could say to stop him. "

"Oh, hell," Lisa said, putting her face in her hand. "I have to tell Eric the truth. I stopped Finn from doing it, but I can't let this go on."

They heard a chime as the office door opened.

Martha sighed with resignation and headed out to the greeting area.

Moments later Lisa sighed as a smiling Eric walked into her office.

"Surprise," he said, brandishing the picnic basket.

"Finn left for Egypt, and I'm free for lunch."

"Hi, Eric. I'm glad you're here. We need to talk," Lisa said sadly, sighing again.

Eric narrowed his gaze. "About. . .?"

"Eric," Lisa said his name, gazing into his eyes. They were familiar, but they were not Finn's. She was never going to be able to spend time with Eric again without being reminded of the other version that she liked better.

Setting the picnic basket on the floor, Eric fished out his phone when it rang. Instead of answering, he sent the call to voice mail, and flipped the silence-only switch on the side.

"Now you have my full attention," he said. "What do you want to talk about?"

"Eric—look. . .you know that night we missed connecting for drinks at the hotel?" Lisa began, waiting until he nodded to continue. "Well the truth is I met someone else that night."

Eric leaned his elbows on the chair arms and touched his fingers together in contemplative gesture. It was his way of shifting all his attention to a problem. And this was definitely a problem.

"Okay. I guess I don't mind a little competition," Eric said. "Who's the guy?"

Lisa shook her head. "That's just it—there's no competition. He's pretty much all I can think about now."

She picked up her drawing pencil, twirled it in her fingers as she considered how much to reveal and how to say it. There was a good chance she would never see Finn again, no matter how much she missed him. Long distance relationships rarely worked. Did she have to go into it that deeply and tell Eric who it was?

"You and I—we never—Eric you're a nice guy, but

not meant for me," Lisa finally said. "I'm sorry. I should have told you sooner, but I was pre-occupied this week."

"So what's so great about this other guy? Is he older than me?" Eric asked, not deterred yet.

"No. No, he's a younger man too," Lisa admitted. "But it wasn't his age that drew me. He's intense, serious minded. And I…it's probably not going to work out, but I can't date you when it might. I hope you don't hate me for ruining your lunch plans. I do appreciate the thought."

"Is he better looking than me?" Eric demanded, grinning at his own question when she rolled her eyes. Damn—he was going to miss her. He really liked her sense of humor.

"No. The man is not really more handsome than you," Lisa said easily. "And he's not as nice or as well off or as personable. I still like him better though. He makes me feel alive again. When you find someone who makes you feel that way, you'll understand."

"Probably not," Eric said on a laugh. "You're the perfect woman. I was planning to marry you."

"That was never going to happen," Lisa assured him as she snorted over the bold statement. "Trust me, I am far from the perfect woman. The perfect woman would for damn sure not be interested in another man."

"Well, maybe if you get tired of him, you can give me a call," Eric suggested. "It's not like you're sleeping with him yet, right?"

Lisa said nothing. There was a limit to what she was willing to admit.

Eric frowned. "So, what? You *are* sleeping with him? I thought you didn't move that fast."

"That's a rather personal question given the fact you and I only had a single, casual dinner date that ended in a chaste, unmemorable kiss," Lisa protested. "You strike me as the kind of man with a booty call list a mile long, so no judgment is allowed. It just wasn't happening between us. I suggest we admit it and move on."

"Seriously—I was planning to marry you," Eric said again.

This time Lisa laughed. "Kissing you was like kissing a friend. We have no chemistry, Eric."

"You have chemistry with the new guy?" Eric asked.

"Yes," Lisa said softly. "And he is not the kind of man you get over enough to go back to dating casually again. Can we still be friends?"

"Sure," Eric said. "Can we at least eat the lunch I brought?"

Lisa laughed softly. "God—you are resilient. I do admire that about you."

Eric shrugged, as he passed her a sandwich and a bottle of mineral water. "Yeah, I wish my brother had gotten a little of that quality. Finn's ex did a number on him. I don't think he's been with a woman since his divorce."

Lisa swallowed. "I'm sure it's only a matter of time. Finn is an incredibly attractive man too, as you well know. All he has to do is be willing to take a chance again."

"Yes, but Dr. Roberts is a skeptic. He puts a wall between him and every woman he meets. The woman would have to crawl into bed with him to get his attention."

Lisa paused with the mineral water at her lips. She lowered it, unable to even take a sip. Her heart rate sped up. Finn wasn't even out of the states yet.

"Do you think that's likely to ever happen to Finn?" Lisa asked, the voice inside her screaming at her to change the subject before the truth accidentally rolled out.

Eric laughed. "Since we're not dating anymore, I guess I can tell you this. I left a note and key at the desk for a friend I was trying to hook Finn up with while he was here. The wimp begged off. I swear when he's back in town I'm going to fix him up."

"Stop there..." Lisa said, holding up a hand. When he did stop, she used the same hand to run over her face. "I can't believe I'm going to do this."

"Lisa...it was just a joke....a brotherly thing. Are you that offended?" Eric asked, sipping his drink.

"No, I'm not offended," Lisa replied, drawing in a giant breath. "It's just. . .the clerk gave me the note you left Eric . . .and the key to Finn's room. I thought it was you because the note was signed by you. And she thought I was the woman. . ."

Eric dropped what was left of his sandwich on the napkin in his lap and leaned forward in the chair. "Are you telling me that you slept with my brother?"

Lisa sighed. "Yes. I slept with your brother. I didn't know it was your brother until you brought him around to meet me. You never said you had a twin. And I . . .he looked like you, at first. I almost didn't go through with it, but it had been so long, and he smelled so damn good. I couldn't help myself. Then he wasn't you, and I was glad he wasn't you. . .I can't really talk about the rest."

Eric leaned back in the chair. "So Finn thought you were Alicia . . .and you thought Finn was me. So just when did you figure it out?"

"Not completely until you introduced us," Lisa said.

"And then. . ." Eric prompted, trying to take in that his brother had slept with his girlfriend.

"And then I went to see him. . .to apologize. . .or whatever," Lisa said, clearing her throat. "He doesn't feel like you, smell like you, or kiss like you. He's edgy, competitive in surprising ways, intelligent in his field, and loves you more than anything. I sent him away and planned to never see either of you again. The guilt was too much, no matter how much I really liked him."

"Well this really sucks," Eric said fiercely. "I didn't sleep with his ex when she offered. I didn't want that between us. Yet Finn slept with my girlfriend."

"No, he didn't. He slept with your booty call woman. And the freaking note was signed by you asking to be woken up. Want to tell me about your relationship to Alicia? Does she always wake you up? Don't try to bullshit me. You're not completely innocent in this," Lisa argued.

"I'm just an average man with great needs," Eric joked, laughing when Lisa rolled her eyes.

"So is your brother. And he made me happy to be the woman meeting them," Lisa said defiantly.

"He could have told me himself," Eric argued, suddenly remembering all the attempts Finn had made to start a serious conversation. He'd thought Finn had been going to say he was renewing his contract. Eric hadn't wanted to hear it. He shook his head and picked up his sandwich again.

"Finn is a dead man. If there is anything left of him after I'm done, you're welcome to him," Eric said, eating his sandwich.

"It wasn't Finn's fault that we continued after our. . .mistake. It was mine. All mine. He was naked when I got there and his ass was. . .never mind. TMI. And you can leave anytime you want now," Lisa ordered.

Eric was quiet for a long time as he continued to eat, frowning over the information as he thought about it. He was disappointed, but not really pissed.

Finn and Lisa.

Maybe it wasn't going to be his favorite idea for a while, but he didn't want Finn crawling back into his shell either. *Damn it—he missed his brother. He wanted him home.*

"If it was so damn great, why did you let him just leave today?" Eric asked.

"I didn't say it was great," Lisa said sharply, finally taking a sip of water. She needed it to cool her flaming face.

"It had to have been great. He's my twin," Eric said firmly, fascinated when the blush spread from her chest to her neck.

"Could you please not talk about Finn and me?" Lisa begged. "It's been hard enough to. . .I miss him. Okay? I miss him. But he's got his work and his contract and—damn it, Eric. I'm sure I don't have to tell you any of this," Lisa finished.

"Make him come home and I'll dance at your wedding," Eric said, almost smiling over the irony. "I'm almost over the worst of the disappointment. Give me a few more minutes here and I'll talk you into marrying him. Finn deserves a good woman too."

"Thanks for the sincerity of your own devotion to a woman you thought about marrying. Glad I'm so easy to get over. By the way, I'm not marrying your brother either," Lisa said, shaking her head.

"You obviously don't understand Roberts men," Eric said. "When we set our minds on something we want, we always get it."

"You didn't get me," Lisa pointed out.

"Didn't I?" Eric asked, smiling as he reached for his sandwich again. "Now I can have dinner with you anytime I want. You're going to be my sister-in-law. To make this up to me, you have to do exactly as I say for the next three months. I want Finn to come home."

"Me too," Lisa said sadly, picking up her own sandwich. "Me too."

Chapter 7

Lisa swung her car into the short term parking lot at the airport.

"I'm wishing we had told Finn the truth already. He would have had the plane ride to adjust. I don't think the airport is the perfect place for our little revelation, Eric," Lisa said.

Eric laughed. "Consider this Finn's punishment for sleeping with you and not confessing to me. I love him too much to do anything else. We'll break the news to him gently and together. Trust me, sweetheart."

"I don't like handling it this way," she said, climbing out of the car.

Eric walked around the car and pulled Lisa into his arms for a reassuring hug. "Come on. He's due any minute and I want to get this over with quickly."

He kissed her forehead as she nodded.

It was one week shy of three months since he'd seen her.

Finn knew this because he'd marked off the days on a calendar, working himself hard until he was too tired to dream of her every night.

He'd lost weight but finished his contract in record time. He had wanted to be home weeks earlier, but in the end bureaucracy had delayed him.

He and Lisa had done an online chat and talked on the phone once a month.

Neither that nor the emails had been satisfying.

She was friendly, but distant too. Technology was not the same as being there.

Now he was unsure and worried, lost in wondering if he was the only one who felt the way he did about the two of them.

Then he saw Lisa walking towards him through the airport crowd, her gaze searching until it found his.

Seconds later she was running to him and he was catching her up. She was sniffling, crying, hugging, and kissing him while he laughed, professing his happiness to see her over and over.

He finally made himself let her go.

When she stepped back a little, Finn glanced over her shoulder, straight into his brother's critical gaze.

"Eric," he said.

"Hello, Finn," Eric said in return, willing his mouth not to quirk. "What do you think you're doing with Lisa?"

Finn let out a breath, only to take in another as he met and held his brother's gaze.

"I fell in love with your girlfriend last time I was home," Finn said firmly. "I'm sorry, bro."

"Sorry bro? That's all you have to say about kissing her in front of me. Well, fuck that shit, Dr. Roberts. Either tell me you're back to stay for good or get on another plane to Egypt," Eric said, crossing his arms.

They were drawing all kinds of attention in the airport, two tall, well-built redheads fighting over an equally stunning, mostly red-haired woman.

It wasn't even all that uncommon in Boston, but the fight that seemed to be brewing among the two males was.

"Oh, I'm back to stay," Finn said stiffly, "but I'm staying with Lisa."

"Finn. . ." Lisa began, only to find his fingers pressed over her lips. Eric might be enjoying the drama, but she sure wasn't.

Finn kissed her cheek and dropped his bag by her feet. "It's okay. Eric has right to be upset. I have to let him have his say. This was inevitable."

"Well I say it was pretty low of you to sleep with Lisa when I never slept with Megan," Eric said.

"One date did not make me your girlfriend," Lisa exclaimed hotly, walking to the two men fighting over her. "I swear one day I'm going to laugh about all this. *Eric, tell him*."

Finn put his arm out to hold her back and it slid across the top of her breasts, effectively drying up her speech as she grabbed his arm against her. When he turned to look at her for her firm grip on him, Finn's gaze was dancing. "God, you feel good. I missed you like hell."

"Stop that," Lisa ordered, pushing Finn's arm away as she heard Eric snicker. The instant arousal she felt for Finn only made her glare at both of them.

"That dare in your gaze is not having the effect you were hoping for, honey," Finn informed her.

Huffing, Lisa turned her gaze on Eric, who was openly laughing now. "Enough of this high school bullshit, Eric. You're a grown-up. Can you act like one please?"

"Fine. Finn? Lisa told me about the two of you the day you left town. I made her promise not to tell you because I knew this tiny moment was the only revenge I had the heart to extract," Eric said. "I'm over it. You can have her."

"So you don't care?" Finn asked.

"Eric cared for about two minutes," Lisa answered for him, making Eric laugh. "We both agreed it was never going anywhere."

"Good—because I'd have to kick my brother's ass if he tried to take my girlfriend," Finn joked, sliding his arm away from her grasp, thinking about how much fun he was going to have with her later. Guilt-free fun.

"One week of. . ." Lisa stopped, clamping her mouth closed when both men laughed. "Bastards. You're both bastards. And I've fallen in love with one of you. God help me."

Finn stepped into her then, swooped to her mouth, catching her off-guard. "Call me that again later, and then please tell me you love me again. God, I've missed you."

Eric reached out and punched Finn hard in the arm. "Stop embarrassing her in public. Lisa isn't that kind of woman."

Finn pulled her close and straightened to his full height, ensuring he was a full three inches taller than his evil twin. "I'm sorry. I never intended any of this, but I need her. Can you get that?"

"No, but what the hell. I just can't believe you took advantage of her mistake. That was so not like you," Eric said. "It could have just as easily been me she climbed in bed with that night. In fact, she thought it was."

"Yes, I suppose it could have been," Finn admitted.

Lisa took a deep breath, breathing in the scent of Finn.

"Never would have happened. I was lured by the smell of Finn. You just aren't him, Eric. We've had this discussion. Move on."

Finn grinned down at her. "I have a meeting tomorrow just to check in, but I'm mostly free for the next three days. I don't officially resume my regular office hours until next week."

"You can crash with me until you get things figured out," Lisa said, "unless you want to spend some quality time with Eric."

"My condo is finally fixed, but you're not bringing those sand-filled clothes into my place. Shack up with your girlfriend. You know you want to anyway," Eric said, taking out his phone to check the message that came in for him.

"When we dump the gambler here, I'll tell you in great detail where I want to be for the next three days. Do you have to work?" Finn asked Lisa.

"Boss," Lisa said pointing at herself. "I gave myself time off to play with you."

Eric looked up from his phone and gave her a look. "Could you two at least wait until you drop me off to talk about your sex life?"

"No," they answered together.

"Here then," Eric said, fishing a key out of his pocket. "Happy reunion. It's the Copley suite."

Finn grinned and took the key from his brother, letting go of Lisa long enough to hug Eric. "I missed you too. Thanks for not hating me."

"Stop getting mushy on me. Just means I won't have to hook you up. By the way, you owe me the perfect woman since you took mine," Eric said.

"Don't get your hopes up." Finn warned. "Why don't you just buy one?"

"Ha. Ha. Very funny. Go back to your sand box," Eric said.

"Not for a while and not unless my wife goes with me," Finn said.

"Wife? What wife?" Lisa demanded, pulling away.

"Ah hell," Eric said, climbing into the backseat of Lisa's car. "Here we go. I told you he'd want to marry you."

"But I. . ." Lisa began, standing outside the car, staring up into Finn's blue-gray eyes.

"Long engagement. I promise I'll be faithful. If you want to live together to see how it goes, I'm willing to do that too. Just be my girlfriend," Finn said sincerely. "I'm even more in love with you now."

"You don't really even know me Finn. I'm older than you and look it. This could wear off in a few months. I want you like crazy at the moment, but anything could happen," Lisa said. "We both know this. We've been divorced before."

Finn stepped into her, kissed her softly, absorbed her moan and lifted her to her toes for an embrace that reassured him the woman in his arms could be convinced.

"I'm going to be the husband you always dreamed about having, and you can tame my beast," he whispered.

Lisa laughed. "Never," she declared. "I'm hoping to have trouble walking tomorrow."

Finn bent her body as he kissed her deeply, his erection straining against the fabric of his well-worn jeans. It was all he could do not to back her up against the car. Three months, he thought. Three painfully long months were finally over.

The car door opened and Eric stuck his head out, looking disgusted. "Geez, bro. I got you a freaking expensive room in a five star hotel. You're seriously going to do that in the airport parking garage?"

Finn glared at his brother, let Lisa go, and walked her to the driver's side.

Then he jogged around to climb into the passenger seat.

"You owe me," Eric said, as they pulled out of the airport.

"For stopping me from embarrassing Lisa in public?" Finn asked. "Okay. Thanks."

"No," Eric said, smiling. "For telling mom and dad about your new girlfriend."

"Okay, I do owe you," Finn said, grinning.

"Yes. They were quite concerned to hear you were going to be the step-father of Lisa's four children. Fortunately, I didn't tell them her last name. So they haven't had time to buy her off," Eric said.

"What?!" Lisa said, her voice raising. "I went along with your plan to torture Finn and you repay me with another shenanigan?"

Eric tilted his head.

"Think about it, Lisa. Anything they don't like about you is going to be easy to deal with once they know I lied about the four kids."

"Finn, I'm never marrying into your crazy family," Lisa said, glancing briefly at a now laughing Finn. "Your evil twin cannot be trusted."

"No debate," Finn said. "Try to get used to him though. At our wedding, Eric will be the best man."

"Always will be, and not just at your wedding, bro," Eric corrected. "Even if you are the one that got the perfect woman in the end."

"Become a nicer person," Finn ordered. "Then I'll see what I can do to help you out."

Lisa snickered. "Eric is pretty nice, except for the damn booty call list."

"If Eric is so great, what am I then?" Finn demanded, turning in his seat to face her, liking her slightly evil smile.

"You—Finn Roberts—are the *best* mistake I ever made," Lisa said, enjoying Finn's laugh echoing in the car.

# # #

WEBSITE
www.donnamcdonaldauthor.com

EMAIL
email@donnamcdonaldauthor.com

TWITTER
@donnamcdonald13 and @scifiwoman13

FACEBOOK
Donna McDonald Contemporary Romances
Donna McDonald Recommends
Donna Jane McDonald

CONTEMPORARY BOOK BLOG
www.donnamcdonald.blogspot.com

About the Author

Donna McDonald is a best selling author in Contemporary Romance and Humor, and lately has been climbing the Science Fiction list as well.

Science Fiction reviewers are calling McDonald "a literary alchemist effortlessly blending science fiction and romance". Contemporary and humor reviewers often write to tell her that the books keep them up reading and laughing all night. She likes both compliments and hopes they are true.

McDonald's idea of success is to be sitting next to someone on a plane and find out they are laughing at something in one of her books. This would of course be while she was heading off to some new place on her next adventure .

Other books by Donna McDonald

Never Too Late Series

Dating A Cougar (Book One)
Dating Dr. Notorious (Book Two)
Dating A Saint (Book Three)
Dating A Metro Man (Book Four)
Dating A Silver Fox (Book Five)

Art Of Love Series

Carved In Stone (Book One)
Created In Fire (Book Two)
Captured In Ink (Book Three)
Commissioned In White (Book Four)

Next Time Around Series

Next Song I Sing (Book One)

Single Title (Non-Series Books)

The Right Thing
Quickies Volume 1
The Shaman's Mate (Fantasy)

Forced To Serve Series

The Demon of Synar (Book One)
The Demon Master's Wife (Book Two)
The Siren's Call (Book Three)
The Healer's Kiss (Book Four)

Made in the USA
Lexington, KY
26 October 2014